Advance Praise for *Worlds of Light & Darkness*

"Contains some real gems. In L. Deni Colter's riveting 'The Weight of Mountains,' a mother and son contend with a prophecy that their family land will 'break off the end of the world and float away.' The decadent cosmic fantasy 'Collecting Violet' by Austin Gragg follows an ancient interpretation of the grim reaper through the process of collecting a soul. And 'Joy of Life' by Alessandro Manzetti, about monstrous white snakes called 'heartbeat hunters,' is sinuous and distinctive."

-Publishers Weekly

"*Worlds of Light & Darkness* brings together a thoughtful and compelling collection of stories that allow each featured author to showcase their styles and talents through a variety of worlds and characters."

-Stony Brook Press

"*World of Light & Darkness* practically guarantees readers they'll find stories to love, no matter what their taste in fantastic fiction."

-Gerard Houarner, author

About the Cover

Our cover is an original piece made especially for *Worlds of Light & Darkness* by renowned illustrator Elizabeth Leggett.

Elizabeth is a Hugo Award-winning illustrator whose work focuses on soulful, human moments-in-time that combine ambiguous interpretation and curiosity with realism. Her clients represent a broad range of outlets, from multiple Hugo Award-winning *Lightspeed* Magazine to multiple Lambda Literary winner Lethe Press. She was honored to be chosen to art direct both *Women Destroy Fantasy* and *Queers Destroy Science Fiction,* both under the *Lightspeed* banner.

She can be found at archwayportico.com.

Explore more Worlds of Light and Darkness:

DreamForgeMagazine.com
SpaceandTime.net

THE BEST OF DREAMFORGE AND SPACE & TIME | VOLUME 1

WORLDS
OF LIGHT & DARKNESS

ANGELA YURIKO SMITH
Editor & Publisher, *Space & Time*

SCOT NOEL
Editor & Publisher, *DreamForge*

Uproar
Books

1419 PLYMOUTH DRIVE, NASHVILLE, TN 37027
UPROARBOOKS.COM

WORLDS OF LIGHT & DARKNESS

Cover illustration by Elizabeth Leggett.

ISBN: 978-1-949671-24-7

First paperback edition.

To my wife Jane, without whom
DreamForge could not exist at all.

To our core team, Jane Lindskold, Mark Zingarelli,
Jamie D. Munro, Lois Yeager, and Leah Segal,
without whom DreamForge could not be what it is.

To our First Line Readers, Contributors,
and—most importantly—subscribers, thanks to whom
we have these wonderful stories to share!

-SN

For all those who came before,
clearing the path for those to follow.
For those who will follow,
may you explore far beyond
the horizons we have discovered.

-AYS

FOREWORDS

WORLDS

FOREWORDS

The Challenge of Inspiring

Many years ago, at Bubonicon, I was scheduled to be on a panel about writing dark versus writing light. One of the other writers listed was Daniel Abraham (whom you may know as one half of James S.A. Corey of *The Expanse*). I knew Daniel had written some pretty dark and creepy stories. (His "Flat Diane" won the International Horror Guild's award for best short story in 2004.) I anticipated we'd be politely arguing opposite sides of the question.

When I passed Daniel in the hallway, I said, "I see we're on a panel later. It should be interesting."

Daniel gave me a slow, thoughtful smile. "I may just surprise you."

And he did. During opening statements, Daniel said, in his experience, writing stories that contain elements of hope, of light, of faith in the future is much, much harder than writing stories whose goal is to evoke terror, distrust, anxiety, tears, and other negative emotions.

After much discussion and trading of examples, the panelists arrived at the conclusion that—despite Tolstoy's often misquoted comment about all happy families being alike while all unhappy families have their own unique forms of misery—the reverse is actually true. Happiness is often unique to the individual. So is what makes someone laugh or feel inspired. Therefore, writing to inspire positive emotions is quite difficult.

Don't believe me? Okay… Here are a few examples.

I'm a beader with an almost irrational fondness for seed beads. Very few gifts make me as spontaneously happy as tubes of seed beads (especially size 8 these days) and appropriate threads and needles. (Okay. Dark chocolate with nuts and black coffee are in there, too.)

My husband, Jim, would look at gifts of seed beads with unadulterated dismay. (And he prefers chocolate creams, as well as lots of cream and sugar in his coffee.)

When we were dating, Jim showed me the movie *Raising Arizona,* after telling me that it was one of the funniest movies he'd ever seen. Poor Jim! I didn't find the movie in the least funny. My reaction was sorrow for the childless family driven to kidnapping, as well as fear for that poor baby. Humor definitely is not a one-size-fits-all element.

However, writing hopepunk, as it has come to be called, does not necessarily mean writing utopias. In fact, hopepunk often works best when presented in a dystopian or horror setting, because these are natural settings against which to fight back, to rebel, to try and make a difference. The editors of both *Space & Time* and *DreamForge* know this, and their selections often delve into the darker realms of the past, present, and future, as well as into realities that never have been.

So, in the pages of this anthology, you'll find quite a few horror stories. In fact, when I started reading *Space & Time* Magazine, I was surprised to find out just how much horror was on offer. My personal favorite of the many fine *Space & Time* selections in this anthology is Eric de Carlo's "Hands of a Toolmaker," which is set in a very subtle, very creepy dystopia.

Nor are the *DreamForge* offerings light and fluffy. My story, "Born From Memory," deals with a cancer patient taking part in a drug trial in the hope that she might find a cure, if not for herself, then for others. "A Sip of Pombé" by Gustavo Bondoni features a ship that might not reach Mars. "Spiral Ranch" by Serena Ulibarri is set in a solarpunk future where cattle are raised on the sides of high-rise apartment buildings, but that doesn't mean there's no room for drama.

Oh, and I must mention that there are stories with cats: John Jos. Miller's "The Ghost of a Smile" and "The Feline, the Witch, and the Universe" by Jennifer Shelby, both of which tales I very much enjoyed.

Anyhow, let's go back to that panel. At the end, the moderator asked for closing statements. Daniel's stuck with me: "I'm Daniel Abraham, and I'm trying hard to become a better writer."

So, as you open the pages of this anthology, be prepared for tales by authors who have decided to take the hard road, the challenging road, to present you with not light and fluffy utopias, nor easy "dark and edgy" tales, but with stories fueled by the belief that it's worth fighting to find the better way, even though, more often than not, your victory will not be the one you anticipated.

—Jane Lindskold, author

Speculative Fiction
as an Act of Hope

Like all human endeavors, writing can be turned to harmful purposes. Storytelling becomes propaganda; narratives are crafted to divide us, to sow fear and distrust for the benefit of those who would reap the power in their lies.

Yet in essence, writing and oral lore—its ancient precursor—have always been an act of hope.

We tell stories to pass on knowledge, to explore the potential of our lives, to comfort and forewarn, and to imagine the meaning of existence itself. None of these acts are fatalistic or embody nihilism at their core. Even those who write with extreme skepticism about the survival of our species do so by engaging in an act that can only profit by the attention of others, find significance only in the passing on of their narrative to those whose actions might make a difference, and on further still to future generations who might heed and understand.

Isaac Asimov was once quoted as saying, "If my doctor told me I had only six months to live, I wouldn't brood, I'd type a little faster." What would he have said, I wonder, if instead he were struck with the notion that he would live forever, but that he alone would be the only human consciousness to survive?

Even then, the need to imagine may have overwhelmed him, and rather than despair, perhaps Isaac would have ended with, "I'd type a little slower." Even the last storyteller would want to leave behind something of us, the musings that would make for an archaeological mystery to whatever curious species finally bridges the gulf between the stars.

When it comes to writing, there is always an imagined future, always the hope of a mind somewhere not only capable of reading what we have to say, but eager to understand the ancestors, the culture, or the creatures who recorded their dreams and dared to envision a meaning for existence itself.

In all this, speculative fiction has a special role to play. In addition to entertaining and exploring the human condition, as traditional fiction so richly does, speculative fiction casts a wide net across possibilities and imaginings that take us beyond our immediate experience.

What happens if we disrupt the ecosystems upon which we depend for life? When will our technology develop a consciousness and a will of its own? What if we extend human civilization to other worlds? Will we always be human or are we quickly becoming something else? Is democracy the future or has authoritarianism returned to stay? What are the consequences, the paths, the alternatives?

Even those who write about global extinction hope for something better.

In a world where we may already have unalterably changed the course of global climate, where nuclear conflict remains within the realm of possibility, and authoritarianism is on the rise, why should anyone be hopeful?

Because becoming better than what we are is what it means to be human. Civilization, science, medicine, and the rule of law are not our natural states. For a million years, technology was defined by flaked-stone tools, the use of bones, and the eventual mastery of fire.

Slowly at first—almost imperceptibly—the incremental advancement of the millennia became the defining strides of centuries. Over time, we have seen that the slope of human advancement is not steady but accelerating upward at an ever-dizzying pace.

Within only the last six hundred years, we have gone from the printing press to the internet. Within the last three hundred years, from the steam engine to the fusion reactor. Within the last century, from the iron lung to messenger RNA vaccines. Today, advancing knowledge and its communication are so swift and pervasive that it threatens to overwhelm the human capacity to reason and to understand.

The rate of change is now so apparent that it induces fear, denialism, and resentment, forcing us to take comfort in old myths and authoritarian sureties. We want to be assured that the world has a place for us and that our lives and communities still matter in an age when men will leave Earth to homestead the planets or build new civilizations in freefall about the sun or in the deepest reaches of space. Will kindness prevail? Will science sustain us? Will friendships and family, dedication and exploration, prayer and empathy, love and perseverance still mean anything in the days ahead?

It can be truly terrifying! What better force to lead the way than speculative fiction? Reminding us always that the ways forward are ours to choose. That we can over-come dire circumstances, share discoveries, uncover truth, create welcoming communities, and look forward to all the unbounded possibilities among *The Worlds of Light & Darkness.*

—Scot Noel, *DreamForge*

Seeking Outliers for Literary Disruption

At the heart of *Space & Time* there is… *heart*. Since 1966, the publication has been dedicated to accepting the outliers. Some of our best stories were the ones rejected by other publishers not because they were poorly written but because they didn't fit anywhere else. They were the square pegs.

This includes horror stories with happy endings, science fiction about flowers, and fantasy stories in factories. We love experimental pieces that change minds. We love the monster's point of view. No topic is taboo except the promotion of hate.

Space & Time started on a $25 mimeograph machine purchased by a high school student named Gordon Linzner. A small group of fans built up around this rough little publication not because of perfect editing, targeted marketing, or the engaging layout. They gathered because this quirky, stapled-together set of pages welcomed underdogs.

The fan base built up because they loved weird fiction. Around the 100th issue of *Space & Time*, Linzner passed the reins of the magazine to new publisher Hildy Silverman. He and Hildy are both still part of the magazine as *editors emeritus.*

It's the willingness to accept experimentation that has been the backbone of the magazine for five decades. Victor Frankenstein was not worried about the *what ifs* when he created his creature. His eyes were on the sky, his mind on fire from thunderbolts as he conceived a new idea. He didn't worry about *what if* because he was focused on *what might be.* Because of his willingness to make mistakes, he gave life to the inanimate.

So, granted, it could be argued that he should have entertained a few *what ifs. What if* my darling turns out to be evil? *What if* my creation turns on me? *What if* no one likes it? But if he had, the monster would have never been created and the world could have hummed along in boring fashion. I'm so glad Mary Shelley didn't let Victor consider *what if.*

Shelley herself would have been a good candidate for *Space & Time.* A woman publishing in the late 1800s was unusual. When the first edition of *Frankenstein* came out on January 1, 1818, it was published without listing her as author. Her husband wrote the preface and the story was dedicated to her father, but the book itself was published anonymously. Mary Shelley was a square peg, but luckily for all of us, the small London publishing house of Lackington, Hughes, Harding, Mavor & Jones saw the great story there and encouraged it to be born.

Space & Time has a place for all kinds of stories from extremely dark to light and happy. The stories shared in this anthology represent a spectrum of these. These are just a few of our favorites during our era of the magazine, not all. If we filled an anthology with *all* our favorite stories, we'd have a full library of work… which, when it comes down to it, explains precisely why we do this—because there are so many square pegs needing a home.

We won't boast that we have all the best stories, poetry, and art (just most of them). We won't claim to be perfect editors. We are winging it here, opening ourselves to the wild winds of the universe with anticipation, asking *what if*. What we will boast of is our willingness to say yes to the weird ones. We like to think of *Space & Time* as the literary home for the hard to classify.

Behind the scenes we have a brilliant team that makes this possible. Overseeing poetry is Linda D. Addison, five-time recipient of the HWA Bram Stoker Award®, HWA Lifetime Achievement Award, and SFPA Grand Master. Gerard Houarner handles fiction submissions and our tireless team of readers. He is the author of nearly 300 horror, fantasy, and science-fiction stories published. Our art director Diane Weinstein was a former assistant editor and art editor for *Weird Tales* magazine and Wildside Press. The new publishers are the husband-and-wife team of Smith. Angela Yuriko Smith is an American poet, publisher, and author with over 20 years of experience in newspaper journalism. Native Australian Ryan Aussie Smith is a publisher and author who produces audio publications for *Space & Time* and other projects.

We hope you will come see for yourself. Visit us at spaceandtime.net and see the latest speculative fiction, poetry, and art. The complete history of the magazine is there, as well as past and current issues in print, digital, and audio. And should you be a square peg yourself, know we especially welcome you. Stranger, you have found your tribe.

—Angela Yuriko Smith, *Space & Time*

WORLDS

Answered Prayers

by Scott Edelman

Whenever I find myself growing sick of this world and of its people, whenever the emotional tribute life demands for my continued existence seems too great a weight for my shoulders, whenever what's taken from me with each breath feels greater than what's being given, I step away in despair from whatever I happen to be doing, wherever I happen to be doing it, hop into my car, and drive until the city is far behind me.

I drive until I end up in some small town, and then, to forget all those thoughts which sent me fleeing... I find a bookstore.

I never stop in the same town twice, and never at a cookie-cutter chain outpost. I want to believe humanity isn't being gobbled up by corporations, that somewhere out there are people who've yet to be compressed into cogs, individuals who still have the power of choice, and if that's a foolish belief in these times of ours, well... so be it. It's a thing I need to convince myself is true, or else... or else I might do something I regret.

Those whom I loved, those whom I still love, those who somehow, against all odds, still love me, deserve the me who believes.

And yet... I tell no one where I'm going, or *even* that I'm going, I just go, and when I return, they for the most part ask me nothing about where I've been. Not even Barbara, who deserves better. Their reticence is because they believe I've become a person whom questions might break. What they don't realize is—I've already broken. Sometimes, when I drive, and sometimes, after I arrive, I can forget that.

And so, I drove again, aware that the frequency of my trips was increasing, keeping pace with the rising frequency of my foul moods. I let my mind wander as the highways narrowed and the towers shrunk in the rearview mirror. Not for the first time, it occurred to me the day wasn't so far off when these impulsive treks of mine might be impossible, for no more of my desired destinations would remain. Cities would swell to touch cities, each alike, sterile, indistinguishable, populated by a coast-to-coast collection of carbon copy stores, with no space left for the oases I needed.

Nowhere left to pause, to reflect, to forget what I've lost so I can remember what I haven't. Because doing that becomes a little more difficult each day.

That last trip was coming. For all I knew, this one might be it.

And what would I do then?

I suddenly noticed I was cruising through a town square, and so lost in thought had I been, I was unsure which town exactly, or just how I'd gotten there. In a park at its center stood the statue of some man beloved to those who lived there, but I didn't recognize him, and doubted anyone not a native would know his name. I slowed as I passed a movie theater, the marquee of which touted a showing of the latest comic book blockbuster, then realized—no, not the latest, as this was not a town large enough that its theater ever got to screen first-run films—and pulled into a parking space in front of the appliance shop next door. As I glanced at the refrigerators and washing machines inside, I could also see a few televisions turned toward the street, each tuned to a different channel. My eyes were drawn to one which showed cartoon animals chasing each other with pies, a scene which brought back in a burst all I'd left behind that day.

Because, for a moment, it also brought back Andy. And then, by making me remember what I'd temporarily forgotten, took him from me.

I quickly looked away.

There, across the street, was the bookstore I'd sought, a place where I could distract myself, if only for an afternoon. I was pleased to see there was no coffee chain logo in the window, no displays of knickknacks which had nothing to do with what I'd come for. No hats, no toys, no keychains, no stuffed animals. Only books, and nothing more.

As I walked over, I could see the owner through the glass, his back to the street. I made out the beginning of a bald spot as he rearranged books on a shelf. I pushed the door open, which rang a tinny bell, and when he turned, his eyes appearing extremely large through the thick lenses of his glasses, the effect made him seem almost surprised at the arrival of a potential customer.

"Can I help you?" he asked.

He gave a slight bow along with his question, but—no—I then realized it was only something I'd mistakenly read into the hunching of his shoulders from a lifetime in the book trade.

I took a deep breath, and knew from the smell, even without looking around at his stock, that what I'd found was a used bookstore. Anyone who knew books, needed books, would know. I smiled.

"You already have helped me," I said. "After all, you're open today."

"Are you looking for anything special?"

"Just browsing," I said. "I'm not after anything in particular."

"Then you'll probably find it," he said. He smiled then, too, amused by a joke I imagined he'd made many times before. "If you need anything, let me know."

He turned away and continued puttering with the books closest to him. I couldn't make out the sense of it as he moved one volume slightly to the left, another up two shelves, but then—it was his bookstore, not mine. Collections rarely make sense to anyone but their owners. And sometimes not even then.

I looked around, studying the shelving which extended in all directions into the distance. I barely knew where to begin. The store seemed bigger inside than its frontage had me expecting, a square footage perhaps attained because it extended behind some of the other shops on the street. I couldn't make out any signage indicating what sorts of books were shelved where, so it was hard at first to decide which way to turn. But then I simply headed down the aisle which seemed by its length to lead the farthest away from the entrance, hoping, if I could locate a nook that few other customers had reached, I might find some hidden treasures there.

I moved left, then right, then left again through what felt like a labyrinth—how he kept track of it all, I can't imagine—losing count of the twists and turns until I rounded a corner which felt as if it was way in the back—though perhaps, as in a maze, I was closer to the front than I knew, and it lay just beyond that wall—to find the science fiction section, though without labels, only the books themselves gave that away.

I tilted my head and started checking out the spines, which based on the author names I could see had no alphabetical order to them—surprising considering how meticulously the owner seemed to be curating the locations of books up front. At first, I couldn't find much of anything I hadn't read before, until I spotted a Philip K. Dick novel the title of which I didn't recognize, and I'd thought I'd read them all—*A Time for George Stavros*. I slipped the copy from the shelf and discovered it to be a well-worn paperback, one obviously read many times. It was about a Greek immigrant and his family. Nothing obviously weird about the story at first glance, which seemed weird in itself, considering the content of everything else I'd ever read by that author.

I was intrigued, but unlike the other books, no price was penciled inside its cover. I thought I'd better find out how much this was going to cost me before falling in love with something I couldn't afford, so I headed back to check with the owner. Making my way to the front of the shop took longer than getting to the back, though it seemed that was supposed to have been the other way around, since my path should have been familiar, only... it wasn't.

Once I was there, standing by the counter on the surface of which there was only a bowl of mints and a cash register, I couldn't spot the owner anywhere and heard no movement but my own. I felt strangely alone.

"Hello?" I called, loud enough I was sure he'd be able to hear me in whatever recess he was working.

"Yes?" came a voice at my ear, and I turned to find the man immediately by my shoulder. I almost jumped, but ever since... ever since what happened... surprises didn't surprise me much anymore.

I held out the paperback toward him, gently slid the cover open, and pointed to where the price should have been.

"How much for this one?" I asked. "You forgot to mark it."

"Oh, that's not for sale," he said, and snatched it from me. And yet... when I looked at his hands, the book wasn't there either, nor on the counter beside us. I looked to his vest pockets, but they were too shallow to have hidden the book. For a moment, I was stunned into silence by his action.

"This is a bookstore, right?" I finally said, once the shock faded from what had just happened. "You sell books?"

"Oh, we sell books, yes. Just not that one."

"But... it was out on the shelves."

"My mistake. With this many books, it happens sometimes. I'm so sorry. But I'm sure you'll find something else suitable."

The man once more seemed to bow, and I once more told myself, no, that's only what the years had made of him.

I grumbled and started back to where I'd found the book he'd taken from me, in the hopes of finding something else which would give me a few moments of forgetfulness, but I couldn't seem to return to the same set of shelves. I tried to remember my previous twists and turns, but nothing worked, and I occasionally ended up at the front of the store again, where the owner would turn and look at me over his glasses. But once I gave up and simply wandered aimlessly, as I'd done the first time, I found a new alcove which appeared inviting.

I stood before another unmarked bookcase and ran a finger along row after row of familiar titles, looking for something which would erase my morning's moods. One book stood out, thicker than all the others—a doorstopper of a volume by Thomas M. Disch, with a title—*The Pressure of Time*—which stirred a vague memory.

I knew that title for some reason, and then—I suddenly knew that book.

It shouldn't exist. It had never been published. It had never even been finished.

I raced to the front of the store, where once again the owner was nowhere to be seen. This time, though, when I called his name and he once more whispered much too closely in my ear, I was ready. As I turned, I took a step back and hugged the book tight to my chest.

"I'm sorry, sir—" he began.

I took another step back as he started walking toward me.

"So, this one's not for sale either? No. Don't give me that. I don't accept it."

He lunged forward and grabbed hold of the book, but I wouldn't let go. I couldn't. He tugged, but I held it so close he couldn't pull it free.

I wasn't going to let him make it disappear like the first one.

He sighed and stepped away.

"How much?" I asked.

He looked at me intently. He removed his glasses and slid them into a vest pocket.

"You couldn't afford it," he said.

"How much?" I repeated.

He named a price. A very high price. It was a lot of money, more than I'd ever paid for a book before. But... something had happened here, was happening here, and I had to know what it was. The rules of the universe were bending, and I needed to bend with them, so I pulled out a credit card. I held it toward him, but he wouldn't take it from me.

"Oh, I'm sorry, sir," he said, smiling. Unlike his earliest smiles, though, this wasn't one I liked. "But you see, we're a cash only establishment."

"Is there an ATM nearby?"

"You'll find one just around the corner."

I nodded and moved to the front door, where I discovered the knob would not turn.

"Sorry," he called out. "Until a book is paid for, it must remain in the store. Besides, we're getting ready to close. You'd never make it back in time. Why don't you come back tomorrow?"

"I will," I said, one hand still on the knob as I looked down at the book. "What time do you open?"

I lifted the book to my nose, took a whiff, and then found myself whispering, "Never mind."

"What's that?" he said.

"I said, 'Never mind.' I won't be coming back tomorrow."

"I'm so sorry, sir, but that's entirely up to you. Now if you'd hand over the book—"

"I won't be coming back tomorrow because I won't need to come back tomorrow. I'm not leaving."

"Oh, no, oh, no, oh, no," he said over and over, his face growing pale. "I'm afraid that's not possible, not at all. That's not how this works."

"I know how this works," I told him. "I've read too many stories about shops like these. Anyone who's read as much as I have has. If I were to leave tonight, by the time I returned tomorrow, you'd be gone. And not just you. *All* of this. Even if I could find this town again, this space would be an empty lot. Or even worse, a Starbuck's.

And no one inside would have a memory that you or your books were ever here. No, I'm not leaving. I'm not letting you trick me. Not when *this* is here. Not when—"

Over the man's shoulder, on one of the shelves he'd spent so much time reorganizing, I spotted a copy of Truman Capote's *Answered Prayers*. Before he could stop me, I went behind the counter, took it down, and flipped through its pages. It wasn't the collection someone had cobbled together from bits and pieces of the novel left unfinished at the time of Capote's death. It was complete. I gripped it tight against *The Pressure of Time*.

"Not when *these* are here."

"You can't do that," he said, stammering. "You can't stay. No one has ever stayed."

"Well, then. Let me be the first."

He made as if to reach for me, and for a moment, I had the eerie feeling he was going to make me disappear the way he had that Philip K. Dick novel. But then his shoulders slumped even further and he let his hands drop to his sides.

"As you wish," he said. "But the store is now closed."

He pushed past me to lock the front door, and then went back to his puttering at the shelves, to what end I could not tell.

"But what about you?" I asked. "Won't you be going home?"

"No, sir, I will not," he said, not bothering to turn toward me as he spoke.

I looked around at the store's spare interior, and suddenly its decor seemed far less pleasing than when I'd arrived. This was no modern bookshop, which meant that in addition to there being no coffee kiosk, there were no tables and chairs, and certainly no comfortable couches on which browsers and laptop users could park themselves. If I were determined to spend the night there, I'd have to find another way.

I studied the bookcases nearest me, where it didn't appear any magical titles had been shelved. I hoped I was right, that the odder titles were only to be found as the aisles wound more deeply into the store. I removed the ones that seemed familiar—familiar in a right way, that is—and formed them on the floor into a rough rectangle to make what could possibly pass for a bed. I then got down on top of them, considered for a moment putting those two lost but found books beneath my head so he couldn't steal them, but then thought... no. Not good enough. I tucked them inside my jacket and zipped it up to my neck, hoping that would be enough to keep them safe, at the same time realizing—if the man wanted them, he could take them, and there was nothing I could do about it.

Nothing, apparently, except refuse to leave.

I thought of what I'd left behind that night, of those who'd wonder where I was, and why I hadn't come home, but nothing seemed quite so important in that moment as what I was hugging to my chest.

I put my head down, uncertain whether when I woke I'd still be in a bookshop. Maybe all would proceed as I'd told the owner it might were I to slip out the front door. Maybe I didn't need to leave the store for it to vanish. Maybe the store would leave *me*. I'd be on the floor of the chain coffee shop, its employees wondering why they found me asleep there when they opened that day. Or I'd find myself in a field, surrounded by the rubble of a building tumbled down long ago. It didn't matter. I couldn't leave.

Not yet.

And I didn't—for when I woke with the sun coming in through the shop's front window hitting my eyes, the shelves still towered above me. I felt inside the jacket, then looked, making sure the man hadn't fooled me in a different way, replacing them with ordinary books as I slept. But no. They were still there. I was relieved.

I stood, and saw the man was still there, too, still puttering at the shelves in the same incomprehensible way, still wearing the same clothes. He'd stayed with me all night. And I wondered... did he, unlike me, have nowhere else to go?

I cleared my throat. The man turned as I got back to my feet.

"Ah, still with us, I see," he said. He nodded at the books in my hand, and returned to a shelf behind him the books he'd been holding. "Are you ready to pay? We still don't take credit cards, though. It's just a short walk to the ATM."

I knew better than to believe him. It was surely a far longer walk than he'd promised, in more ways than one. Was it even *possible* to pay? I knew too well what would happen if I left to get the funds. And even though I was tempted for the first time in my life to become a shoplifter, even though an urge rose within me to act the thief, even though in the world outside these walls I knew I could have easily won out over the slight owner... I knew there was no way I was getting out that door. Not with anything he didn't want me to take.

"Where's your rest room?" I asked.

"Need I remind you again that this is not how this is supposed to go?" he said, managing to sound both stern and exasperated at once. "The facilities are for customers only, and you, technically, are not yet a customer. You haven't bought anything."

When I explained to him what would happen next if he refused to point me in the right direction and how neither of us would like the result, he relented. But after that need was taken care of, I suddenly realized how hungry I was. I regretted in that moment this was not a modern bookstore, one which wasn't sure whether it wouldn't rather be a cafe, for here there was nothing I could eat save the mints by the cash register. I popped them in my mouth and sucked them to slivers until my stomach hurt more than when I'd begun. There was no water fountain either, so I returned to the restroom and drank from the faucet. That would have to do, to hold me until... until what exactly? I had no idea. I dried my hands, walked past the owner, and dove back into the shelves, delving as deeply into the winding narrow paths as I could, staying as far from the man as possible.

I foraged and found, mixed in with books I knew too well, books I'd never gotten a chance to know at all, and neither had you. Books that shouldn't be. There was *The Mystery of Edwin Drood* by Charles

Dickens, all of it, with the true ending, the one known only to Queen Victoria, whom Dickens had told of it before he died without having written it down. And there as well were *Our Married Life* by L. Frank Baum, *The Last Dangerous Visions* from Harlan Ellison, and Thomas Hardy's *The Poor Man and the Lady*, never published, never read, until I was being given a chance to do so. I tried using my phone to get more information about them, because I couldn't remember which had been left unfinished, which had been completed but lost, which destroyed by time or burned by an uncaring relative. But I could pick up no signal, no matter where I stood in the shop. Whenever I happened to move near the owner as I wandered vainly, he looked at me as if I were foolish to even try.

And there was Jane Austen's *Sanditon*, and there was Kurt Vonnegut's *If God Were Alive Today*. And Herman Melville's *The Isle of the Cross*. And Sylvia Plath's *Double Exposure*.

The day passed quickly, for I was dizzy with excitement. And, unfortunately, somewhat dizzy with hunger, too. I piled each treasure I'd found by the front door, knowing I couldn't take them (yet), knowing I couldn't stay forever (yet), under the watchful eyes of the owner, who made no move to stop me from my task. At one point, as I looked at the mound that grew by his front door, I became puzzled.

"You haven't had any other customers today," I said. "Or yesterday either."

"Oh, there have been customers," he replied. "Do not think yourself unique."

"But what about the bell?" I said, pointing to where it hung above the door. "I would have heard it ring, as it rang for me. And I would have heard their voices."

"You were simply much too far in the back to have heard any of it," he said, nonchalantly, his back to me. "My customers came. They did their business. But unlike you, they did what they were supposed to do. They came… and then they went."

He turned then and moved from behind his counter. He nodded toward the door.

"Are you about ready to pay?" he asked. "It's getting on to closing time again. And you should really go."

I shook my head. I was getting a headache, so it hurt for me to do so. As he locked the door on us once more, I dropped to the floor for a second night of sleeping on a block of books. I wanted to stay awake to see what he would do then, what he ate (for surely he ate), where he slept (for certainly he slept), but instead, weary from hunger, and from inhaling the centuries as I sifted through the books no one remembered or cared about in a search for those which had been truly lost, which had never been born, I fell asleep, this time more quickly than the night before.

On the third day, I woke, the sun once more in my eyes, and I went through the same morning routine as the day before. I ate mints from a bowl—a bowl whose level never seemed to diminish even as it never seemed to be refilled—until my stomach ached, whether from the hunger itself or from too many mints I could no longer tell. I drank from the faucet, ran damp fingers through my hair. And then, after making sure my hands were entirely dry, I once more walked aisles which twisted and turned and took me such distances the store could not possibly have contained them, and each time somehow led me to shelves I'd never seen during my earlier wanderings in the shop. Had those alcoves even existed until I searched for them?

There I continued to discover the impossible. I found Plato's *Hermocrates*, *The Scented Garden* by Sir Richard Francis Burton, August Strindberg's *The Bleeding Hand*, Malcolm Lowry's *In Ballast to the White Sea*, and Frederik Pohl's *For Some We Loved*. As the day passed, I'd carefully bring them to the front of the store and pile them with the others, a pile the owner, to my relief, left untouched. When I had no energy to continue and paused there, gathering my strength, he looked at what I had done, and then looked at me sadly. And I believed that sadness was genuine.

"Even if you left, and even if you came back, there's no way you could afford all of those," he said. "No one could. They are beyond price."

"I know that," I said. But I'm not sure that I did. I sat down on the bed and gazed at the stack made up of what I had found, a stack which had now grown several feet high. He sat beside me.

"You can't stay here forever, you know," he said. "Because I can't stay here forever."

"Maybe you're right," I said. "But in this moment, I can't think of anywhere else I'd rather be."

"How about... there?"

He waved toward the front glass, and I turned and looked out a window I hadn't bothered looking through since I'd arrived and had begun finding books which existed nowhere else in the universe.

Across the way, I saw the movie marquee I'd passed—was it only two days earlier?—by which a man atop a ladder was changing the title of the film playing there. I watched as down came the large black letters for the theater's recently completed run of SUPERMAN LIVES starring NICOLAS CAGE, and up went the announcement of that day's new movie: FRANCIS FORD COPPOLA'S MEGALOPOLIS with WARREN BEATTY.

The appliance store across the way, in front of which I'd parked, now seemed to be selling only electronics, and on one of the huge televisions in the window I spotted the opening to an episode of *The Twilight Zone*, only when Rod Serling stepped out, he was far older than I'd ever seen him, older than any of us ever had. And my car was gone, replaced by a three-wheeled vehicle which would surely not have been roadworthy in my world. Behind it was what appeared to be little more than a giant glass bubble, and to the front, something that still had the basic structure of a car, but no wheels at all, and huge fins. In fact, none of the cars looked like any I'd ever seen, except maybe in dream.

And the buildings! I saw towers higher than any that had ever existed except in unrealized blueprints, with bridges way above my head that connected the upper floors. A dirigible was moored to the top of an immensely tall skyscraper.

There were people, too, and I tried to make out their faces through the glass, to learn who would walk such streets, but with night falling, they became little more than smudges. Would I have recognized them if I could have made them out? Were they, too, a completion of something lost? Was Stephen Crane out there? Christopher Marlowe? Keats? Shelley?

I yearned to go out and see them, see it all, and almost reached forward and touched the doorknob again, but knew that if I did, and if the door should open, once I passed outside, none of it might be there. All might be as I'd left it days before. And even if it were changed, even if the promise of my vision was fulfilled, I might then not be able to get back in. Though... would I even want to?

But I was tempted, almost beyond resisting. And so, I slept again, only in part because of my fatigue. Mostly, I needed to avoid that temptation. If I slept, perhaps it would sleep as well.

For the first time, when I woke, the owner wasn't at work endlessly reorganizing his books, but standing over me. I stared into his upside-down face, sat up, rubbed my eyes. I tried to see whether the outside world was still as he had shown it to me the night before, but the sun was too bright.

"Is it so bad, where you come from?" he asked as he looked down at me.

It was an unexpected question, one I couldn't bear to answer directly.

"There's a hole in my world," I said. "These are the only things I know which will plug it up."

"But you can't stay here like this. You won't survive. And I have to go. There's a schedule I must keep."

"Then go," I said.

I turned from him and wound my way to the back again, where

on unlabeled shelves which could not possibly exist, I found Hunter S. Thompson's *Prince Jellyfish.*

And James Joyce's *A Brilliant Career*, Stephen King's *The House on Value Street*, and Richard Brautigan's *The God of the Martians*, too.

Books that couldn't be, but in that place, were.

While deeper in the back than I'd ever been before, I heard the ringing of the store's doorbell, the first time it rang since I'd arrived four days before. With no other customers ever having shown, I at first thought the sound meant the owner had left, perhaps hoping to have snuck out while I was beyond his hearing, but then I heard the murmur of voices, two voices, and realized a customer had indeed arrived—the first to arrive since I had, regardless of the line the owner had been trying to sell me.

Curious, I put down my books and headed to the front of the shop, a trip which this time seemed nearly instantaneous and had me wondering how I'd never found that combination of twists and turns before. When I rounded the final corner and found myself in the front area, I was confused—partially by the speed with which I'd gotten there, but also because of what I took at first to be my own reflection on the glass, rather than an actual third person there with us. As I struggled to comprehend why the face before me seemed so familiar, how it could be both like and unlike my own, I froze. Then something broke within me, and I could speak again.

"Andy?" I said, my voice cracking, splintering the name as I realized who and what I was facing. "Is that really... you?"

It couldn't be, but it was. My son, once a child, and fated never to be anything more, now as large as me, as large, as they say, as life. My son—who I'd once found broken beneath his shattered bicycle by the side of the road, abandoned by the driver who'd hit him and could possibly have saved him, now—an adult.

My son—alive.

I ran to him, half afraid that when I hugged him, he'd vanish. But he was solid, and only the return of his embrace kept me from falling to my knees. I cried as I'd been unable to cry for a long time.

"It's OK, Dad," he said, with a voice impossibly deep, the voice of a man decades older than he'd ever been. "I'm here."

"But you can't be here," I said. "You're dead. I lost you."

Even as I said this, I realized the foolishness of those words. Of course, he could be here. All stories would find their endings in this place. Why not his?

"Nothing is ever dead," said the owner, echoing my thoughts. "Nothing is ever lost."

"You've got to leave here, Dad," said my son. "You can't stay in this place. You'll only die."

"I already died out there," I said, looking into eyes that were mine, that were his... that were hers. "I died when you died. Does what happens next really matter?"

"It matters to me."

"Then come with me. Leave with me and let's go there together."

"Dad, that's not the way this works—"

"That's what *he* claimed." I tilted my head toward the owner, not pointing, because I couldn't bear to take my hands off Andy. "He said there were rules to places like this, rules I had to follow. But I don't care. The only way this is going to go is the way I want it to go. The only way I'll leave is if we leave together. I'm not losing you again."

By my son's look, I could tell he believed my threat. No, not threat. *My promise.* But whichever it was, he saw it was real. Andy had always been able to tell when I was telling the truth and when I was merely trying to put one over on him, even when he was a kid. So he knew. He knew I wasn't going anywhere. Not without him.

He nodded at me and the owner in turn, then spun and started walking toward the door. I followed, pausing briefly by stacks of books I'd so carefully collected over the previous days. The titles and authors called out to me, promising endings previously unknown, endings I alone could get to read. But there wasn't anything here I needed. Not any more. Of all the lost endings the universe had to offer, there was only one I needed.

I walked after my son, ready to resume the truncated story that was my life.

But as I stepped over the threshold, though Andy had been mere feet ahead of me, outside, once I was on the other side of the doorway, I was alone.

He was gone.

The scene on the street was as it had been four days before—the movie theater with its superhero cinema, the appliance store with its teasing cartoons, even my car—save for the tickets which had apparently been slid under the windshield each of my days away. But as for my son… he was once more lost.

I turned back to see an empty shop, a handwritten FOR RENT sign in the window, and nothing on the other side of the glass but a few empty shelves.

The counter, with its bowl of mints—gone.

My pile of books unwritten by the authors meant to write them—gone.

And the owner of the store—gone, of course, as well.

But where—where had Andy gone?

I didn't trust that what I saw inside was actually there (or not there, considering what I'd once been led to believe when looking out) and must have blanked out for a moment, because the next thing I knew, I was inside, broken glass at my feet, my voice echoing in the large empty room—though not so large as it once had seemed—as I called out Andy's name.

There was no answer.

I returned to my car, used the parking tickets to wipe the blood from my fingers. And drove. I don't know how long and how far, but I eventually made it home to Barbara, who I told, well, not quite the truth, and who accepted the last tortured explanation I hoped I'd ever have to give her.

But still—where was my son?

I only knew that he was out there somewhere, no longer crumpled by the side of the road. I had to believe that when we stepped through the door, we each returned to our own separate worlds, and he was now where he was meant to be, where no books are lost, no dreams unbuilt, no lives unfinished. It's a world I can't reach. But it's there.

As for me, I no longer take long drives in search of small towns and their hidden treasures, and no longer have to explain to Barbara for having taken them. Knowing those towns, those treasures, are out there is enough.

It has to be.

From DreamForge #5, March 2020

Scott Edelman is author of 100+ published
short stories and has been a finalist for the
Bram Stoker Award eight times. During 13 years
at the Syfy Channel, he served as editor of Science Fiction
Weekly, SCI FI Wire, and Blastr, and was a four-time
Hugo Award finalist for Best Editor. He is host
of the Eating the Fantastic podcast.

Pioneer

by Mark Gallacher

Mars Site 3 Archive, #371 21 August 2110.
Max Grade, Mission Specialist
Personal Journal Entry: Sol 10

My father and my grandfather were both working fishermen, working off the West Coast of Scotland on a six-berth boat called *The Reliant*. Storms that would have been unrecognizable just over a century earlier frequently crossed the Irish Sea, battering the coast with brutal intensity.

Both men were diehards in an industry that was increasingly automated and robotized. They took pride in the physical hard work and hazards of the job. They gladly shared stories of their working lives, recounting tales with unhurried pleasure, as if they were making strong nets from fine rope, often with a glass of whisky to ease their flow. Despite all the technological leaps and bounds, in an ever-shrinking world, storytelling was still treasured.

Both men had married highly educated women, which gave them a certain local notoriety, as if there was a proclivity for the seduction of intelligent, cultured females.

I still have cousins, aunts, and uncles who claim my grandfather,

Old James as he was known, drowned at sea, regardless of the number of times I have corrected them. It is a testament to how family narratives can be more powerful than the events that created them.

My father told me on several occasions that Old James was dead before he hit the water. The whole crew saw it, boat pitching in a storm. It happened so fast Old James didn't even have time to cry out. He died, tipped over, and the sea took him.

His body was found the following day and the autopsy revealed a massive hemorrhage in the brain. No water in the lungs. He was almost certainly dead when he hit the water.

My father quit fishing after that, retrained at college and became a schoolteacher. But people still used his fishing name: James Younger.

"Just call me James," he would sometimes say, knowing full well that he would take James Younger to the grave.

I think he named me Max just to make sure there would be no more naming nonsense. But my friends at school called me Mac J, which morphed into J-Max when I moved to the USA to take my Master's in Geology. My mother laughed when she heard J-Max for the first time and said the name made it sound like I was a rapper. My father moaned when he heard it. But the name stuck and he never corrected anyone when it was used it in his presence.

Old James. James Younger. J-Max. What will I call my son, should I be lucky enough to have one? Will he look up at the stars and planets the way I have looked at them?

My father and grandfather were sea travelers. They witnessed bone-shaking storms, delicate winter sunrises, bright stars in the deep darkness of cold night. Far from any shore, they saw ghostly meteors cross the vast firmament. They knew the old wonders and signs, more ancient than recorded history.

My father was the most fervent dreamer of the two men. He loved astronomy and he dreamed of Mars the way some men dreamed of unspoiled wilderness.

My father also spoke of Mars the way some men recounted their former dreams of youth, voices burdened by time and personal choices, or quietly, with sudden grief, like a slackening and pulling— a tidal sadness shaping the heart's rhythm.

At a certain age, a man's life has a kind of heft, with which he can gauge his success or failure. The roads not travelled measured in relief and regret. My father reached that age with a certain quality of stoicism. It is what it is.

But best of all, my father sometimes dreamed of Mars with a boy's delight and when he showed me the books and the pictures he had collected, hundreds of hi-res images of vistas and craters, of NASA landers and rovers, immaculate graphs and animations, close-ups of drilled rocks and those first tantalizing signs of water on the steep slopes of highlands overlooking vast plains, he spoke with breathless reverence, he spoke with wonder.

He showed me Mars Site 1.

"A bloody near disaster from Day Two. The whole site swallowed up by a planet-wide sandstorm. Luckily, the crew managed to take flight and return home. They called it *The Longest Stopover in History* in the news."

And in hushed tones, he pointed out Mars Site 2, unoccupied because the Mars Mission 2 crew never arrived. Their ship suffered a fatal structural failure and broke up halfway between Earth and Mars, spinning away in the great void, lost forever. No time for goodbyes or messages for loved ones. Gone forever.

"It's all there, Max. Robots on standby in the Living Domes. They call the robots serfs. Did you know that? All the equipment. The serfs. The rovers. The automated water distiller. The ice excavator. The food stores. The nuclear power source still running. It's a ghost site."

"Why don't they send another crew?"

"Politics. Superstition. A lot of people think it's in the wrong location. They think the next site should be here. About ninety kilometers farther south. That's probably going to be Mars Site 3 in about twenty years' time. You'll see it. Me too."

"Maybe I'll be an astronaut and go there. Maybe it'll be me."

"Why not? I reckon you can do anything you set your mind to."

The moons of Jupiter and Saturn could also excite my father's imagination, but all his passion was for Mars. It was Mars where life would be found. It was Mars where the next step in human colonization would take place. It was Mars his boyhood dreams returned to in the cradle of his sleep.

I was not an only son. I had an older brother, Peter. It seemed at first that Peter had won the DNA jackpot as far as our family was concerned. Fiercely intelligent and academically gifted, his early life was full of promise. And for a while, his career as an engineer was in the ascendant.

But he was also an alcoholic. His addiction took ten years to ruin his career and marriage and another ten years to kill him. In between, his drinking broke the unbreakable bonds of family, until they were a thin sliver of memory and love.

I had no such academic gift. I had to work laboriously at school and university. Small steps. I did have my mother's love of art and poetry. And for a brief while, I thought I might become a writer. But I loved science and exploration too, and my father encouraged all things scientific in our house. Eventually the pull of science was stronger than the pull of art.

But watching my brother, I learned one thing quickly. I was going to have to work hard and I was going to have to be alert to the dangers of any kind of alcohol or stimulant.

So, my journey to Mars began with my father's serious "Why not?" It's as simple as that. The greatest journeys start from the simplest of steps.

We talked about our conversation over the family dinner that night. My older brother laughed out loud. My father raised his glass, to toast me. "And why not? What's to stop Max from becoming an astronaut and flying to Mars?"

My mother did not laugh or wave the notion away. She looked at us with her clear, intelligent gaze. "Wonderful," she said. "Fill your boots."

Why do I write about such things, millions of miles from home, on another world, at Mars Site 3?

Well, Mars is a cold and dim-lit place, and looking out across the blood red plains and dry vistas, I am inevitably drawn to memory, and the cradle of all memory is home. It is a particular kind of longing and remembering, special to Mars.

I have discussed it with the other team members and they have had the same kind of experience. We call it Earth-dreaming. A sad reverie that overtakes you as you watch Mars's brief blue sunset fade on the horizon and your inner gaze turns to Earth and home. Our fragile blue origin in the cosmic darkness.

Mars is the new world that sings of the old. And even when memory is not stirred, our dreams are lit with the green brightness of childhood, the blue vividness of youth, and all our bright tomorrows not yet made yesterday.

I write about these things because Peter is gone, my father is gone, and my mother is gone. All gone and none to know I stand here on the Red Planet.

And when I stand at the observation bay window and look out at the Red Plains and rolling hills of Mars, I whisper in love and gratitude:

Look, Father. Look, Mother. I made it. On Mars.

From DreamForge # 2, June 2019

Mark Gallacher is a Scottish writer and poet who lives in Denmark with his wife and two sons. His stories have been shortlisted twice for the Fish Short Story Prize, longlisted for the 2017 Retreat West Short Story Competition, and published in New Writing Scotland and in print and online magazines.

The Ghost of a Smile

by John Jos. Miller

I quite enjoy my work.

I get to travel a lot and I meet some very interesting people and the hours aren't bad at all. I am but one of many who do what I do. I haven't been at it for very long, at least as compared to some who have been on the job for a very long time indeed. I don't think about my beginnings much. I was birthed in a gesture of kindness, a helping hand offered in a time of need, and I grew into an image painted or drawn or carved on wood or stone. I thrived upon and was given form by the written word and was empowered by belief that grew out of love, because words have power as do the beliefs shaped by them.

I am a psychopomp, but for the living, not the dead, because the living are more often in need of help. I am guardian and guide. I am the mystery in the night, the seemingly random road taken that leads to wonder.

I am the ghost of a smile.

Richard Logan looked up into the London sky, so bright and sunny just a moment before and now pelting large, cold drops of rain that would soon soak him to the skin. The pedestrians surrounding him on the narrow but busy street between the tube station and the British Museum were opening their umbrellas, but Richard, new to the city and not used to the sudden vagaries of London's weather, wasn't carrying one.

He was a dark-haired, serious-faced young man, not yet thirty, with long-fingered hands that looked like they belonged to an artist. And in a way, they did. He was an American surgeon on exchange with a London hospital and was on his way to take his first look at the British Museum when the sudden downpour hit. Pedestrians surged around him as he stood for a moment looking about, and then his eyes lit on the small, unprepossessing shop before him. Inside its display window facing the street was an array of old, dusty books. The shop's nature was confirmed by its window's archaically ornate gold leaf lettering, so badly treated by time that he could barely read it: Old Books and Manuscripts.

Murmuring to himself, *You never know,* Richard went up the three stone steps that had been polished to a dull sheen by the footwear of centuries of customers and threw open the creaky door. A small bell jangled as he closed it.

He let his eyes adjust to the dimness as he stood in the entrance. It looked, Richard thought, much as he'd imagined an antiquarian London bookstore would look. Books crowded sagging wooden shelves, were piled in odd corners and upon random tables, filling every nook and cranny of the irregularly shaped room. He took a deep breath and caught the scent of paper well aged and imbued with the countless smells of the generations of their owners. Pipe tobacco of university dons, perfume of fine ladies. Lurking spices of near-every type of national cuisine. Richard smiled as he moved through the room and caught a subtle whiff of marijuana wafting off a stack of vintage *Rolling Stone* magazines piled on an end table set beside a comfy leather reading chair whose upholstery had worn through on both arms.

All this place needs, he thought, *is a plump older gent dressed in baggy tweeds with a pince nez teetering on the tip of his nose.*

"Can I help?"

He started at the voice. She'd come from an inner room as silently as a cat and he half-turned, looking over his shoulder. He floundered helplessly for a moment, then gestured toward the street.

"Oh—I was just… the rain…"

He saw the immediate dismissal in her eyes and felt a sudden stab in his heart for the second time in moments.

They were, he thought, the most beautiful eyes he'd ever seen. Violet, with flecks of green jade and honied gold. She had long black hair and a fine-boned face. She turned from him and moved away through the cluttered room with feline suppleness.

"I mean." He was suddenly desperate to regain her grace. "I collect books. Love them. Always have."

She had gone behind the waist-high counter and arced an exquisite eyebrow at him. Richard approached the counter, feeling like an idiot. He was by no means a player. He had a certain innate shyness, but mainly he never could find time for women. From less than an illustrious background, he'd had to work his way through college to supplement the scholarships he'd accumulated, because his single-parent mother had three other children and was in no position to help him with the bills. He also had no desire to start life a hundred thousand dollars in the red, so he'd lived frugally and concentrated on his goal of becoming a surgeon. He'd always loved fixing stuff, making things whole again. He'd focused on his career like a laser because to him there was no higher calling than mending people.

But he wasn't lying to her about the books. They had been his friends all his life. A confirmed scrounger through old bookstores, he had the patience to browse through hundreds of volumes and the eye to sift the gold from the dross. It was the one hobby he allowed himself, and now that he was actually making real money, he had deeper pockets to indulge his desires.

"Do you have anything special?" he asked suddenly.

"Special?" She seemed doubtful. "What do you mean?"

"Oh, you know. Unusual. Scarce." He didn't want to say expensive. No, definitely not that. He could withstand the indifference in her gaze, but he never wanted to see contempt in it.

She looked at him for a moment, then slowly nodded. She gestured to the glass counter behind which she stood.

Richard looked down, eye ranging over a couple of old, mostly battered volumes given the honor of being kept under glass. His gaze glided over them for a moment, then stopped, came back, and rested on the red cloth cover with the faded embossed gilt oval illustration centered by three additional lines of gilt along the cover's margins.

"Can I see that?" he asked, pointing.

She looked at him, momentarily frowning, then shrugged. He wondered at her brief hesitance, but she took the volume out and laid it on the counter before him, and as he flipped it open, he stared in disbelief.

First, the signature. Clean, flowing in a fluid, looping style, in the purple ink the author favored: "To My Friend Jennifer, yours always, Lewis Carroll." Then Richard's eyes flicked to the bottom of the page to see "MacMillan and Co." and below that the year "1866."

"*Alice's Adventures in Wonderland*," Richard said in a soft voice like Galahad stumbling upon the Holy Grail. "A first edition."

But, of course, he knew that it really wasn't. It was the first unsuppressed edition. The real first had been published the year before, but John Tenniel, the artist, had been bitterly disappointed by the quality of the printing and had Charles Dodgson—the author's real name—recall the entire run and make the publisher issue another. Very few copies of that true first run had somehow made it out into the world—twenty-two still existed. For all practical purposes, the second printing was generally accepted by collectors as the first. And that edition was by no means common, having had a run of only a few thousand copies, most of which had vanished over

the years. Few of the survivors were still in the original binding state.
Even fewer had been signed by Dodgson. And fewer yet had been
signed by him as "Lewis Carroll."

"Jennifer must have been a child," Richard murmured.

"How do you know that?"

He looked up into her eyes, which were regarding him intently.

"When Dodgson signed copies of *Alice* for adults, he always
signed as Best Regards or Best Wishes or whatever from the author.
Unless he knew the owner well, in which case he used his real name.
He only signed as 'Lewis Carroll' for kids."

She nodded slowly, and Richard felt that he had scored some
obscure points in an even obscurer game that was being played
between them.

"She was my grandfather's great-grandmother," she said. "I was
named for her."

"Jennifer." He was a bit taken aback by this. "It's been in your
family that long?"

She nodded.

"And you're selling it?"

"It's what we do here," she said.

He looked back down at the book.

"It's in terrible condition," she said, not exactly employing the
hard sell.

Richard nodded. He'd noticed that right off, even before he'd
opened it, but the thrill of discovering the signature as well the date
had driven that from his mind. It looked as if it had gone through a
conflagration. The front cover was in decent condition for a book
that was a hundred and fifty years old and the beginning pages were
all right. But the last third had been damaged by both fire and water,
with the destruction growing worse throughout. Richard inspected it
gingerly. Some pages were touched by damp, some singed by fire.
Near the end, only a few lines of the last few pages survived. The
back cover was only a charred fragment.

"It happened during the Blitz," she explained. "My grandfather's house got hit by a German bomb."

Richard looked at her.

"Everyone survived, but," she shrugged, "they lost much of their collection. They salvaged what they could."

"What do you want for it?" Richard asked.

"Three thousand pounds," she said steadily.

"Done."

He could not read the sudden look in her eyes.

It had been a month since Jennifer Barnstable had sold *Alice* and there was still an empty place inside her. She wondered how long it would last. She suspected that it would be there forever.

She'd been stunned by his quick acceptance of the price she'd quoted. It was certainly high, given the volume's condition. But there was the signature. And the personal attachment. She was almost furious that the young fool had accepted her outrageous price without a murmur of protest, but then she realized that her anger was actually directed at herself. Yes, it was a bookstore. Yes, they sold books. Yes, that book was on the shelf. But she'd never expected someone to come in off the street and whisk it away like that. She cursed her stupid self-confidence, because deep down she knew that she'd thought that he'd never pay that price, that she was playing some kind of mysterious game of truth or dare with him. And he'd won it. An offer accepted is an offer to be honored, no matter the cost or the remorse after the fact.

Jennifer stood behind the counter and looked down at the empty spot in the glass case that she hadn't the heart to fill. It might, she thought, remain empty forever.

The bell above the door jangled as someone came into the shop. He paused in the doorway, closing his lowered umbrella. It was raining, just like that day a month ago, just like it had seemed to be every day since she had given *Alice* away.

"This time," he said as he collapsed his black umbrella, "I came prepared. I'm getting used to your weather."

It was him, Jennifer realized. Richard Logan. She remembered the name on the black Amex card. Doctor Richard Logan.

She tried to conjure up some resentment toward him in general, toward this unexpected reappearance specifically, but found herself unable to do so. After all, it wasn't his fault. He was just a random customer, with the innocent face of a blameless puppy and eyes that…

Jennifer looked down at the brown paper-wrapped package he'd laid on the counter.

"What's this?" she said.

"Open it," he said, with, Jennifer thought, more than a trace of smugness.

Frowning, she removed the wrapping with deft hands, and when the first bit of red cover appeared through a final layer of tissue paper, she knew instantly. It was *Alice*. But *Alice* whole and well again. Not new-looking. She recognized every slight imperfection of the front cover and quickly, though carefully, turned the pages. It wasn't tarted up in buckram or red morocco with fine marbled end papers and raised bands across the spine. The new parts of the book were mated perfectly with the old. The repairs were seamless. If Jennifer hadn't known where they began, she couldn't have spotted them. The back cover matched the front perfectly and had the same moderate signs of aging.

"Do you like it?" he asked her.

Jennifer could only stare for a moment. Then she asked, "You did this?"

He laughed, a little self-consciously. "Good lord, no. I actually do dabble in book repair, but I wouldn't trust that book to these hands." He held them up. "I mean, I know my way around the human heart pretty well, but I found an old bindery in Bath to restore this particular patient."

"It must have cost a fortune," Jennifer said, half to herself.

He shrugged. "It's what I do. I fix things. But I know to call in specialists when they're needed."

He looked quite pleased with himself, Jennifer thought. As well he should. She felt momentary jealousy that he could afford to do something she and her family never could, but quickly got over any resentment. That was the way of things, wasn't it?

"Well," Jennifer said, slowly, touching *Alice* gently on the cover, "thank you for showing me this. I'm happy that—"

Suddenly she couldn't go on.

His face changed expression and he shook his head. "No—you don't... It's *for* you," he said. "It belongs here, to you. I just... fixed it. You see, we don't own things like this. We're their custodians. When the time comes, we pass them on. To your children, perhaps."

Jennifer was stunned. "I can't take this from you."

He seemed genuinely bewildered. "Why not?"

"Well—I don't have any children." The utter absurdity of it hit her. "I don't even have a boyfriend."

The look in his eyes suddenly changed again and Jennifer felt them catch hers and hold. "Someday," he said, "you may. Have both."

They looked at each other for a long moment that stretched and held and then Jennifer saw something move on his face. His eyes widened and there was such a look in them—

Jennifer realized that his gaze had flickered fractionally away from hers, over her shoulder and past her. She glanced in the mirror that was situated at the end of the counter that allowed her to see most of the room behind her, put there as a half-hearted gesture to ward against shop lifters. And she saw it, too.

There, sitting atop a dusty bookshelf, well toward the shop's rear, was a large, fat, orange- and white-striped cat, smiling a huge impossible smile, and as they watched for a moment that seemed to last almost forever, it gradually faded until it was just that smile, and then that too drifted away on the dusty air.

• • •

I am a psychopomp for the living. I furnish the ticket that can take you to your heart's desire, but you have to figure out how exactly to use it. I am the road unexpected. The mystery in the night. The ghost of a smile.

I do quite enjoy my work.

For Joseph and Nicole,
with all imaginable good wishes,
from (to borrow a phrase) the Author

From DreamForge #4, December 2019

John Jos. Miller is a science-fiction author known for
his work in the long-running Wild Cards shared universe series
of original anthologies and novels, edited by George R.R. Martin.
He has also published nine novels, and nearly 30 short stories
and eight comic book scripts. "The Ghost of a Smile" was written
for two friends of John's and appeared in a chapbook
that was offered to the guests at their wedding,
a fact which makes the tale all the sweeter.

The Spiral Ranch

by Sarena Ulibarri

Two cows were missing from the Spiral Ranch. Piper tapped the Pasture 7 control screen and activated the LASSO app to check the headcount against her wrist unit. The app confirmed: two fewer than yesterday. She swiped over to the com and dialed Pasture 3.

"Hey, Jayce."

His voice came through the speaker a moment later. "Yes'm."

"You have any extra cows over there?"

"Uh, no, ma'am."

"Any missing?"

"Don't reckon so. Why, what's up?"

Piper pushed her hat back from her sweaty brow and scratched her head. "No reason."

They'd rotated the herd up from Pasture 6 three days before, and all the cattle had been accounted for then. Piper hefted herself up onto the wall—an inward-bowing lip that let in fresh air and sunlight but kept the cattle from stumbling over the ledge—and peered down at the street eight stories below. No cows were splattered on the sidewalk. A couple of reggae buskers played on the corner and some tourists pointed cameras toward the skyscraper. Piper lowered herself back onto the grass. Maybe something had gone wrong with the tracking chips. She walked up the slope and around the curve until she hit the gate leading to Pasture 8, doing a manual headcount on the way. Still two short.

The logs on the robotic milking station showed both of the missing cows had been milked the night before, but not this morning. The moveable slats that made a cattle guard around the cargo elevator were open and seemed to be functioning fine, so it was unlikely the cows had taken a ride down to another pasture. Besides, the LASSO app could detect any active chip within a two-mile radius. Wherever the cows were, they weren't in the building.

She checked the fallow pastures all the same, but to no avail, so she headed to the slaughterhouse. The Spiral Ranch was primarily a dairy producer, but they had small-scale meat processing as well, hidden in the basement so the people of Austin could pretend it didn't exist. It was Piper's second-least favorite part of the building.

She found Monique down there, singing century-old show tunes while she loaded packages of beef into delivery bots. Monique's logs revealed no records of the missing cows, even when Piper checked for deleted or manipulated files. They were just... gone.

Up to the corporate office, then. Piper's *least* favorite part of the Spiral Ranch.

She climbed the stairs from the slaughterhouse up to the lobby, and caught the public elevator there, riding to the top next to a few restaurant patrons. The elevator doors opened on a wide breezeway. The lattice of the rooftop garden crisscrossed green overhead, vines climbing down the walls on either side. The tourists turned left toward the restaurant, and Piper turned right toward Adrianne's office.

She pushed the button next to the frosted glass office door. The button turned green, but Piper hesitated a moment before she turned the wrought iron flower doorknob, steeling herself for what was likely to be an unpleasant interaction.

Adrianne sat behind a glass desk, arguing with someone on a holographic screen. Floor-to-ceiling windows stretched behind her, and flowering trees too tropical for central Texas lined the interior wall. Piper's boots left scuffs on the immaculate white tile floor. She hung back awkwardly until Adrianne managed to close out the conversation and the screen disappeared.

"What was that all about?"

Adrianne crossed her legs, dangling one high heel off a toe. "Just more investors threatening to pull support unless we can improve our public image."

"What's wrong with our public image?"

Adrianne raised an eyebrow and let out a mirthless laugh. "Really? You didn't see that smear video some reporter did, accusing us of animal cruelty and excess waste?"

Piper shrugged. "It ain't true."

"In any case, I need to set up a new advertising campaign to combat it, and the investors are shooting down *all* my ideas."

"You could make an ad telling people how we've reduced the price of milk and cheese in the city by more than two-thirds."

Adrianne scoffed. "In a city that's sixty-percent vegan."

"How about how we're a major energy producer, both solar and methane—"

"Every damn building is an energy producer!" Adrianne rubbed a hand across her face. "I'm sorry. Um, what was it you came in here to tell me? I'm real busy."

'Course you are. There was a time when Piper might have stopped into her office just to chat or make evening plans. But those days, it seemed, were long gone. Piper and Adrianne had been good friends back in college, and had drawn up the plans for the Spiral Ranch together. But that relationship had devolved since becoming boss and employee. Piper wanted nothing to do with all the paper-pushing, and Adrianne seemed to want nothing to do with the animals.

"I can't afford to have my inventory disappearing," Adrianne said after Piper told her about the missing cattle.

"I just thought you should know."

"Maybe there's something wrong with that app of yours. I've been looking into alternatives we might want to upgrade to. If you have some time, I'd like to go over them with you."

Piper bristled. She'd coded the LASSO app from scratch and she was proud of it. It was running just fine. She stood, slapping her hat against her thigh. "I'm real busy."

The next morning, two more cows were missing. Her searches and inquiries proved as fruitless as the day before, so when night fell, Piper stayed behind. Jayce had stopped by to do a repair on the manure collector. After he'd packed his tools and set the clam-shaped machine rolling on its course again, he hesitated by the elevator.

"Staying late, boss?"

"Think I'm gonna camp out and see if I can solve the mystery of the disappearing cows."

"Want me to stay with you?"

Piper shrugged. "Only if you want."

He stepped into the elevator and Piper assumed he was gone for the night, but he reappeared about an hour later with a couple of roast beef sandwiches, two sleeping bags, and a guitar.

The sun sank in a dull orange display. Piper lay in the grass of Pasture 7 with her head propped on a rolled-up sleeping bag, swatting at the occasional fly. Some of the cows kept grazing, but most folded their legs beneath them to sleep. Jayce picked a slow, amateur rhythm on his guitar. From somewhere down the street, a live band rocked out for an energetic crowd.

"Why don't we have cameras?" Jayce said suddenly. "So's to watch what happens to the cows at night, I mean."

"You really want cameras watching your ass work all day?"

"Not really," Jayce said. "But cameras are everywhere else."

Piper shifted on her roll-pillow. She'd been the one to convince Adrianne that cameras were a waste. She disliked the constant surveillance and data mining that were ubiquitous to modern life. "Never needed them, I guess. LASSO keeps track of the cows, tells us their vitals, better than a camera would."

"'Til something weird happens."

"'Til something weird happens," Piper agreed.

After another long silence filled only with Jayce's next attempted song and the shuffling of the cattle, Jayce said, "Think it's aliens?"

"What's aliens?"

"What's taking the cows."

"What kind of fool question is that?"

Jayce looked hurt. "It ain't a fool question. Didn't you never hear about them cattle mutilations in Colorado?"

Piper raised an eyebrow at him.

"Back in the twentieth century. Lots of cattle were getting cut up right in the field, surgical-like. No one knew who was doin' it. Seemed like aliens."

"It's damn near the end of the twenty-first century now and we still ain't found no aliens," Piper said. "If they're around, I don't know why they're being so sneaky and picking on cows."

"Fair enough," Jayce said. "But no one did ever figure out who was slicing up them cows."

"No, I remember now," Piper said. "It was the government, wasn't it?"

"What would the government want with cows?"

"There was some toxic spill or nuclear accident. They were testing the cows to see how dangerous it really was, without telling anyone."

Jayce shrugged. "Could be the government, I guess, but I thought they shut down all the nuke plants along with the coal."

"I don't know who it is," Piper said. "But I'm going to figure it out."

Jayce eventually fell asleep, snoring inside his sleeping bag. Piper kept hers as a pillow, crossing her arms to keep warm as the night cooled. Her toes itched, but she refused to take off her boots. If something happened, she needed to be ready.

Near two in the morning, the sounds of live music faded away, replaced with a chorus of cicadas. Piper was fighting to stay awake when a new soft buzz joined the night noises. She sat up, tuned her ear to it. The cattle staggered to their feet, pawed the ground, bumped into each other. A pair of glowing red eyes peered over the pasture wall.

Piper jolted. The whirring grew louder, and then a large drone darted into the pasture. The cattle panicked. Piper tossed her sleeping roll at Jayce and he snorted awake.

"What the…" He jumped to his feet and narrowly avoided a stampede. "I told you it was aliens!"

"It's not aliens," Piper said. "It's twenty-first century cattle rustling." She snapped pictures with her wrist unit. It was an old police drone, but any identifying marks had been scuffed off. These drones had been common in the skies of any major city about a decade ago, but they kept getting shot down, captured, or hacked, so they'd been decommissioned and auctioned off. The drones were supposed to be strong enough to pick up a small car. This one positioned itself over a cow and a set of claws appeared, reaching down like an oversized arcade game.

Jayce grabbed a rope from next to the elevator and edged toward the drone. The propellers whacked the rope away. He steadied his feet, tossed it again.

"Gotcha." The rope caught around the body of the drone. Its claws clenched around the cow's torso and lifted. These were dwarf cattle, about half the size and weight of their flat-ranch predecessors, but still a good five hundred pounds a head. The drone snatched it up like it was a plush toy. Jayce dug his heels into the grass, but the drone buzzed toward the open air gap, the cow mooing in protest.

Piper homed the LASSO app in on that cow's chip. The rest of the herd clustered in the farthest corner of the pasture. Jayce held strong, but the drone pulled him off his feet and he slid across the grass toward the ledge.

"Jayce, let go!" Piper ran after him. Drone and cow disappeared into the night. He let the rope slide out of his hands just in time to thunk against the wall.

She yanked him to his feet. "Come on. The LASSO app has a range of two miles. We can track where it's going." He stumbled after her toward the elevator.

She tapped her boots in impatience, checking her wrist unit as the cargo elevator snailed its way to Pasture 1. The cow's chip was still in range, but getting fainter. The elevator door opened and the two of them burst out and ran down the stairs to the lobby. Outside, her electric motorcycle hummed to life. Jayce climbed on behind her. She zoomed off, transferring visual of the LASSO app to her bike's console with a shout. Her hat flew back, caught around her throat by the leather chin strap.

Just past Sixth Street, she caught sight of the cow, floating placidly through the air between buildings. Its bellowing moo echoed through the quiet streets and it released a patty that splattered across a restaurant's sign. *That's not gonna help our public image,* Piper thought.

"They're heading for the river," Jayce shouted.

Piper looked back to the road. Sure enough. She dipped the bike into a dangerously sharp left turn. The drone crossed the river, widening the space between them. Piper considered the roadways. If she followed them, it would be another half a mile before they could cross.

"Hold on!" She bumped the bike up a sidewalk and across a pedestrian bridge.

Twice more she lost sight of the drone, but the cow's location kept blipping on her screen. West of the city, where the buildings disappeared and the Carbon Sequestration Forests grew thick, the drone disappeared from sight and the blip on her screen showed it was headed deep into the forest. She pulled the motorcycle off to the edge of the road. Driving across a pedestrian bridge was one thing, but forging through a forest was another. It was a hearty bike, but not an off-roader.

"It's them radical occupiers, ain't it?" Jayce asked.

"Has to be." Piper dropped the kickstand and stepped off. Jayce followed.

"I've got cousins that sympathize with them," he said. "Always telling me how the government stole the land from them to control food production."

"Guess they want to start their own herd." Piper examined the terrain on the map, but the resolution got fuzzy a mile or so in, right where the drone was heading.

Huge swaths of formerly agricultural land had been turned into Carbon Sequestration Forests in the mid-21st century. It was part of a global re-forestation program to counteract dangerous CO_2 levels in the atmosphere, and helped move agriculture into city centers, where crops were now grown in closed-system vertical farms and community rooftop gardens. Even before the massive bee die-out that caused most of the remaining flat farms and ranches to fail, agriculture had already been moving cityward to reduce transportation costs. Piper remembered the shortages and riots from her early childhood, when her own family had to give up their small ranch and move into one of Austin's new arcologies. There were still people who claimed both the bees and the CO_2 levels were just conspiracies, like Jayce had said.

The drone whirred overhead, going back the way it had come, now with no bovine cargo. "Feeling up for a hike?"

"You're not going in there?" Jayce whispered.

"This is our chance to find out exactly where they're hiding out. We can take their GPS coordinates straight to the police."

"They got guns, Piper."

"That's why we need to be all sneaky-like. You don't want to join me, you can stay here and keep a lookout."

His mouth opened and closed a few times before he said, "Yeah. Yeah, okay, I'll come with you."

They hid the bike a few yards into the trees, then picked their way through the underbrush as best they could with only the full moon filtered through the branches and the glow of Piper's wrist unit. It got sluggish and glitchy the farther they trekked into the forest, as though the signal were being jammed. A device that didn't have the customization and firewalls Piper's did probably would have shut down halfway there. The cow's blip reported high adrenaline levels, but other than that, the animal was fine.

Jayce grabbed her arm and pointed. Piper followed his eyeline to a thin wire she was inches from tripping. They backed up, hyper-vigilant for other traps. From nearby came the familiar lowing of cattle. A few yards over, the trees broke enough to reveal a small clearing, with all five of the missing cows grazing between jagged tree stumps. Another blip appeared on the LASSO app—a sixth stolen cow heading in.

Jayce lingered back, but Piper crept closer, avoiding a few more trip wires, and took pictures. The drone whirred into sight. The cattle scattered and men emerged from a shack. Piper ducked behind a juniper.

A man with a thick horseshoe mustache tossed a lasso around the cow's neck while a man with a curly mullet used a handheld controller to release the drone's claws from around the cow. A third man, bulky and muscular, gave the animal some kind of shot. The drone settled into the field and lay like a giant dormant spider. Piper licked her lips. With the right equipment, she could hack it, easy.

A border collie looked her direction and began to bark. She picked her way to where Jayce waited, and the dog kept barking but didn't follow. By the time they made it back to the bike, she had sore feet and a fair number of scratches and burrs, and at least one tick.

She swiped through the images on her wrist unit, most of which were dark and fuzzy. "Let's hope this will be good enough for the cops."

Jayce frowned. "I don't think we should go to the cops."

"What? Why not?"

"It's like to take forever that way. They'd probably pick off an entire herd before the paperwork even got filed."

Piper nodded. "Fair enough."

It would also bring a lot more public attention to the ranch, which would just aggravate Adrianne's problems. The sky was beginning to lighten—dawn already. Fatigue fogged her brain, but ideas were beginning to coalesce like clouds on the horizon.

"Okay, no cops. Not yet anyway." Piper kick-started her motorcycle. "Let's see if we can beat them at their own game."

Jayce went in to work, but Piper called in sick, leaving the message before Adrianne got in so she wouldn't have to talk to her. She slept through the morning, then gathered the equipment she needed in the afternoon. That night, she scanned into the Spiral Ranch, locked and armed the lobby doors behind her, took the public elevator all the way up to the top, then climbed the spiral staircase to the rooftop garden.

The open-air garden mixed decorative plants among the vegetables the restaurant used, and it offered a fantastic view of the city. Piper hung her hat from the corner of an ornate bench and waited for the drone, with a tablet on her lap containing a program she'd put together that afternoon.

A corner of Adrianne's office window was visible through the lattice flooring. The lights were still on. *Was she really working this late? This investor thing must really have her spooked.*

When the drone whirred into sight, Piper was ready. She latched onto its signal, then directed it to veer right. It veered right.

"Easy as pie," she muttered as she lowered the drone into the garden. She crouched over it. With a few tweaks, she could keep control of it while she sent it back into the forest to retrieve the cows.

The propellers whirred suddenly to life and Piper ducked out of its way barely in time as the drone darted back to its original course. She scrambled for her tablet. By the time she'd recalibrated it, the drone had reappeared, cow in claws. The drone died for a second, dropping two stories. "No, no, no." Piper leaned over the ledge. The drone caught, rose, and headed away from the Spiral Ranch. Piper latched onto its signal again, and it jerked, swayed, not sure which commands to obey. It veered dangerously close to a nearby high-rise apartment building. Piper held her breath. The cow bellowed in panic. Then the drone veered back toward her.

And crashed straight through Adrianne's floor-to-ceiling window. Piper raced down the staircase and across the breezeway. Adrianne's frosted door was also shattered, so she stepped through the frame.

Adrianne looked from the drone to Piper with a horrified expression. The cow staggered to its feet; the drone claws opened and closed against the floor as though reaching for the cow. Glass powder crunched under Piper's boots. She leapt onto the sputtering drone, yanking wires and smashing circuits until the lights stopped blinking and it lay still.

"What the hell is going on?" Adrianne demanded.

The cow mooed and circled the office. The safety glass had shattered so finely it covered the cow's hide like snow. It was relatively unharmed, but definitely spooked.

Piper climbed off the drone and opened her mouth to explain, but Adrianne cut her off. "No, you know what? Get this animal out of my office first."

This "animal" is the root of your livelihood, Piper wanted to tell her, or have you forgotten it's not all paperwork and advertising?

She patted the cow's rump and led it out to the cargo elevator, down into Pasture 7. Back upstairs, Piper stood in the doorway, catching her breath. Adrianne shook bits of shattered glass out of her chair.

"Just what the hell do you think you're playing at?"

"The missing cows." Piper gestured toward the drone. "This is what's been taking them."

Adrianne pinched her nose. "And you thought crashing it through my window was the best way to get rid of it?"

Piper couldn't bite back the sarcasm. "*Obviously.*" She strode over and tried to heft up one side of the drone, but it was too heavy, so she gave up and headed back toward the door without it. "The cow's okay, by the way."

"Don't turn your back on me."

"Why?" Piper rounded on her. "You've turned your back on the whole point of what we built here. You sit at the top of your glass tower, completely removed from the ranch."

Adrianne took a long breath and spoke in a lower voice: "There are a lot of details involved in running—"

"You were supposed to lead school groups! Teach them about livestock, about where milk comes from and how we process methane energy. You were supposed to keep it local and simple, not be pandering to investors and trying to franchise out to every other city. We were supposed to be a community pillar and cultural heritage site. But we're nothing but an architectural novelty. You won't even step your dainty shoes in a pasture anymore."

That had been building for a long time. Adrianne blinked at her. "Franchising? What are you talking about?"

Of course *that* was the only part of Piper's rant that Adrianne noticed. A company in Pennsylvania wanted to do a Spiral Ranch knock-off; Piper had assumed they'd tried to franchise and Adrianne had asked for too much, but based on her current confusion, maybe they'd side-stepped her all along. Though she'd turned down an offer to work for them, she'd recently been reconsidering.

"Nothing. Nevermind. This isn't the right time to talk about it. We need to—"

The alarm sounded. Lights flashed and Adrianne's wall-screen showed a schematic of the Spiral Ranch, the point of violation blinking red at its base: the lobby doors on the ground level. "They're here," Piper said. "I should have known they'd come after I disabled the drone. Can you lock them in?"

Adrianne tapped furiously at the screen for a moment, then shook her head.

"Great, looks like I have to do the dirty work again."

Piper tore down the staircase four steps at a time, slamming the doors open at each pasture as she passed them. She had no plan, she just knew this was her herd, and she would be damned if she let them be carted off into the forest. All the pastures that were supposed to have cattle were fine, until Pasture 3. It was empty, and the gate leading down to Pasture 2 hung off its hinges.

She hesitated at the door to the lobby. No one should have been able to get to the Pastures by either stairs or elevator without an employee badge, but *someone* had made it through. Piper eased the door open a crack, heard a man's voice, and pulled it quietly shut. After a deep breath, she pushed it open again, peering through the smallest sliver she could manage.

"Sorry for the disturbance, officer," the man was saying to the screen in the wall. "We're gettin' them cows back under control now."

The man was nothing more than a Wrangler-clad silhouette against the screen, but she knew that voice.

"Jayce, you son of a—" Piper muttered under her breath.

But then he cleared the screen, turned to another man lurking in the shadows, and said, "Okay, I told 'em what you said. Stop pointing that gun at me now."

The man with the handlebar mustache didn't lower his shotgun. "I might if you'd'a cooperated from the beginning."

"This is my job, Mack. These are my friends."

"What, the cows?"

"No, you smog-head. Them girls who run this place."

With a ding, the elevator opened and one cow clomped out. The man with the curly mullet herded the cow toward a livestock trailer, which was backed right up to the lobby door. The muscular man leaned out of the elevator. "How many more?"

"'Bout ten."

Muscles groaned. "This is so obnoxious." He stepped back and the elevator doors shut.

Piper smirked. The cargo elevator skipped the lobby and went straight from Pasture 1 to the slaughterhouse. The rustlers would have to transfer the cows one at a time into the public elevator to get them down here. That should buy some time, anyway.

"What's going on?" Adrianne hissed at her ear. Piper jumped, eased the door shut, and pushed Adrianne back.

"Just go upstairs and call the cops."

"What?"

"Just go. And stay up there where you're safe."

Adrianne's scowl reminded Piper how she had insulted her for hiding up in her glass tower just a few minutes ago. But she only said, "Come with me."

"No, I need to make sure they don't leave, track them if they do. Go. Hurry!"

Adrianne fled up the stairs and Piper rubbed a hand across her face. Charging into the lobby seemed like suicide, but maybe she could cut off the cattle rustling at the elevator. She climbed the stairs back to Pasture 2. A border collie kept the agitated cattle clustered toward the front of the pasture. The elevator opened and Piper ducked down behind one of the cows. Moving that fast and that low was a good way to get yourself trampled—they may have been dwarf cattle, but they'd still break ribs and cut nasty gashes if Piper found herself under their hooves. Muscles kick-shoved two cows to drive them into the elevator, then followed them in. The doors snapped shut.

Piper grabbed a handful of seaweed feed and started the whoops and clicks they used when rotating the cattle to a new pasture. She shoved the seaweed at one cow's face. The cow licked a long black tongue toward it, but the dog snarled and snapped, not letting any of them follow Piper. You can't bribe a dog with seaweed, and apparently "Go on, git," wasn't a command it understood. *Running out of time.* She could already hear the whir of the elevator on its way back up. Only—*wait, no.* That wasn't the elevator.

The robotic manure collector puttered past. Piper glanced from the clam-shaped robot to the ledge above the elevator. Like most of these ledges, a bird had built a messy nest there. Only a few days before, Jayce had joked that they should heft the manure collectors up there to get rid of the nests. He'd even measured to prove that it could fit.

With the dog yapping at her heels, the cattle mooing and stamping, Piper kicked over a water trough and stood on it. The bird fluttered off with an indignant squawk, and Piper plucked the nest down and set it gently by the milking station. A couple of taps on the control screen brought the manure collector to a halt, and then she crouched down, hefted the smelly robot, and perched it on the ledge. She had just enough time to race back to the control panel and hit "go" when the elevator doors opened.

Muscles saw her, shouted, "Hey!" and then the manure collector rolled right off the ledge and onto his head with a clunk. He toppled unconscious to the floor. The robot landed tracks up, the storage compartment broken open and mess oozing onto the floor. She shooed the cows away from the elevator, then opened the slats of the cattle guard to keep them from crossing. Muscles had a pistol in a holster on his left hip. Piper grabbed it, stepped into the elevator. She'd been five when her family had finally turned over their land, sent their animals up to Nebraska and moved to the city, but her father had taken her once a year to a shooting range, saying it was an important skill to preserve. She'd never believed him until this very moment.

When the elevator doors opened, Mustache Mack had his back turned, but Jayce yelled "Piper!" and Mack swung around, pointing his shotgun at her. She stepped out of the elevator and pointed the pistol back at him.

"Just return the cattle, and we won't tell the police anything about this," Piper said.

"You're in no position to negotiate."

"I know where your homestead is."

His gaze flickered for a moment. "I don't want to have to kill you."

Jayce looked to the trailer, backed against the front doors, where Mullet was busy shoving the cattle up a ramp. Jayce licked his lips, then tackled Mack from behind, arm around his neck. Mack's gun fired at the ceiling, raining tile and insulation down on them. Jayce let go in surprise, long enough for Mack to gain his footing and point his gun at Jayce.

"Guess this is just as good. You make any wrong move, girlie, and I shoot him."

"You're not gonna shoot me," Jayce said.

"I just might, cuz. You ain't making full use of both of them knee caps."

"This is your *cousin*, Jayce? Why didn't you say anything when— when—" She faltered.

"Thought I could talk some sense into him," Jayce said. "'Stead, he kidnapped me, used my employee badge to get in here."

"*Kidnapped*," Mack snorted. Gun still on Jayce, his eyes flicked to the pistol she held. "Where's Wayne?"

Must be the bulky smog-head upstairs. "He's still alive. For now. Why are you doing this?"

"Cows ain't supposed to live in skyscrapers. We just want to bring agriculture back to the land, back to the people."

"By stealing our cattle."

"Way I see it, we're liberating them." Mack said. "You know, we could use someone with your expertise. Pretty impressive, the way you hacked that drone. You could join us."

He stepped backwards. She was the one with her back to the wall, and he had only a few steps to make it to the trailer. Could she actually pull the trigger if he made a run for it? Piper had no way to know if any help was on the way.

"We want the same thing you want," Mack said.

"No," she told him. "The Spiral Ranch may not be the best way, but we can't go back to the old ways, either. The land has to heal, re-grow."

He took another step back. "That's just propaganda, and you know it."

She stepped forward, closing the distance between them. Someday, maybe people would spread out, start living horizontally again instead of vertically, but right now was a fallow time.

"Let's go, man," Mullet yelled. He herded the last two cows into the trailer and latched the gate.

"I can't let you take our cattle," Piper said.

"Then I'd say we are at an impasse." Mack cocked the gun. "Too bad. I—"

He didn't get to finish that sentence. The manure collector robot dropped out of the shotgun hole in the ceiling and knocked him out cold. Jayce caught the weapon before it hit the ground but let his cousin fall. Piper looked up to see Adrianne waving down at her through the hole.

"What did you do?" Piper shouted. "Crawl through the air vent?"

"Oh, hell," said Mullet, racing around to climb into the truck. Jayce and Piper sprinted after him, but before they made it outside, lights flashed on the street and two police cars pulled onto the sidewalk to block the trailer.

"Well, look who it is," the officer said to Mullet. "Johnny-boy, I thought we had an agreement I wouldn't be seeing you again." She handcuffed him and led him to the car.

The second officer stepped into the lobby, looking from Jayce and Piper to the unconscious man on the floor, and wrinkled his nose at the manure robot, now definitely damaged beyond repair. Jayce slowly lowered the shotgun and leaned it against the wall. Piper lifted her hands, the pistol dangling from her index finger by the trigger guard.

The elevator door dinged open then, and Adrianne stepped out, tugging her blouse down and standing tall despite the fact that she was covered in grease and manure. Bits of fiberglass clung to her disheveled hair. "Thank you so much for your quick response, officers. I'd appreciate if you'd get these intruders off my property as soon as possible. There's another upstairs."

After the cops dragged the unconscious criminals away, they took statements and had Piper, Jayce, and Adrianne fill out some lengthy forms. "And here I thought those reports about flying cows were due to some new drug," one of them said with a chuckle.

"They still have half a dozen head out in the forest," Piper said.

"We'll look into it." The officer pointed his stylus at her. "Do *not* go out there again. You hear me?"

Piper swallowed, nodded. A tow-truck came for the truck and trailer. Cattle filled the lobby; a few of them wandered out along the street. After the police left, Piper approached Adrianne. She looked like hell. Bits of her hair had torn out of their clips and stuck out in all directions. She'd lost both shoes, and manure splatters spread across her sky-blue skirt.

"Guess you *are* willing to do some of the dirty work," Piper said. Adrianne gave a weak smile. "I'm sorry I said all those things, before. I... I didn't mean nothin'."

Adrianne shook her head. "No, you were right. About some things, anyway."

"There's another ranch up north, they wanted me to go up there, build a LASSO system for them, show them how we run things." Piper looked at the floor. "I ain't gonna do it."

To Piper's utter shock, Adrianne laughed. "Let's talk to them together, see if we can work out a deal."

"Really?"

"You've got the tech and knowledge they need. And a franchise opportunity sure would make my investors change their tune. I just wish you'd *told* me, Piper. I'm sick of people trying to steal things from me. Stealing my cows. Stealing my reputation. Stealing my partner."

Piper grinned at that. She hadn't felt much like a partner in this for a while.

The short summer night was coming to a close. The sky flushed yellow, and sunbeams reflected off the city's many mirrored windows. Piper reached for her hat, but remembered it was still on the roof, if a breeze hadn't sent it flying.

Jayce came down the stairs with the border collie, declaring that the dog was his now and he needed to take it home. Piper shouted at him that the dog would be helpful to round up the cattle still wandering the lobby and the street, but he was already gone. She sighed.

"Lot of repairs to do today," Piper said.

"And cleaning." Adrianne picked at her soiled clothes.

One of the cows snuffled at Adrianne's hair. Piper patted its side. "Help me get these girls back where they belong?"

To her surprise, Adrianne agreed. They hung a "Temporarily Closed" sign on the lobby door and got to work.

From DreamForge #1, Founders Issue

Sarena Ulibarri is a fiction writer who lives in
New Mexico. Her fiction has appeared in various magazines
and anthologies, including Lightspeed, Fantastic Stories
of the Imagination, Weirdbook, and GigaNotoSaurus.
She is editor-in-chief of World Weaver Press.

An Infinite Number

by David Amburgey

My therapist wants me to write to you as if you are alive.

She wants me to tell you how much I love and appreciate you, tell you all the things I never got the chance to say. Only I never got the chance to tell you anything, nothing you were ever able to understand. You died in the dark, on August the second, in the fourteenth week of your life. You died for no reason at all except that sometimes, infants just die. No father can be ready for that. I wasn't.

In truth, I told you so many things while you were here. None of them meant anything to you: to you my words were just warm noise. But it meant everything to me. You woke us up at all hours of the night, and if I'm honest, I never wanted to be the one to soothe you back to sleep. Now, I'd give anything for you at three in the morning. I wish I had never put you down.

This is getting hard to write, so I'm just going to get to the point.

I read a book about us.

In this book a physicist says that our universe could be just one of many universes, that there could be infinite combinations of particles expressed in an infinite number of ways. Your daddy doesn't understand it all, exactly. But if it's true, then this, out of all the possible versions of my life, is one of the worst. And that makes me so happy because if that's true, then it means that on the morning of August the third my girl woke up chubby and happy all across the multiverse.

An infinite number of you learned to walk, and talk, and make us all laugh. An infinite number of you loved, and lost, and put your need for me into the past. An infinite number of you worked an infinite number of jobs and lived an infinite number of lives.

I spend every night lost in the permutations of you, you-that-are-not-lost.

This is the worst possible universe, but I still got fourteen weeks of you. There's no way to qualify that quantity. I will always keep loving you, and if you're out there, and if we're out there, our love for you will always be an infinite number.

From DreamForge #5, March 2020

David Amburgey is an aspiring writer in Scarborough, Canada. A graduate of the University of Toronto with a BA in History and English Literature, he is currently working on his Stonecoast MFA in Creative Writing, with a specialization in Popular Fiction. In his free time, he volunteers with a creative writing mentorship program for teens in his community.

Sing! & Remember

by Lauren C. Teffeau

My stylus never pauses as I transcribe the simple but earnest words of the villager before me for my report. "And what happened after that?"

"The lindworm attacked, that's what. Killed my neighbor, her entire family." He watches me for a reaction I cannot give.

I hum your words to myself. I've been interviewing people all day, commandeering the humble common room of the sole inn in Harnsey, a village at a crossroads that appears only on the most detailed maps of the Brance. The rough-hewn tables and benches are better suited to mugs of ale and bowls of stew and good-hearted conversation, but they serve me well enough. After all, the Order's business is not one of comfort, not when we're often all that stands between monsters and the people we've sworn to protect.

Every witness spoke of the same serpent-like creature that was behind so much devastation just four days ago. There hasn't been a lindworm attack in this area for decades, but it still looms large in the collective memory. And no wonder, considering the destruction they can wield with a swipe of their claws or their sturdy tails.

Each sighting must be carefully documented, including witness accounts, property damage assessments, and other costs incurred so we can better allocate resources in our eternal fight against the cursed beasts from the age before that still haunt the land. And my job is to see it done. May it be enough.

The man cranes his neck, looking over my shoulder. "Say, what's that noise?"

"You said it looked like an overlarge snake except for its face?"

He turns back to me, his eyes a hard sort of green in a tanned, well-weathered face. Life in this part of the Brance will do that to you. "Almost feline. Oh! And claws, like a hawk's." His eyes widen in disbelief then affront. "Are you… humming?"

"What? Oh yes. I do that sometimes," I say absently. "Don't mind me. Now what—"

He makes a slashing gesture with his hands—abrupt enough my fighting instincts waken from where they've slept these past months. "Humming without concern to the people who died here? And with your Order to blame." He shakes his head, disgusted.

I owe this man no explanations, but I will not tolerate his criticism. "Sir, need I remind you my Sisters destroyed the creature that attacked your neighbor?"

"Too little, too late. Five people gone—a huge loss." Margins matter out here, especially at harvest time, though that's hardly our fault. He fixes me with another disapproving look. "You're doing it again. Show some respect!"

"I am," I say sharply. "Just not to *you*."

While we glare at one another, Sister Elzanne and Sister Avera join us. They greet me with a civil nod and wait their turn to be interviewed. We may share the streak of white hair that adorns our crowns and marks us as Sisters of the Zasita Order but that is all, I realize, as a slight curl of dislike lingers on Sister Avera's lips. She eyes the crossbow slung across my back with disdain, perhaps knowing how long it has gone unused in my current role as a scribe with the Order.

No matter. I return my attention to the villager, last of the eyewitnesses and verging on the least useful. "Is there anything else you'd like the record to show?" My voice, once warm with inquiry, is now coolly flat like the plains that spread out south of here.

He sputters for a moment, torn with the desire to castigate me further even as he mentally reviews all he's told me. "No, Sister," he says finally. "That's the truth of it."

I set down my stylus and force my face into something approaching sympathy. It's hard to tell—everything feels so distant these days. "I am very sorry you had to endure this. Such creatures don't belong in this world. My report to the Order will help ensure this won't happen again."

Then, still humming, I wave Sisters Elzanne and Avera forward. Both of them are easily ten years younger than me, still eager to confront the world's enemies after their time at the Academy with their swords sheathed at their sides. I feel the same call, but you know why I now serve the Order in other ways.

The heavy doors creak closed behind my last interview subject. It's early enough in the afternoon, the rest of the locals are still hard at work, leaving the three of us alone in the establishment.

"I need to take both of your statements for the official record."

Sister Elzanne crosses her arms and leans against the table. Road-weary perhaps. "We came, we killed, with nary a scratch. What more is there to say?"

Sister Avera nudges Elzanne's shoulder. "Look, she's writing it down."

"I take my responsibilities to the Order seriously, Sister Avera." That they are not doing so at least Sister Elzanne seems to realize by the sudden scowl darkening her face.

She straightens and looks me in the eyes, at least in this moment, as an equal. She must be the leader of the pair, in either age or temperament. "The Order sent us here as soon as they received word of the attack. We traveled to the fields along the outskirts and fought and killed the lindworm that burst from the ground nearby. We

worried it from either side until I could perform the killing blow."
Beside her, Avera mimes slitting her throat. "Is that *thorough* enough
for you, Sister?" Sister Elzanne prompts me.

I nod as I commit the last of her testimony, softly humming your
words. Always your words. "What do you make of one of the villagers'
assertion that it was a much larger lindworm that attacked them?"

"That a dead monster will always look smaller compared to the
one they've conjured in their heads, but they wouldn't dare admit as
much to a... representative of the Order," Avera says.

I am a Sister same as her, but Sister Avera is making it clear she
won't call me that, not with a scribe's stylus in my hands.

Sister Avera gives Elzanne a loaded look, as if she cannot imagine
someone like me can see right into her foolish heart, straight to the
arrogance both youth and good fortune foster. Their partnership
seems an easy one. What will happen when one falls before the other?
When Sister Avera loses Sister Elzanne, the way I lost you? She won't
be so smug then, I think.

Perhaps she'll be the one to go first, overconfident and eager to
meet death, never realizing there's a future beyond the fight. Or
perhaps she does and refuses to greet it the way I have, still humming
your song under my breath—sometimes daring full-throated song
when I'm alone—to keep the music alive for you.

"Are we done here?" Sister Avera asks, her voice verging on a
whine. "I'm hungry."

I give them both a nod. "Thank you, Sisters, for your time." With
my tablet and stylus tucked in my satchel at my side, I make my way
up the stairs to my room on the second floor of the inn to finalize my
report.

Their whispers reach me, like the darting strikes of a viper. Sister
Elzanne exhorts Sister Avera to lower her voice, that I've earned my
white hair same as them.

"But she's always singing to herself. As if we can't hear it!"

"Perhaps she's been knocked in the head too many times."

"Nonsense," Sister Avera replies. "When's the last time she's seen battle?"

"Some Sisters must leave active combat for various reasons," Sister Elzanne says mildly.

"She couldn't handle it?"

"That or an injury, perhaps. Keep in mind those assigned crossbows and other ranged weapons are often paired with swordswomen. Perhaps she lost hers."

"To refuse another partner is to refuse the fight." I can almost hear the sneer that surely graces Avera's face at such words.

Or envision Sister Elzanne's arched brow when she replies, "And if you lost me, would you be so eager to replace me, I wonder?"

"If it meant keeping my pledge to the Order, I would," Avera insists.

Sister Elzanne chuckles. "Hmm. I see I need to teach you some manners the next time we spar."

My hums drown out the rest of their words as I close the door to my room, uncaring of everything except my memories of you.

Sunlight dappled the rutted wagon road between Darvet and Venzor. A fragrant breeze off the mountains to the north kept us cool as we marched along. Springtime in the Brance does afford some pleasantries.

You asked me *what rhymes with honor* that wasn't wander or squander or yonder. I rolled my eyes at your antics. You'd always figure it out on your own, no matter what I'd say, and make it beautiful. "We should have taken that farmer up on his offer of a ride."

"And share space with squawking chickens the whole way? No, thank you." You grinned back at me. "Besides, it's a beautiful day. What good is traveling the world if we don't stop and enjoy it every now and again?"

"I didn't join the Order to travel." I joined it to fight monsters.

To battle back the creatures for the good of the rest of the world, my Sisters at my side.

"Maybe not, but you have to admit it's a nice bonus." You spread your arms wide and looked up as if you could embrace the sky. "And on a day such as this, it makes all our hard work a bit more bearable, yes?"

I smiled in spite of myself. You always were good at getting me to do that. "But what if we're too late?"

"Ahh." You gave me a look that cut right through me. "*That's* why you're so grumpy. Don't worry. If it were urgent, the Order would have told us as much in the briefing."

We had been instructed to travel to Venzor after crocutta were sighted in the region. A vicious species of wolf that preyed on all fauna in an area, hunting in packs. Potentially devastating, given Venzor's over-reliance on their sheep and goats for foodstuffs and trade goods.

"We have plenty of time." You turned mischievous. "In fact, I finished another stanza last night. Want to hear it?"

"If I say no, will you actually keep your infernal lyrics to yourself?"

"Of course not. Torturing you is half the fun."

Every mission of ours is commemorated in your words from our first assignment together to our latest task in the Southern Reaches seeing to a jaculus infestation. I made the mistake of telling you how endearing it was, and there hadn't been any peace from your rhymes and practice with meter and tempo since. Things I didn't have the patience for then, but I mark the moments by them now.

"Don't you have enough material to fill three epics at this point?"

You shook your head, suddenly serious. "Ours is still a story without an ending. I want it to go on forever."

Sister Elzanne and Avera are gone the next morning when I join the innkeeper in the common room for breakfast. They've probably been sent somewhere else—hopefully into another scribe's jurisdiction.

I hum into my mug of tea, bubbles tickling my nose. A strange mood I'm in.

I must check in with the Order's section leader in Darvet to the north, but there's no need to hurry. I can take my time. I can even take the time to walk the site once more, try to quiet the lingering voice in my head that insists we have overlooked something.

Once the Order's coin is in the innkeeper's hand, my cloak and satchel and crossbow across my shoulders, I return to the fields where a monstrous beast burst from the ground and ripped a family to shreds.

According to local lore, the lindworms usually live underground, which explains why sightings are so rare, and when they do appear, it's a portent of some kind. None of the villagers would dare tell me what they thought this one signified. The Order would frown upon such superstition anyway. It is our sacred responsibility to send such beasts into oblivion. One day, by the might of the Sisters following in my footsteps, maybe even extinction. But we cannot be everywhere, no matter how we try.

You know that better than me.

One vulture makes a perch on a fence post that somehow remained standing while the rest bordering the field were torn asunder. Stalks of barley bent and broken, leaves still spattered with the same blood that darkens the ground. Bedrock and topsoil have been churned about. The villagers have worked hard to fill in the tunnels the creature made, leaving their footprints and the battered land behind.

A bird screeches overhead, throwing into sharp relief just how quiet it is. I've even stopped humming. I start your song from the beginning. It's always helped me think, did you know that? It's lonely out here, so I sing in my raspy voice, a shadow of yours no matter how many times I said otherwise. I knit the words together from your beloved verses as if by singing them aloud I can summon you from memory. How I wish it were so.

I follow the tracks of the monster as it attacked, joined by Sister

Elzanne and Avera's bootprints as they met it and dispatched it into the next world. Ichor and scales mark those areas, close to the tree line. A breeze stirs the branches, and I notice a hole the width of a barrel torn through the underbrush.

All the villagers I'd spoken with made a point of saying the carcass Elzanne and Avera delivered was much smaller than the one that had killed their neighbors. My Sisters had fought the beast that confronted them on this very field, but what if there were more than one? Lindworms tend to be solitary, but would my Sisters have investigated to ensure as much? I shake my head. See the thoughts your song conjures?

With apologies to you, I stop singing and release my crossbow from the straps on my back. The weight of the weapon settles into my hands, into calluses time hasn't yet worn smooth.

Without looking, I slide a bolt from my quiver and cock my crossbow, my gaze on the woods, the secrets it's hiding. Or not. Won't know until I venture forth and learn the truth.

Slighted by her own for things out of her control
Sister Kalira carried on, despite her weary soul
Jassan's song on her lips, ever reverent
Determined to see to her latest assignment

Your lyrics were always more sophisticated than my simple rhymes, but it's the only way I know how to keep the song alive for you.

Sister Avera would be rolling her eyes at my plan, I'm certain. And you… You would tell me I'm being overly cautious for following up, overly foolish for going alone. But you'd be at my side nonetheless. You're at my side now, aren't you?

I hum under my breath to keep you here where you belong as I stalk towards the tree line.

• • •

Filled with victory from the beasts they'd slain
Sisters Jassan and Kalira were on the road again
Jassan with her broadsword at the ready
And Kalira with her crossbow ever steady

Your sing-song voice—a blade's edge away from bursting into laughter at any moment—needled me as I tried and failed to keep a straight face at such a ridiculous verse. Not your usual quality. But that didn't matter when your purpose was to drive me mad. Passing the time, you'd call it, practice, whenever I complained.

How could I argue with that when you were painstakingly chronicling our exploits so we wouldn't be lost to time like so many of our Sisters since the Order's founding years upon years ago? You started the stanza from the beginning, your voice strengthening with each word.

Motion from the left side of the road caught my eye, the skin on the back of my neck prickling like those moments just before a fight.

"Enough!"

You wiped the hurt from your face when you saw I had my crossbow out and pointed at the shadows that had gathered just beyond the tree line.

A whisper of steel as you eased your sword from your sheath. "What is it?"

"I thought the briefing said the villagers saw the creatures on the southern edge of Venzor." If that were true, how had they made their way this far north so soon? We wouldn't have a chance to set up blinds, monitor their movements, and decide the best course of attack, as we originally thought.

You shrugged, your gaze locked on the trees. "You know how reliable witness accounts are." The crocutta's signature high-pitched call shattered the air, silencing the birds, as they took notice of us, sensing our purpose in that place.

"We'll draw them out, face them on the road," I said with a frown, already calculating all the things that could go wrong. "In the forest, there's too much interference. I don't want to chance hitting you."

You nodded tightly and turned to me, your dear face hungry for the fight to come. Then you opened your mouth:

> *With an understanding that comes from sacrifice*
> *Sisters Jassan and Kalira well know the price*
> *Of victory*
> *Of infamy*
> *Of history*
> *Made on the throw of a dice.*

My first bolt punches into the lindworm's underbelly. Not so rusty, Sister Avera.

Its screams scatter the birds roosting in the tree limbs overhead as I cock my crossbow. My next bolt flies into its torso before it finds me in the underbrush. A single swipe of its foreleg, claws extended, knocks aside a young tree, sending it thrashing down to the ground.

I'm already moving, getting off two more bolts before the creature slithers after me, looking like a reptilian hunting cat from the waist up. When I first spied the enormous lindworm's foul den amongst tree roots, human bones, and a mix of soil and its own excrement, I realized I never expected to find what I was looking for in Harnsey's woods. Or perhaps more precisely, I didn't particularly care either way. I only wanted to do *something* to clear my mind of my Sisters' judgment, my heart of your absence. To determine whether or not I'm capable of feeling anything again that's not mired in loss or bitterness.

Crashing through the underbrush, my training comes back to me from where it's lain dormant these long months apart. Each of your stanzas propels me forward, creating a large enough lead I can bury three more bolts into its chest, my arms flexing with the strain of re-cocking the crossbow each time. The blood dripping from the lindworm's sides, the quickening of a fight... A language more immediate than those found in your stanzas or my reports. I've missed it so. But you know that, your song my lament.

I wrench my left ankle on tree roots, bark my knees in a mad scramble up a stone embankment. Run headlong into brambles, their thorny reach determined to foul up my crossbow. My bolts run low, along with the clearance to use them.

My lead bleeds away. The lindworm swipes at my cloak, jerking me back before its claws tear through the material. I'm still free, but it won't last. Nothing does—how well I know that now.

Maybe I *am* no longer fit for the fight. Sister Avera's disdain wasn't misplaced because I would rather die here—a product of my foolishness and folly—if it means I'll be reunited with you.

The next strike sends me tumbling, my crossbow knocked out of my hands, numbing pain shooting up my right forearm at the impact. I swipe leaf litter out of my eyes, draw the dagger I keep in my boot. A last resort. But I didn't earn my white hair for nothing.

The lindworm bares its fangs. I wait for its strike, dart left, then whirl back, my dagger seeking its throat. If the creature's teeth and claws find me before the dagger finds its mark, I tell myself at least I'll no longer be alone.

My bolt felled the crocutta snarling in front of me before it could lunge. "That's the last of them." It collapsed with a pitiful whine, the rest of the pack scattered and dying. I pushed myself into motion, gathering up my bolts where they'd flown, deep in gristle, blood, and bone, as well as the ground or the occasional tree trunk.

If there were more of them, we'd be ready, no matter how much my arms shook from the exertion from so many shots, from such an unexpected battle, no matter our training.

I wasn't paying attention to you. You'd be scraping your blade off in the grass, wiping it clean with an oiled rag before sheathing it. Perhaps even writing down a few observations or snatches of rhyme in that journal you always had hidden away in the pocket of your cloak. That's what happened after every encounter. I let my mind fill in the blanks as I wrestled a bolt from the still-warm chest of a crocutta, its black tongue lolling out between its grinning teeth.

"Kalira... " you said in a pained voice.

I turned and saw you as you were, not how I assumed, pale with blood loss, a puzzled look on your face as you fell to your knees. I didn't understand what was wrong, then I saw the gash across your upper thigh, so deep we both knew what that meant in an instant that felt like forever as I rushed over, gathered you in my arms, and laid you down on the road, your lifeblood painting a starburst around us. "No, no, *no.*"

"I'm sorry," you told me as I pressed down on your thigh as if my hands could stop the slippery warmth from escaping.

"What? *I* should have been faster. I—"

"No, Kalira. This wasn't your fault." You struggled against tears, against the certainty of death, as you looked up at me, begging without words to make it easier to let go. But I wouldn't, not ever, not without a fight.

"You said ours was a story without an ending. I need you here to help me finish it, Jassan. I can't do it without you."

You coughed, gripped my hand, and said with the barest hint of a smile, "Now you'll finally have your peace and quiet."

"Quiet perhaps, but never peace," I replied, but you were already gone.

It's the pain that tells me I haven't passed on into the next realm where we'll be reunited. Some of my Sisters don't believe in such things, but I do. I don't know how I'd spend my days if I didn't, not with you gone.

Scattered images and impressions follow. Wet heat saturating my robes, the tree branches waving farewell overhead, inexplicably Elzanne's disapproving stare, and a male villager shouting and whispering, sometimes both at once, as I drift in and out of awareness. Visions too sensible for hallucinations, too disappointing for the afterlife.

I must remain tethered to this world a bit longer, I'm afraid.

"Sister Kalira, foolish woman, are you with us still?" Sister Elzanne, most assuredly.

"You found me?" I ask in a harsh voice. A wagon of some kind groans underneath me.

"You're lucky Sister Avera left behind one of her daggers else—"

"Luck?" I repeat the word, hoping for it to make sense. "Luck, made on the throw of a dice."

"Is she singing again?" someone else whispers. "Perhaps we gave her too much pain medicine."

No. There's no medicine that can treat what pains me.

When I wake again, I'm back in Harnsey's inn, bruised all over with my right arm splinted and bandaged, a foul-smelling poultice secured against my side.

Someone stirs in my periphery, and Sister Avera approaches my bed.

"How…?" I make a weak gesture to my injuries, surprised at how much energy it takes.

"The villagers saw you return to the fields. When Elzanne and I heard, well, we couldn't let a mere scribe show us up in our sacred duty."

"She's no mere scribe. You saw the lindworm she slew, half over the size of the one we fought together," Elzanne says sharply as she joins us.

Sister Avera nods, chasten. "A poor attempt at humor. Your pardon, Sister Kalira."

So, I'm a Sister to her now. I suppose that is something. The rest…

"We've done as the Order instructed in seeing to your injuries. A villager has offered to take you to Darvet to continue your care as thanks for your service here." She gives me a sad but genuine smile. "I'm sorry we cannot linger."

"No need to explain, Sister." They're probably already late traveling to their next assignment and the people who need their protection.

She waves Sister Avera out of the room. Before Sister Elzanne shuts the door behind her, she turns back to me. "I now know why you sing, Sister Kalira. While you were unconscious..." She shakes her head. "Just don't let grief dull your blade."

I arch my brow. "My bolts fly true."

Sister Elzanne gives me a sharp nod. "So they do, Sister. So they do."

My simple rhymes can never replace you
But I've learned one thing is still true
With whipcord waxed, my bolts sharpened
Wits no longer dulled despite a heart still broken
I can fight without it feeling like betrayal
So I'll sing and remember our story and hope I do justice to the fable
And my friend, no matter how painful
So we can go on forever
Not a fitting tribute, but the best I am capable

From DreamForge #1 Founders Issue

Lauren was born and raised on the East Coast, educated in the South, employed in the Midwest, and now lives and dreams in the Southwest. When she was younger, she poked around in the back of wardrobes, tried to walk through mirrors, and always kept an eye out for secret passages, fairy rings, and messages from aliens. She was disappointed. Now, she writes to cope with her ordinary existence.

A Sip of Pombé

by Gustavo Bondoni

The antique Land Rover, fifty years old if a day, bounced over the rutted track, between trees that had been intentionally left untrimmed. Samuel Kyanbadde would have preferred to launch much earlier—his nerves had become more and more frayed as the days passed—but the delays mounted as niggling issues came up. In the end, the Russian had put his foot down: either the launch happened before the end of the week or they'd miss the window.

Armed guards stopped them at the last checkpoint, but smiled and waved when they recognized Samuel sitting in the passenger seat.

A gap opened in the jungle. Two rockets came into view and his stomach jumped. He turned to his companion in the back seat. "They've taken off the camouflage netting!"

Happy Odongo didn't smile. The serious young man almost never smiled. "We must really be going, then."

"Isn't it great?"

"If they managed to get everything working, it is."

Samuel studied the vehicles. It was the first time he'd seen them without the dense camouflage designed to shield them from spy satellites and *especially* from Google Earth. The Americans and Chinese only occasionally watched Uganda, but Google was omnipresent.

He felt dizzy for a moment. They looked much taller without their disguise. As the Land Rover approached the nearest one, he couldn't help feeling that the giant booster was going to topple onto his head at any moment.

The President himself met them at the barracks. He was wearing a shirt in the western style with the top three buttons open. He smiled his politician's smile and shook their hands respectfully. "You two are heroes. By tomorrow, the entire world will know your names."

One way or another, it was true. Either two Ugandans would be on their way to Mars, violating every missile proliferation agreement in existence, or they'd have died horribly in an explosion too large to cover up. Their names would be released in both cases—only the context would differ.

"Thank you, sir."

They walked off to join the Russian. The project leader looked like a giant snowman: a round torso all wrapped in white and with an equally round head, clean-shaven and pale-skinned. The ensemble was topped by a wide-brimmed pith helmet. He smiled at them and rubbed his hands. "So, the day is finally here. How are you feeling?"

"We're fine," Samuel said, before Happy could ruin the mood. "We can't wait to get up there and show everyone that we're not backward savages."

"They won't think that. Imagine it. This will be the first mission to Mars that leaves directly from Earth and not from some moon installation or Lagrange point. It's the most technically advanced attempt humanity has ever made. We'll show them."

Even Happy refrained from reminding the man that they already knew all that. They both had degrees in astrophysics—Happy had a doctorate from Oxford—but the Russian always seemed to treat them like children. Still, it was hard not to like him; he was completely obsessed with getting his planned mission to Mars, and today, it was he who was acting like a child, bouncing around like a kid patiently waiting for Christmas gifts.

"Let's get you into your suits."

They walked into the barracks building, which had been converted into a dressing room for the astronauts. Samuel chuckled. This was probably the only space facility in the world where getting a malaria-carrying mosquito in your suit was not only a real risk, but specifically listed as a pre-flight check item.

It would serve, wooden floors and all. There was no need to keep up appearances. No one was going to broadcast this takeoff live. It had to happen in complete secrecy. Hell, if anyone found out about it, they'd come here and shut it down. They'd also take the Russian away and quietly shoot him: the man only cared about getting a Mars mission up, but attempting to sell rocket designs with deep space capabilities to the North Koreans probably hadn't been a great idea, no matter how politically innocent the man was.

Once suited, the two Ugandans rode up the elevator. The Russian chattered the whole way. "We swept both rockets for bombs today. They were clean. The insurgents don't seem to have gotten through. We might even have been able to keep them from finding out about this."

"I'm much more worried about the Americans shooting us down," Happy replied.

"No. No. Everything will be fine. You'll see."

Their rocket was called the *Kabalega II*, in honor of the man who'd fought the British —one of the most noble and perseverant of African freedom fighters— in the very place where the spaceport was located. *Kabalega I* was standing four hundred meters away on another pad. It was going to launch first, carrying their rover and the Mars habitat. Their own rocket contained the transit ship which, if everything worked as planned, would become their orbiter.

The Russian strapped them in and connected all the hoses himself while the technical team looked on with bemused smiles. It was a mark of the esteem he was held in that no one corrected his mistakes until, after an emotional good luck speech, he left. Only then did the techs reconnect the hoses and recheck the straps. One of them furtively handed Samuel a flask containing pombé, the local beer, brewed by his ancestors since before the British had decided to come looking for the source of the Nile.

They shut the hatch with a solid thunk, and the noise of the insects and the birds was left on the outside.

Samuel, born and raised right there in Bunyoro, always missed that sound when it wasn't present. It had been the soundtrack for his entire life except for the stint at the University of Arizona and then, later, at MIT. But other than those seven years, the buzzing and chirping had been a constant companion.

He wondered if he'd ever hear it again.

Ignoring the chatter over the radio, Samuel looked out of the single porthole. All he could see was the tip of their sister rocket and a cloudless sky.

He wondered if he would survive. All the odds were against it. Even if the Americans and the Chinese had been deceived by the official story that the Ugandan government was modernizing the Kagadi Hospital, or the unofficial one that the government was building a high-tech subterranean prison for rebels, the likelihood of survival was slim.

The land grab in space had reignited tensions that had seemed buried in the early years of the century. Back then, space cooperation had been a unifying force, a check on the nationalist ambitions of the major players in the Great Game.

But then the world had polarized. Authoritarian régimes on the extremes of the political spectrum had turned their eyes skyward and seen endless resources in the asteroid field and even on Mars. Their dreams had been fueled more by desire and demagoguery than by science, but it was enough to rekindle a race toward the outer reaches of the system. And enough to create a state of near war on Earth.

Fortunately, there were more immediate concerns. He and Happy were perched atop one of two heavily modified and strengthened N1 rockets—boosters that had originally been designed to take Soviet cosmonauts to the moon. The failure of the N1 had been the main cause for the Americans reaching the lunar surface first. These tricky rockets had exploded one after another. And now he was strapped into one.

The Russian had assured everyone that the rockets—with his modifications—would work. But the truth was that the boosters had only really been tested underground and the flight characteristics of the giant vehicles in atmosphere had only been tested in simulation. In the computerized fluid dynamics programs, they had worked flawlessly.

Of course, if the foreigners hadn't bought Uganda's cover stories, it was all moot. The rocket would be blasted out of the sky as soon as one of the anti-missile satellites could be brought to bear. The Chinese were unpredictable, the Europeans timid, and the Russians simply didn't care, but the Americans would shoot first and ask questions, lots and lots of questions, afterward.

The countdown reached two minutes and Samuel glanced over at Happy. He had his eyes closed and was moving his lips.

Praying? It might not be a bad idea. Samuel himself held out until the countdown reached ten before closing his own eyes. Then the shaking started, followed by crushing acceleration. He didn't open them again until he felt the first stage disengage. There was no question of hearing the updates through the radio, the noise was tremendous, but he felt the metallic clank and the small explosion used to jettison the used-up rocket through his backside.

"Kampala, this is the *Kabalega II*, everything is nominal," he reported.

"Nominal for you, perhaps. We've got every major government

asking us what the hell is going on. And how CNN got a crew here so fast is anyone's guess."

"Well, I'll let you deal with them. We're getting into Mars trajectory burn position in thirty-five minutes. How are our base and rover doing?" It wasn't critical that the base and rover survived, of course. They had enough fuel to return. But it would be a terrible disappointment to go all the way out to Mars only to shrug, take a few pictures, and come home. Especially considering that he'd have Happy for a shipmate all the way there and back again.

"Everything looks good so far. They tell me the Russian had to be carried away. He was so surprised that it actually worked that he fainted."

"Comforting thought. We have a few million more kilometers for him to fail at something."

But they were on their way. A launch explosion in a fully fueled rocket was the only thing Samuel hadn't been trained to deal with. It was clear to everyone that, if anything happened, he was expected to die heroically in the explosion.

News followed them across the solar system. The enraged Americans had sent the Sixth Fleet to perform exercises and maneuvers off the coast of Tanzania. The Chinese had cut off all financial aid to Uganda, while several European nations had denounced the launch in the U.N. Of the countries with people on Mars, only India had remained silent. After all, the reaction to their own space program decades before had been the same.

The most interesting reaction of all was that of the Russians. While not exactly condoning the launch, they did make a point of mentioning that it had been made possible by Russian technology, and that if any other country needed such technology for their own space programs, they knew whom to call. Fortunately, no one mentioned the role of a certain Russian head engineer in all of this.

The President of Uganda—dressed in traditional ceremonial robes—spoke at the emergency meeting of the U.N. He explained that Ugandan rockets were meant for peaceful uses only. He told the assorted angry white faces that Uganda had as much right to the solar system as any other nation on Earth. More, in fact.

Uganda was a nation synonymous with exploration. At one time, it had been a central part of the mystery of the Nile. A blank space on the map. When men made reference to "darkest Africa," Uganda was part of what they were talking about. It had drawn European explorers like honey drew flies.

Whether those men—Livingstone, Stanley, Burton, Gordon—had done more harm than good was open to debate, but one thing was certain: they'd taught the Ugandan nation that determined men, working on solid principles, could overcome obstacles and shine light on the unknown. The country had learned their lesson well.

"And besides," the President had concluded defiantly, "the launch window is closed and you can't stop them. The men are going to Mars and, barring a technical problem, they will be landing there. You'll have to learn to deal with that fact." And he'd walked away.

Watching the live—well, somewhat distance-delayed broadcast—Samuel had applauded. Happy, of course, had been less sanguine.

"You know what this means, of course."

"That the Europeans and the Americans have been rightly told off?"

"That the Europeans and the Americans on Mars aren't going to come help us if something goes wrong. They'll want us to fail, so they can tell all the other governments thinking of doing something like this that Mars is too dangerous for anyone but the big boys to consider. That way, they can carve it up amongst themselves."

"Don't be silly."

But Happy, like pessimists everywhere, seemed to be right all the time. A few days after the president's speech, Brazil announced its intention to hit the next launch window using Similar N1 technology licensed from Russia. Argentina then shocked the world by saying that it was reviving its Condor project and that it would brook no outside interference in its manned space project. A number of Asian nations followed suit, led, predictably, by North Korea, who'd been waiting for the opportunity all along.

"We're not going to be popular at all, now," Happy prophesized.

Again, the man was correct. Uganda became the subject of sanctions as the First World attempted to make an example of them. Arms inspectors swarmed over the launch site. The Lord's Renaissance Army issued a statement demanding that control of the country be given over to them, and that, if the West had only supported them in the civil war against the government, none of this would have happened in the first place.

Amazingly, the government survived. The program had caught the people's imagination, and they stood staunchly behind their leadership... and became global pariahs.

"Good morning," Samuel said.

"It's not morning. And I doubt it will be too good."

Samuel wondered how Happy had been selected for the mission. The man's personality made him a prime candidate to become a murder victim even if one didn't have to be locked up with him for nearly seven months. A quick psychological screening should have eliminated him.

Of course, there weren't all that many Ugandan astrophysics PhDs who'd volunteered for a mission to Mars on unproven Russian rockets, so he'd probably been Hobson's choice.

"It will for me. I'm coming to the end of *War and Peace*," Samuel replied impassively. "Should have it done before the next sleep cycle."

"I can't believe you'd subject yourself to that. It's all Russians whining about being Russians."

Samuel didn't even bother to correct him. Happy had spent the entire mission to date, all three months' worth, using what spare time he had to amass high scores on the ship's Tetris emulator and thinking up new ways in which the mission could go wrong.

Samuel's ancestors had never been cannibals—the tribes of Bunyoro had committed different atrocities—but men like Happy made him understand what might drive someone to bite the flesh off a vanquished foe.

But he contented himself with one thought: only four months to go.

The report from Earth did not bear good news.

"I hate to admit it, but you were right," Samuel said.

"Of course I was right."

"So, are you satisfied?"

"I'd rather have been wrong," Happy replied glumly.

"Yeah. Me, too. But too late for that, now."

The object they'd picked up on the long-range scan, the one Happy had immediately decided was an American missile, had turned out, after consulting with Earth, to be... a missile. No one planet side had taken responsibility for it, but it had been launched from L4, which limited the number of suspects considerably.

"What do we do?" Samuel said.

"Let me think. We have a few hours before it hits." He set himself in front of the flight computer and began punching in numbers. Samuel knew better than to interrupt him.

"All right. There's good news and there's bad news." Happy looked as if the news was all bad, though.

"Start with the good news. I've been giving myself an ulcer thinking about all the possible ways the news could be bad."

"The missile won't hit us."

"Wow. That actually *is* good news." Samuel had been prepared for a death sentence, which made everything else wonderful by comparison.

"The bad news is that we now have a choice. What planet would you like to see: Mars or Earth? We can't do both."

"What?"

"The missile is on a perfectly calculated trajectory, but it must have spent all its fuel. I doubt it can maneuver. We have plenty of fuel to move out of its way. But once we burn it, we can't use it for anything else. That means we won't have enough to brake on Mars, accelerate away and brake again in Earth orbit. I tried everything. Slingshot maneuvers, moon gravity assist, everything. It doesn't work out."

"You mean they weren't trying to kill us?"

"Maybe they'd love to… Maybe it's a nuclear warhead and they will. But they must know we'd have to be incompetent to get hit. They just want us to move out of the way and fail. So now what?"

"What do you mean, now what?"

"I mean what I said. You're the mission commander. Which planet are we going to grace with our presence?"

"How much time do I have?"

Happy checked the display. "None." The answer appeared to bring him a certain amount of joy.

"And we'll die if we go to Mars?"

"Unless our equipment works as designed? Yes."

"I don't care. We came all this way. Onward."

Happy said nothing. He just leaned over the controls and began to program instructions very, very quickly.

"We made it!" Samuel said, as the computer confirmed that their orbit was both stable and following the trajectory that would allow them to reach the habitat module on the planet.

Even Happy had nothing negative to say. Against all odds, the ship was in orbit around Mars and, if the telemetry could be believed, the habitat had landed and was working correctly on the surface.

But perhaps the spirit of Happy had simply been relocated. Thirty minutes after he informed Kampala of their arrival, they received a message from mission control. "Orbiter *Kabalega*, congratulations on your astounding achievement. We're delighted that you have arrived safely. It's a proud moment for everyone in Uganda, and our exploratory spirit is vindicated.

"We have also received a recommendation from the United Nations that you don't descend to the surface. The international community feels it would send the wrong message; therefore, we cannot give the order for you to land. We will shortly be sending you a new set of flight parameters so that you can return to Earth quickly and safely. The Chinese government has agreed to supply you with the fuel you lost earlier. Be patient; it will take some time to figure out a refueling procedure."

Samuel was stunned. How could they do this? Why had the Ugandan President suddenly caved to the international interests he'd taken such glee in thumbing his nose at previously? Had the situation back on Earth truly gotten that bad?

He put his head in his hands and sobbed for nearly ten minutes.

It was Happy who broke the silence.

"They didn't order us not to land," the other man said quietly.

"What?"

"They didn't order us not to land. They told us what the U.N. recommended, and they told us they were sending over new flight course parameters and some nonsense about refueling, but he didn't tell us not to land."

"So? It was implied. He told us he couldn't give us the order to land."

"He doesn't need to. We were given orders to evaluate the situation once we got here, and we haven't been given a single order to contradict that. Since it's your job to evaluate the situation, I'd like to know what you feel the situation is."

"Everything is in good shape for a landing."

"Then that is what we'll do." It seemed to Samuel that Happy nearly smiled, but the other man got hold of his emotions quickly. "Besides, I'd much rather die horribly of radiation exposure on Mars than go home and get shot for disobeying orders."

"Those aren't our only options!" Samuel scolded. But his heart wasn't in it. Right then, he could have kissed the sour bastard.

Fifteen minutes later, he had programmed the lander's trajectory. They had to get into the ship within the next hour and twelve minutes to hit their window. That meant that he had a long wait before he could communicate with Earth. Their current orbital position put them at near maximum message travel time, nearly half an hour.

Five minutes before the lander disengaged and began its flight down to the red surface, Samuel began his transmission. "Thank you for informing us of the situation in the United Nations and for sending us the new return solutions. Nevertheless, after evaluating the situation per our standing orders, we have decided to press forward, to Mars."

"I told you we were going to die," Happy said. The man seemed to get a great deal of satisfaction from the fact.

"We're not dead yet," Samuel responded.

"You are correct, we're still about eighteen hours away from that."

Samuel sighed. He wanted to argue, but there was no way he could fix the oxygen scrubber, which had, a mere three days into their planetary stay, gone up in smoke. The air inside the habitat would soon become unbreathable and they'd die. Simple as that.

The next launch window to their orbiter was five days off. The spacecraft might as well have been on Earth for all the good it did them. "I'm going for help."

"Help? The only base in range of the air tanks on our rover is the Chinese settlement. They haven't answered a single one of our radio messages. And we don't know the terrain." Seeing that Samuel was suiting up anyway, Happy insisted, "Even if you make it there, you won't make it back."

"Look, I'm going with you or without you. So you need to decide what you're going to do right now."

Uncharacteristically, Happy chose that moment to chuckle. "Well, since I've come all this way…"

The rover was a near-direct copy of the model the ESA was using in the Polar regions, and like most European things was much more safety oriented than fast. But under Happy's skillful guidance—the man might have been unbearable, but he was an excellent driver—they navigated the boulder fields and arrived at their destination in just under four hours. That meant they actually did have enough air to get back!

A baffling sight met them. Four people in suits of three different designs, two red and one each of bright white and off-white, were furiously packing a six-wheeled truck-like rover the size of the Ugandan Mars Habitat. Samuel identified it immediately, he'd seen it in countless photographs during his training: the Russian *Laika* heavy utility vehicle. What was it doing at the Chinese base?

As soon as they saw them, the frantic work came to a screeching halt. The four astronauts stopped to stare, until one of the red-suited figures reacted. He stepped forward and stood beside the Ugandan rover waiting for them to descend.

Samuel, his head spinning, did so. He strode to the red suit and saw the unmistakable oriental features of the leader of the Chinese mission. The red-suited man put his index finger in front of his helmet.

"Excuse us…"

The man waved his arm agitatedly and repeated the gesture. It almost looked as if he was asking Samuel to be silent.

"The reason…"

The man removed a firearm from a holster, pointed it at Samuel's helmet and made the sign with his finger yet again.

The Ugandan shut up.

Seemingly satisfied, the man gestured with the weapon for Happy and Samuel to walk forward toward the enormous Chinese camp, a palatial facility which made the Ugandan habitat look like an abandoned water tank. He led them to the airlock at gunpoint, and the other red-suited figure rushed ahead to open it.

They were silently ordered inside. The gun never wavered, and Samuel never even dreamed of trying to take it away. The man looked deadly serious.

On the other side of the airlock, the leader of the Chinese expedition unclipped his visor and took a deep breath.

"Remove your helmets." He ordered, waving the gun. "Do not speak."

Samuel and Happy complied.

"Now, are your radios disconnected? Nod if they are."

The Ugandans nodded.

"Good," the Taikonaut replied. He smiled, holstered the weapon and gestured. "Then, on behalf of every other human on the planet, I'm delighted to welcome you to Mars. We've all been admiring your bravery from afar, and it's an honor to finally meet you."

"Wait, what?" Samuel stammered. "Why did you threaten us with the gun?"

"It seemed the simplest way. I apologize if you were frightened."

A woman's voice cut in. "We couldn't answer your radio communications. We've all been ordered by our governments to make no contact with you and offer you no aid. Even the Russians. But we've been monitoring your progress, listening in on your chats with Kampala. We knew you were in trouble."

They turned to see a short-haired woman with ice-blue eyes sitting cross-legged on the floor. She was wearing a white T-shirt with the NASA logo emblazoned on it. She absolutely, positively had no right to be where she was.

"I'm sorry, I don't understand."

"The radio is the problem," the Chinese commander explained. His English was excellent, with a British accent. "Everything said over the radio on the surface, even over local channels, gets picked up by one of the NASA orbiters—we think it's MAVEN III—and beamed back to Earth through the Deep Space Network. So we couldn't respond, not even to tell you that you were welcome here."

"But she…"

"It's a delicate situation. The Russians are the only ones whose government has no problem with them talking to all the rest of us. So we use their truck to get around. Of course, the Americans and the Euros are perfectly friendly, but only the Russians are allowed any contact with the Chinese. No one is really supposed to be talking to the Indians, but ever since you came onto the scene, they haven't been policing that, which is why you saw Nehru loading the truck."

"Nehru? An Indian on the Chinese base?"

The three astronauts who'd been loading the truck entered through the airlock and Samuel looked at each in turn. There was another taikonaut, a Russian, and the cream-colored suit… Indian?

"As I said, it's delicate. When we first arrived, a sandstorm crippled our main generator. We were told by our government to die honorably. And we would have, except that Salenko," he nodded towards the Russian, who'd taken his helmet off to reveal a face as grizzled as it was famous: the first man to walk on Mars, "arrived with his truck and a couple of mechanics and a generator. We had no warning, no radio contact. He just showed up and saved us. That was when we agreed to extend the same treatment to any human being on this world, regardless of nationality. None of the expeditions would still be alive without the help of all the others.

We've all been at the edge of death. Of course, we can't advertise the fact. And we definitely can't call you over the radio to tell you that. The Americans are listening, and they're also watching, but all they see is a Russian truck getting a lot of mileage."

"And you all agreed to this?"

"Almost everyone did. Unfortunately, our political officer failed to survive the discussion. It is very sad, but he died a hero of the People's Republic."

Samuel let that sink in. It was an admission, but it was also a warning. A warning that the men and women living on this planet had cut certain cords with the mother world, and that the same would be expected of the Ugandans. Or else.

"But what are you all doing here?"

"We were loading the *Laika*," Salenko said. "We were going to save you. It sounded like you needed it. If we'd known you were brave enough to risk the journey between your base and this one, we wouldn't have bothered." The big Russian placed the container he was carrying on the ground and enclosed them each in a bear hug. "Welcome to Mars, my friends."

Samuel was overwhelmed. "I don't know what to say."

"Don't say anything. Just don't report on what's happening here," Salenko replied. "I personally don't care. If I ever go back to Earth, I'll be too famous to shoot for treason. But the rest of these guys could be in deep trouble if you talk."

"We wouldn't dream of it," Happy said. "With our luck, we'd land in China and they'd shoot us in your place."

"Anyone alive on this planet is very lucky indeed," the woman said. "Forty-one people who tried before us, and three from a British expedition that we couldn't get to in time, bear witness to that. We won't let anyone else die on our watch, even if we have to openly defy our governments to do it. We're all agreed on that."

Samuel felt tears well up but he refused to give them free rein. "Then count on us to help."

"Good, because the first people you're going to need to help are yourselves."

"I'm sorry. What?"

"You can't stay here indefinitely, of course. We need to get you back and to get your scrubbers fixed, and we need to do it before anyone suspects what's going on here. And you'll need to find a convincing way to tell the world how you managed it on your own."

Samuel shrugged. "I'll tell them only the casing was broken and it started working again when we sealed it. It's a typical launch and landing failure." He chuckled. "And they can't really come here and check it, can they?"

"They might ask us to do it for them," Nehru interjected. "But don't worry. We'll lie for you. I assume your hothouse supplies are alright. You can survive here if we give you the air?"

"Yes. It should work."

"That brings us to the next question," the American woman said. "We're technically traitors for helping you. In all our countries, treason is punishable by death. Some of us might want to return someday."

The atmosphere, celebratory a moment before, suddenly chilled. Salenko broke the silence. "I think what she's trying to ask is whether we can count on you, even in the face of the questions your government might have about what happened here. Will you lie for us?"

This time, the silence stretched uncomfortably. Unusually, it was Happy who replied. "I'll lie for you. We can't go back to Earth anyway, so I see little point in sucking up to them."

Samuel chuckled. "My pragmatic friend is right. We're with you to wherever this might go."

"Good. If your actions match your words, we'll even tell you what we have in mind for the future of Mars. You might be surprised."

Samuel studied the faces around him, each a hero in their own land. "I'm sure I will."

The tension drained from the air and they each received another round of back slapping and hugs.

Salenko started. "Oh, I almost forgot. We have a gift for you. We began brewing it when we heard you were coming."

"Brewing it?"

The man opened the case he'd laid on the floor and pulled out two containers. He handed one to each Ugandan. "Here, drink this. It's pombé. We investigated what the alcoholic drink where you come from is. We had to pool all our resources for the ingredients, so I hope you like it."

Samuel took a sip. It was the worst pombé he'd ever had.

"It's fantastic," he replied with a smile, and took a long drink. The flavor might have been terrible, but it tasted of friendship. And he couldn't keep the tears back any longer.

From DreamForge #3, September 2019

Gustavo Bondoni is an Argentine writer with 200+ stories published in 14 countries, in seven languages. His latest books are Ice Station: Death and The Malakiad. He earned second place in the 2019 Jim Baen Memorial Contest and a Judges Commendation (and second place) in the 2018 James White Award.

Born from Memory

by Jane Lindskold

"I can't remember," I said, "and it's making me crazy. I can't rest. I can't relax. I can't move on. Until I know, I'm stuck."

I was talking to Gabe. I guess you could call him my shrink. He'd been the first person I'd met after I'd come around in the hospital and realized that my life had changed forever.

Gabe sighed and ran his hand through thick, impossibly golden hair. He'd been trying to convince me just to let go.

"All right, Lydia," he said. "There is an alternative."

"Hypnosis?" I suggested dubiously. "I've tried it. It doesn't seem to work on me."

"Not hypnosis. There's a possibility that you can seek out that missing memory."

"Huh?" I caught my reflection in a window pane and realized that I looked remarkably like a goldfish. I could have sketched myself that way, a quick caricature that would eliminate all those necessary, unnecessary details that get put on driver's licenses—brown hair, brown eyes, 5'5", just a little heavy—and still been perfectly recognizable as me, startled to pop-eyed, open-mouthed astonishment.

Gabe went on saying unbelievable things. "What would you say if I told you that strong emotions give birth to a world of their own—a distorted image of the places in which the emotions were originally experienced."

"I'd say that was impossible," I responded, but immediately knew I didn't believe my own words. At a gut level, what Gabe said felt right.

Gabe must have seen my uncertainty, because he replied to my thought, not my words. "We all know it's true, don't we? Places with which we have strong associations feel deeper, richer, more substantial. Even though we can't see this other world, we can feel it."

I chewed on my lower lip, considering. "Is this like the 'vibes' people talk about feeling at a murder scene or something?"

"Something," Gabe agreed. "A lot of those claims are just people letting themselves get over-stimulated by the idea that something significant happened at a given location. This is the real thing. It's true that strong emotions are more often associated with something bad, rather than with something good. That's why a single negative event can overshadow a lifetime of positive associations."

"I don't get what you mean."

"Here's an example... A newlywed and her husband build a home. They live there. Raise a bunch of kids. Celebrate all sorts of great things. Then, one day, he has a heart attack in the family room and dies in his favorite chair. The widow insists on moving, says she feels haunted."

"And?"

"She is, but not by her late husband. She's haunted by her own shock and horror at finding him dead, by the ruination of all her dreams regarding their future together. That's what she can't escape."

"I follow you..." I considered. "The memory I've lost... It isn't negative. I mean, I don't think it's negative. I hope it isn't. That's why I'm so stressed. Until I know..."

"Not all the memory structures are negative," Gabe said. "Some of the most powerful structures are created by experiences so intense you can't really remember them afterward. The emotions pour into you and overflow."

"If that's how it works," I protested, "some scrap of the memory should remain. I can't remember anything."

"You're thinking of this 'overflowing' as if you're a pool or basin. Actually, you're more like a channel. Imagine these intense emotions as a gully washer that comes sweeping through, carrying everything in front of it and leaving nothing behind."

"All right. But you said that there's a landscape built from memories. How does that happen if the memories are washed away?"

"They're washed from you," Gabe said with angelic patience. "I didn't say they were washed from there. They're washed to there, copied or imprinted on the landscape. Pick whatever terms you're happy with. What's important is that, if you move quickly, you should be able to find the missing memory."

"Should?"

"That's right. Structures born from memory are chancy. Some last for a long time. These are usually associated with the sort of places that are constantly recharged with strong emotions."

"Funeral parlors," I suggested. "Hospitals. Airports."

"Churches," Gabe added. "Sports arenas. Schools. They're disproportionately intense. A home or even an apartment building is going to be smaller, harder to find. You'll need a guide."

"You? I wouldn't want to inconvenience you. Anyhow, I should be able to find the place pretty easily. I know exactly where I want to go."

"I doubt you'd be able to navigate the landscape as easily as you think," Gabe replied. "The landscape's not just made of your memories. It's made of all the memories associated with a given location. Good memories, bad memories, happy memories, bittersweet… they're all there, layered on each other like…"

He paused, searching for a metaphor.

"Like an onion?" I suggested.

"I was thinking of one of those fancy desserts, like a baklava or a napoleon. Or one of those cakes with at least fourteen layers and cream in between."

"Mmmm…"

"Give it up," Gabe urged. "Try to move forward. There could be pastry in your future yet."

I shook my head. "I can't. I've tried, but I can't."

"If you insist, then I'll introduce you to a dragon who might help you."

"Did you say 'dragon'?"

"I did." Gabe sighed and tousled his hair again. At least he wasn't pulling it out at the roots. "Dragons hunt where dreams collect. They burrow in the rubble, swallow what they find there."

"Did you say 'swallow'?"

"I did. Dragons eat accumulated emotions. We're lucky that they do. Otherwise, the bleed-through would drive crazy anybody with the least bit of sensitivity. That's why even a place freighted with emotional significance eventually goes back to neutral."

"I guess that makes sense," I said, thinking of tours I'd taken to historically significant places, how they'd seemed sort of vanilla. I'd always credited that to my lack of sensitivity—which is a pretty odd thing for an artist, especially one who had more than her share of what is often termed "artistic temperament."

Gabe was still explaining. "Dragons savor their finds as an oenophile savors a rare vintage—and like the oenophile, they destroy what they most treasure."

"That doesn't sound good."

"It isn't, at least for you—not if that memory is as crucial to your peace of mind as it seems to be."

"It is. If I can't find out what happened, I'll go crazy. It's important."

"Lydia, I know I'm the one who brought this up, but there's a reason I don't want you to try this. Humans are nothing more than dense bundles of memories. I'll ask Arcadia not to eat you and he won't, but…"

"There might be other dragons and they might not be as restrained?"

"There *will* be other dragons and, as soon as they get your scent, they're going to come looking for dessert."

"Oh…" I shrugged. "What do I have to lose?"

"A lot. You're worried about the absence of one memory. If you're not careful, you're going to lose them all."

The dragon Gabe summoned to be my guide was called Arcadia.

"Isn't Arcadia a place?" I said. "Like in Shakespeare, a sort of rural paradise?"

"Yeah," Gabe laughed. "Arcadia is a specialist in dreams of rural bliss. You might say he's eaten more dreams of Arcady than anyone else."

Arcadia reminded me of a lizard or dinosaur rather than a dragon. My mental image of dragons includes wings. Arcadia didn't have any. My personal opinion was that a dragon should be more flashy—metallic scales in hues of gold or silver or flame, perhaps. Arcadia was a mottled dull brown that would blend in perfectly against rock or desert.

I wondered if Arcadia craved those dreams of rural paradise precisely because he was so dully colored. Maybe he felt more beautiful when rich greens and floral bowers flashed through his system.

Yet, despite his muted coloration, Arcadia was beautiful in his non-classical dragon fashion. His head was almost deer-like, with large, liquid eyes that shifted from light to dark brown depending on his surroundings. Where a deer's ears would be, he had two curving horns that pointed forward. His torso—he didn't really have a separate neck—was crested with spikes that extended down to its base. His tail resembled a gradually tapering boa constrictor. His three-clawed hind feet were enormous, enabling him to balance upright briefly, although not to walk bipedally. His front feet were much smaller, the taloned digits positioned so he could use them like hands with two thumbs and three extra-long fingers.

After introductions were completed, Gabe invited Arcadia to sniff me all over. The dragon did so, then sneezed.

"Arcadia will use your scent to take you directly to the cognate of the area where you lived most recently. He'll also take you to the right location. After that..."

"It's up to me?"

Gabe nodded, then turned to Arcadia. "Ready?"

The dragon nodded, a sort of pushup motion that involved the entire front of his body. He stared at the space directly in front of him, his eyes darkening almost to black. His nostrils flared. The spikes along his torso raised vertically, making me glad I hadn't suggested I ride on his back—something I had thought about, so we wouldn't get separated.

The air in front of Arcadia waivered, the way it does over a hot electric burner. Then it began to peel back, revealing a barren cityscape that looked as if it had been ravaged by an earthquake. Cold air wafted out. Shivering, I realized that icicles dripped from the rubble. There was spray in the air that stung like sleet.

"It's cold!" I gasped.

Arcadia chuckled. "Thou hast heard the phrase 'frozen in memory'? There is truth to it."

Gabe handed me a heavy coat and hat. I was already dressed for hiking. Then he helped me set a large pack upon my shoulders. Lastly, he thrust a furled umbrella into my hand. I wondered why I'd need so much gear just to find a memory but, looking through the opening Arcadia had created, I understood. In this destroyed landscape, going even a few blocks would be tough.

"I had no idea it would be so... so ruined!" I said, looking around the dragon's smooth brown flank and through the opening.

"My brethren, my rivals," came Arcadia's dry, rasping voice. "My sisters, my people. They have been hunting here. Thus the damage."

He lifted his head and the curved horns moved, questing like antennae. "The others are not nearby at this moment, but they may be close enough to scent you, little seeker. Dost thou still wish to go forth?"

"More than ever," I replied as stoutly as I could. "Gabe warned me that memories do not last forever, even here."

"Less long," Arcadia agreed, "when my people are about. I shalt not be able to attend upon thee as closely as we had hoped. I must go where I can scout out—perchance distract—those who will surely catch your scent. Are you ready?"

"Let's go!" Pausing only to give Gabe's hand a firm shake, I stepped forth. Arcadia trundled alongside, standing a little over me. His underbelly was lighter than his upper, patterned like light on water.

Our first steps splashed us into what looked like a river framed by half-ruined buildings. The surface underfoot was slick, part water, part ice, so that with each step I slid, crunched, and splashed. Arcadia, with his clawed feet, did better than I, but the heavy, ankle-high hiking boots Gabe had insisted I wear kept my feet dry and gave as good footing as could be hoped for. After several steps, I realized we were standing in the middle of what had been a roadway, although there were no vehicles anywhere in sight.

"I almost know this place," I said, craning my neck to look up and around. "That building in front of us, the one with the blue awning. It reminds me of the Grande Hotel. The one next to it, though... The one with the old-style fire escapes. I don't know it."

"It was a department store," Arcadia replied. "Torn down some five years ago. It still features in people's memories so, for now, it remains."

"I think I remember hearing about that store," I mused. "People were divided as to whether its removal was urban beautification or loss of a landmark. Looking at it now…"

"A place here does not always look as it does in the present world," Arcadia reminded me. "Memories overlap. A memory from one season conflicts with that of another. If they are strong enough, memories may distort the size, even the shape of a structure. Look there, down beyond the hotel. Do you see the green building?"

"I do. Don't know… Wait! That's the hospital, isn't it? I wouldn't have known it if I hadn't spent so much time there. The features seem to shift, as if we're somehow seeing all sides of it at once."

"The hospital, yes," Arcadia agreed. "Shaped by so many memories that one image could not hope to contain it. Beyond it, do you see the tall building with water gushing forth?"

"I do. It's not in very good shape, is it?"

"No. Dragons have been there, and recently. Flowing water shows that. When we devour memories, water flows, carrying the detritus away. Sometimes, new memories rebuild a place. Sometimes, not. I shall climb aloft to see if I can discover where the dragons have gone. Do you recognize enough to direct your own search?"

I looked side to side and was about to say, "No, I don't," when, with a sinking feeling in my gut, I realized what I was looking at.

"Oh, dear god…" I managed, my voice so tight and strained I hardly knew it. "You brought us very close. Do you see that heap of rubble, down from where the department store was? That's my old apartment building!"

"That is where you need go then," the dragon said, turning away.

"But there's nothing there!"

"How wilt thou know," Arcadia asked, "unless thou lookest?"

I had the feeling I'd disappointed the dragon by turning coward. After all, I was the one who had insisted on coming here.

"You're right. Be careful, now."

Arcadia's horns curled tight in what I realized was the equivalent of laughter. "I shall. From my memories, I will draw white doves if need arises to send thee a message. Go now. Balance swiftness with caution. Perhaps all is not lost."

He swiveled his long torso, splashing away along the water- and ice-filled channel that had once been a busy street. I shook my head, hard. Somewhere it still was a busy street. This place was memory and distortion—not reality.

I began climbing the slippery, ice-crusted mound of rubble that had once been my home. As I struggled, several times sliding back almost to the street, I remembered how I had come here.

Three years earlier, I had been diagnosed with a rare cancer. That was the bad news. The worse news was that what I had was so rare there wasn't even a treatment protocol. The worst news was that they gave me about two years.

Then the good news came. The daughter of a really rich man— some sort of software entertainment magnate—had been diagnosed with the same cancer. No fundraisers for Mr. Bucks, no banquets with thousand-dollar tickets. He just started throwing money toward finding a solution. Problem. The researchers needed test subjects. Like I said, the cancer was very rare. They found me. I was offered a job as guinea pig.

I took it. On odd days, I hoped they'd actually find a cure. On even days, I settled for believing I was doing something useful. Maybe they would find a cure for me and Melody and the rest. Maybe they'd be too late for me, but they'd learn enough to save someone else.

I'm not going into details about those years. If there were memories I would choose to forget, those would be the ones. I hadn't liked needles before. Within a few months, I liked them even less. Wait… I said I wasn't going there and I'm not, not except for the part that matters…

Mr. Bucks was really good to me and the other guinea pigs. In most cases, we were all relocated to the same city so we'd be close to the hospital that was the center of the project. He and his family already lived in the vicinity. The few who couldn't relocate for one reason or another were flown in on chartered jets.

Our patron offered us a choice of accommodations within easy reach of the hospital. I asked for a place with a studio where I could paint when I felt well enough. To my astonishment, I was given the entire top floor of an apartment building. It was remodeled so that there were several studios, each positioned to take advantage of natural light at different times of day, so I could take advantage of any chance moment. A private elevator was put in. I even had a live-in nurse caretaker.

I did paint when I felt well enough, which wasn't nearly as often as you'd think. Still, I probably painted more often than I would have if the cancer hadn't made it possible for me to quit my day job. I mean, I was good. I'd even had some gallery showings, but I wasn't making a living. I was seriously aware of the irony.

We lost people from the team almost from the start. Mack had been diagnosed too late and was already weak. Cynthia got some rogue infection. Tansy reacted badly—not to the drug being tested, but to an unpredictable synergistic reaction between it and her blood pressure medication. Others, after months of needles and tests and more tests, ups and downs, and, worst of all, the poisonous hope that came after each trial, only to be dashed again, dropped out, preferring to die slowly and peacefully, drugged to the gills in some hospice.

Mr. Bucks may have resented their retreat—but maybe not— maybe it just made him even more grateful to those of us who kept on with the trial. He continued to pay the dropouts' expenses, just as he'd promised, even though Melody got worse, becoming thinner and weaker, the slender figure that looked so beautiful in the photos I'd seen of her (remember, she was the daughter of a very, very rich man and fair game for the tabloids and fashion magazines) becoming gaunt and ragged.

I don't know what I looked like. I'd asked that the apartment be decorated without mirrors or obviously reflective surfaces. I avoided catching my reflection by chance—one good thing about being an artist was that I could pretty much guess where these would be.

Last time I'd heard, Melody wasn't doing well. During trials, we'd often been roommates. Lately, I'd heard she was living in a sterile room, protected from any chance of infection. I hoped she was okay. I'd expected her to be a brat, a spoiled child of privilege, but she was one of the rare ones who learned from watching those around her—including, so I guessed, her own mother, a shallow, self-centered creature who made Jenny Churchill look like Mother Teresa.

Melody and I had been on about the same progression curve, so when I heard how poorly she was doing, I decided the time had come for me to complete my final painting. I'd been working on a tribute to all of those in the test group, a project I'd started after Mack had died. I knew the galleries wouldn't like it. They'd call it "sentimental," dismiss it for being too photorealistic. I didn't care. I was long past the days when I had obsessed over my artistic legacy. The closer I drew to closing my eyes that final time, the less legacy seemed to matter.

I'd collected photos from all the members of our test group or from their families. The doctors, too, and the nurses and techs and researchers, for they had done the remarkable. A few, knowing us for the doomed, had withheld their hearts. Most, however, had given us all they had—wept even more readily than we had, celebrated every small victory. I knew that each and every one of them at some time or another had struggled with the belief that they were failing us. We guinea pigs might have put our bodies on the line, but the medical staff had offered their souls. They belonged as well.

Now, as I struggled up the slippery slope, wondering in some corner of my mind if what was keeping me from making forward progress was my own fear at what I might find—or fail to find—I concentrated on the painting. I'd placed us in a setting inspired by Seurat's "A Sunday Afternoon on the Island of La Grande Jatte."

You might know it as the painting featured in the musical *Sunday in the Park with George*.

I hadn't used Seurat's impressionistic style, though, because I wanted everyone to be perfectly recognizable. I'd spread the figures over several canvases, so that no one need be diminished. If the piece was ever displayed (and I doubted it would be), the canvases could be hung side by side, creating the illusion of being one piece. Once I would have used a huge canvas and a scaffold, but I was beyond such exertions.

Nearly on hands and knees, I made my way closer to the top of the rubble heap. Icy water misting down from above was making bad footing worse. Belatedly remembering the umbrella Gabe had given me, I unfurled it. It was bright red, the color—not of blood, that's darker, as I knew all too well—but of poppies.

"Fitting," I said to no one in particular. "Poppies are for remembrance, no matter what Ophelia said about rosemary. There are other battlefields than Flanders."

A shaft of light pierced the mist, reflecting off the umbrella's dome and casting a brilliant glow on a heap of rubble in front of and above me. That was my first thought at least.

"No, it can't be that. The angle isn't right. What then?"

Poppies, a little voice said in my mind. It sounded like Melody, before she'd gotten so weak that all she could do was whisper. *For remembrance.*

I furled the umbrella. If the red light vanished, then... But it didn't. It remained, shining on top of what I suddenly recognized as the cage of what had been my private elevator.

Using the furled umbrella as an alpenstock, I reached the summit. I squeezed between bent girders and bits of concrete to get inside the elevator cage. The pack Gabe had insisted I carry was too bulky. I shrugged it off and tossed it in ahead of me, then I pushed through.

I had half-expected a miraculous transformation, but nothing happened. Foolishly, I stood, trapped inside a cage of my own choosing. Of course, that was the moment Arcadia's white doves swooped down.

Their voices were just like you'd expect doves' voices to be, half coo, half gentle femininity. "Dragons come! Dragons come! Arcadia has done, all he can do. The rest, dear, Lydia, is up to you."

Crouching, I tore into the pack, hoping for something I could use as a weapon. I found a folded blanket, packets of trail mix, matches, a bottle of aloe salve, a flask of water, and extra socks. Nothing that would help against creatures the size of Arcadia, creatures that ate buildings. I swigged water from the flask, considering…

That splash of poppy red seemed to promise that something was still here, something for me to find. Good. No matter how ruined the building seemed to be, I was going to take that as my guiding light… Fleeting scraps of something read long ago crossed my mind, something about the symbolism of umbrellas. Protection and authority. The dome of the sky. A miniature universe.

The elevator cage was somewhat crumpled, but I had enough room to open my umbrella. I wedged it so that it caught the sunlight filtering through the rubble, tinting my private universe the same translucent red as the splash of color that had brought me here.

Red sky at night, I thought, *Lydia's delight. Red sky at morning, dragons take warning!*

Closing my eyes, I reached out to where the elevator buttons should be, not permitting myself to think that I hadn't seen them earlier, when I'd first entered the ruined cage. I'd pressed them so often, often by memory, so then…

I felt them. Smooth, slightly raised, the bumps of Braille alongside. I pushed the button for up and felt the elevator begin to rise. A gentle ping announced the first floor, second floor, third, fourth, then, finally, my own… Only when the elevator stopped and I heard the doors slide open did I move. Eyes still shut, I walked forward, focusing hard on my memory of my apartment as it had been the last time I had seen it.

When Mr. Bucks had the floor remodeled for me, hallways had been eliminated wherever possible to ease the passage of wheelchairs. The elevator opened into a wide foyer that, in turn, opened to the largest room of the apartment. This had been the one I'd been using as my studio toward the end. The finished panels of the tribute painting were hung, unframed, on one of the walls. There was a gap in the middle of the bottom row. That painting should be on the easel near the window...

I forced myself to look, afraid of what I might see. Afraid, more, of what I might not see.

"I had no idea I looked so bad," I said aloud. My voice sounded strange, like I was in a small, enclosed space, even though to all appearances I was in a large open one. "No idea..."

The figure who sat in the wheelchair in front of the easel didn't react to my voice. She kept painting, her head alternately craning forward and pulling back, as if finding an acceptable range of vision was difficult. She looked a wreck: skin both slack and bloated, scalp hairless, shoulders hunched. She looked about ninety, although I knew she was barely thirty-six. Only her hands and arms were steady. One held the paintbrush, the other the palette on which paints were arrayed. She was painting with a focused determination that said she knew time was running out.

I found I could move closer. Now, at last, I could see what I had come to learn. The picture on the easel was of two young women. One—prettier by far—wore a pale ivory dress with pink rosebuds and lace at wrist and collar. Her hair—a rich auburn that owed nothing to a bottle—spilled loose over her shoulders, almost to her waist.

She was sitting on a picnic blanket spread beneath a birch, leaning against the tree's trunk, reading out loud from a book of verse. Her audience was seated in front of an easel, wearing paint-smeared jeans and a well-used smock. There was a resemblance between the painter and the wreck in the wheelchair. They even wore the same smock.

Me. Of course. The other woman was Melody. During the early days of our treatment, when we were weak but not hopeless, she'd promised me that she'd take me to her favorite spot on her parent's estate.

"You'd love it there. It's so peaceful. You could paint and I'll read to you or something." Her voice had turned wistful. "Think of it. No pinging monitors. No needles. No medicinal smells. Birdsong and the chatter of water over rocks."

"And the chatter of you," I'd laughed. Melody loved to talk. She even had things worth listening to, remarkable in a girl of only twenty-two.

We'd never make it there. Not in reality. But that was how I wanted to remember us. Not as we had met—sick, dying, increasingly decrepit—but as we had hoped we would be. Surely the dreams were at least as valuable as reality.

But had I finished? That's what I needed to know. Like many artists, I had my own sheaf of superstitions. Mine was that, although I roughed them in, I never finished the eyes before the painting was done. It creeped me out to see apparently living eyes peering out of a partially completed canvas—and I'd learned that it made it almost impossible for me to scrape away and restart, because somehow the piece was already alive and it felt like murder.

So, had I finished the eyes? Mine were done. They would have been easier, since I was in profile, focused on the canvas, but Melody? Her eyes were a particularly distinctive shade of green, not brilliant emerald or hazel, but akin to one of the darker jades. I'd anguished over getting it right…

The painter me was blending paint, trying a bit, shaking her head with frustration. Not right… not right… And I could feel how tired I was getting. Soon my hands would begin to shake and I could never manage anything as detailed as eyes when they did.

And I knew with the absolute certainly of the dying that I wouldn't have another chance.

"Lydia?" A voice from the other room. Carrie, the admirable woman who had been my nurse companion. "Shouldn't you take a break, dear? You've been painting for quite a while now. Maybe a little tea?"

"All right," I called, my voice cracked and hoarse, like something from a horror film. "Oolong?"

I chose oolong because Carrie was a tea snob. We'd been given a very fine blend by Mr. Bucks. I knew she'd make sure the pot was preheated, the water the perfect temperature. It would give me time...

That was the last thing I remembered. What I remembered next was being in the hospital. Apparently, when Carrie had come in with the tea, she'd found me unconscious. I couldn't make anyone understand what I needed to know. And then, in the night, I'd died.

Please, Lydia, I begged myself. *You have maybe five minutes. Don't waste them. Don't let Melody be uncompleted. If she's got to die, let her live at least in memory.*

The painter me at last seemed satisfied with her colors. She started laying them on, not quickly—there was no time for quickly, because there was no time for a mistake. Deliberately. Green. Then shading. A rim of slightly darker green around the iris. A pupil—that had to be just right. The whites. Detail on the lids and rims. A touch-up on the lashes.

The painter's hand fell limp. Brush and palette slid to the floor. Melody stared out of the canvas, as alive as she never would be.

I realized I was weeping, but with happiness, not sorrow. I had my memory back. I hadn't failed. I might not have beaten the cancer, but I hadn't failed. The room that had been my studio faded from around me, as my right to memory ended.

When I opened eyes I hadn't realized were shut, I found myself surrounded by dragons.

Humans, as Gabe had said, are little more than bundles of memories. So, it turns out, are dragons. There are differences, of course. Humans make memories. Dragons hoard them. They don't destroy them—Gabe was wrong about that, but then, even angels aren't perfect.

Dragons take memories into themselves, digest them, remember them, make them into something with scales and tails and, sometimes, even wings.

I have wings. They're bright as poppies.

And I remember.

From DreamForge #1, Founders Issue

Jane Lindskold has published over 30 novels and countless short stories. She grew up in Washington, DC, got a Ph.D. in English with concentrations in Medieval, Renaissance, and Modern British Literature. She settled in New Mexico in the '90s.

Tea with Gibbons

by Tyler Tork

When she died, his wife turned into a flock of starlings. She loved the exhilaration of flight, and it was an easy setup to maintain. The birds grew Link seeds to feed to their chicks, and the old and sick could simply be de-linked. It made her hard to talk with, but that was nothing new with Maureen.

Decades later, when Jeffrey's original body finally became too painful and expensive to keep going, he knew that option wasn't for him. After a final get-together with friends, he'd shut the tired old thing down. All its memories and patterns had long since been duplicated in the cloud so he didn't lose anything important, but now he needed a new sensorium.

After four months of searching, he hadn't yet found a satisfactory replacement. "I have no center," he complained to Schel. He'd rented a gibbon to meet an old friend at an outdoor cafe in Sydney. "I miss the consistency. I miss the routines." His lips didn't move, since a gibbon's vocal equipment wasn't up to producing human speech, but a Link call worked just as well across a table as across the world. "I liked sleeping."

"You always were a stodgy old thing." Schel had also worn a

gibbon for the occasion, a female. She was usually more of a dog person, so perhaps she was plotting to get him into bed.

Jeffrey had mixed feelings about that. It had nothing to do with Maureen—they hadn't spoken in years, and their marriage had legally ended with the death of her OB. And he had no objection to Schel as a partner; they'd slept together a few times while her OB was alive, and a couple of times after her spaceplane accident, when she was living in a mech.

No, it was mostly that he'd never done it using a body other than the one he'd thought of as his own. Thinking about being with Schel now, in these bodies, made him uneasy; it seemed perverse.

"I guess I'm a traditionalist," he said, answering her as well as commenting on his own thoughts. He took a slice of apple—he'd always had scones with his tea, but the fruit on a nearby table had smelled delicious, and was. Schel smelled nice, too. The sun was warm, the cobblestones wet from a recent rain, and the streets uncrowded, with ninety-five percent of humanity in sim. Wasting their time, in Jeffrey's view, playing with bits instead of engaging with the real world.

Schel scooted a little closer on the curved bench that circled their table. "You could be a human again. The latest bodies will last centuries, with very little maintenance."

Jeffrey sighed. "They take so long to grow, though. I should've started one years ago."

"Why didn't you?"

She put a hand on his back, sifting through the long hairs there. Jeffrey tensed for a moment, but it felt wonderful, so he didn't move away. "I don't know. I never was comfortable running multiple bodies, and it'd be annoying to be a baby and have to be cared for. The times I did rentals, I felt like I wasn't really me. And maybe I was in denial. I thought I'd have longer." If only it were possible to get a human body already grown... but of course, it would have a personality of its own, a complex enough mind to expand into the cloud when Linked, not serve as a peripheral. Maybe in a century or two, mechs would be good enough, but not today.

Schel's other hand joined the first on his back, and she pulled the band of his shorts down a little to access more area. "Lots of people get along fine with just rentals. Including me. There's always a new experience, and travel is a breeze. In fact, I'm toying with the idea of emigrating to 82 Eridani. If you do decide to commit to raising a new body, you could wait and do it there. We'd have to be offline for twenty-five years, but if we get together a group to go, at least there'd be people we knew once we got there. We'd bring culture to the Dannies."

"I'm sure the colony's created plenty of their own culture by now." Still, it was an interesting idea. Jeffrey shifted to bring a new portion of his back into her reach. The Eridani colonies probably could use a little adult supervision—from the infant he would become when he arrived. There was useful work to do there. "I'll think about it."

"No rush. In three or five years. I haven't used up this solar system yet." Schel reached out a long arm for her cup, raised her head and pursed her lips to drain it, then held it to her face to lick the inside. "Nice tea. I could come back here. Are you almost done with yours?"

There was a little left in the pot, but Schel seemed to be getting restless. "I can be done."

"There's a lovely park a little way down the road. Lots of trees. Have you ever brachiated?"

"Have I ever...?" He recognized the Latin root, but the cloud supplied the definition before he had to think further. "Swung from trees?"

"It's like flying, except you don't have to be a bird-brain to do it." Schel hopped down and reached for him. "You'll love it. And there are lots of private places in the branches. We can talk more up there."

Jeffrey hesitated a moment, then reached out and let her draw him gently to the ground. She kept hold of his hand as they walked down the sidewalk, bow-legged, past a duck pond, a small farm tower, an op-con place in a narrow storefront, an art supply depot. At their slow pace, mechs strode past, towering over them. Jeffrey, feeling cheerful, waved to a group of kangaroos going the opposite direction. They didn't wave back, but maybe there was no one inside.

"Have you been a dolphin?" Schel asked suddenly.

"No."

"No, you've just been sitting in the cloud getting stale, haven't you? All right for some, but not for us. Dolphin, definitely. My treat. If I do go to Eridani, first I want to try some things that aren't available there yet, and it's nice to have someone to try them with."

"You're trying to corrupt me."

"I'm helping you make an informed choice. Come on." She squeezed his hand. "Death has a lot to offer."

From DreamForge #2, June 2019

Tyler Tork is author of the historical science-fiction novel *Doctor Dead* (Rampant Loon Media, 2015), the nonfiction *One-Hour Author Website* (self, 2016 & 2017), and short stories in semi-pro markets. He's a Clarion graduate, under contract with Oghma Creative Media for several fiction and nonfiction books.

The Weight of Mountains

by L. Deni Colter

We stopped near land's end, Mama and I, under the branches of a tree like none I'd ever seen. It perched there at the edge of our world with roots that might go through to the other side and branches that must brush the stars above at night. Mama sat cross-legged in her canvas trousers and work shirt, same as I wore, same as most folks of our land did.

The enormous coil of rope leaning against the tree had awaited me when we arrived. I stood taller and broader of shoulder than both of my older brothers who'd attempted this thing before me, and still, carrying it would be difficult, though not my greatest struggle. I wondered what doubts my brothers wrestled with when they'd stood in this place, about to begin.

I picked at one end of the rope until a thread came loose. Pinching it between my fingers I pulled it free. Spun in some circular fashion, the rope would unwind bit by bit into a thread long enough to stretch to the core of the world. I circled the tree with the thread and tied it to the great trunk.

"Once you pick that rope up," Mama said, "you can't set it down again. Maybe not ever, Cinder."

"I know, Mama." I sat near her, not ready to take the weight onto my shoulder yet; worried that I might never feel ready.

She looked down at her ankles. Her dark hair covered half her face, light at the temples where it had turned gray after my eldest brother undertook this journey. Her bronze skin shone in the last of the daylight. "I lost them all, and for what?"

"I lost them too, Mama."

She looked up. "Then why won't you change your mind?"

I rested my forearms on my raised knees. "Because we were chosen for this. I owe it to our family that went before. To all the people counting on me to bind our land to the core."

I'd spent my whole life *not* telling her how much I wished Old Man Umber had never spoken the prophecy all those years ago when he was still a young boy, foretelling that our land would break off the end of the world and float away. Naming my father's mother as the first of our line to try and save it. My grandmother, then my father, then my two older brothers had tried and failed.

"You're young," she said. "Wait one more cycle." She looked at me with such pleading my heart ached.

"I'm a man grown, Mama. Twenty cycles of seasons. I've had a lifetime of knowing this day might come."

"Then I'm going too," she said. Her eyes held that steely look she got when determined. She'd followed me to land's end, repeating her arguments as if I'd hear something new in them. She'd never said this before.

"You can't come, Mama. Only Daddy's line." The boy-Umber had seen that as well.

"My mother-in-binding, my palm-bound mate, and my two oldest boys all chose this over family. When you go, I've got no one left."

"You've got your life."

"All of you were my life."

"I have to go, Mama."

She made no response except to stand when I did.

I bent to the enormous rope, turning away so she wouldn't see my fear when I committed to it. My spine compressed as I hauled it onto my shoulder, my neck muscles strained. I heard her harsh exhalation, a silent sob at my back. I willed strength into my knees and started for the border. Mama matched me stride for stride. I hoped with all my heart that she bluffed; that she'd stop when we got there.

One short, difficult rise later and the boundary of land's end lay before us. It looked nothing like I'd expected. The green grass of my homeland truncated sharp as an amputated limb into the nothing-ness of endless yellow desert. I walked to meet it and the thread from my rope unspooled behind.

Please don't, I thought as I reached the edge, but Mama didn't hesitate. I stepped into the deep, hot sand. She stepped across at my side.

From one stride to the next, she shrank to my knee and dropped to all fours, her clothes falling away behind. Her body sprouted thick, dark fur with buff stripes at the sides. Her head narrowed, triangular and pointed now. Her teeth and claws grew long.

"Oh, Mama." It came out in a whisper, but relief that she lived overcame despair at seeing her changed to a gulo. Whatever power had changed her, I had to admire the irony that it chose a creature as stubborn, ferocious, and protective as Mama had always been.

Together we passed over a border we could never cross again. I didn't want to look back, but did anyway. Desert surrounded us; home had vanished. The only tie to it was the thread trailing across the sand. Mama already panted in the heat, the long hair on her new body warming her more quickly than me, though the desert sun overhead would wear on me soon enough.

A few strides past the border, a cabin came into view. It seemed we approached it with unnatural speed. I couldn't determine if we moved toward it or if it moved toward us. An old woman waited for us on the porch that I would have sworn empty a moment ago. She sat in a rocker of wood so weathered that all color had bled into the dry heat. Her feet were propped on a railing of branch and log, still in bark, and so derelict she might push it over with a hard shove. Smoke drifted from a pipe jutting straight out from her mouth.

We halted at the porch steps. She nodded her assent and we climbed up to join her. I took a seat on a rough bench opposite her rocker, my back to the railing and the desert, my shoulder near her bare and calloused feet. Mama lay down at my side, still panting, her long teeth exposed.

The creak of the rocker pumped through the still air. The woman, shriveled and yellowed as an old apricot, puffed on her pipe, the blue-gray irises of her eyes sharp in the soft decay of her face. Mama watched her, head up, alert. The old woman removed the pipe.

"I welcome you to the crossing."

If some traditional answer was expected, I'd never learned it and so I gave none. Perhaps this was as far as any of my family had ever made it due to nothing more than not knowing a required response.

"Who have you loved most in your life?" the old woman asked without further preamble.

If this proved the easiest of her questions, then my test would be difficult indeed, but I knew that in this place nothing but truth would do. I looked to my mother and thought of her sacrifices. I thought of Appleonia, the maid whose love had nearly kept me from my duty when my mother's had not. I thought of my father, who'd instilled duty in me by example of his own strength and love. I thought of my older brothers.

Nothing stirred in the desert around me. Each grain of sand seemed poised for my answer. I wondered if this place had looked the same to the others or different to each person who came here.

"Myself," I answered. My mother turned her black, beady eyes to me in surprise.

The old woman puffed a breath of smoke.

"What secret did you keep from everyone you know?"

Again, something easy to know, difficult to tell.

"My fear."

She waited for the rest.

"My fear of this task. I don't want to do this. I don't want to be a living tether for my land, tied for all time to the core. I'm scared it'll tear at my limbs. I worry it'll be a torment for all eternity." I kept my arms relaxed, my feet still, but my stomach churned at the imaginings I'd harbored all my life.

Mama pawed softly at my foot. At least I'd been able to keep it from her until now. The third question came while I still fought to settle my stomach from the second.

"Do you believe you'll succeed?"

The easiest question by far. "No." I shook my head. "My family was stronger than I am and they failed. I don't know why they didn't succeed, but I suspect fear will be my undoing."

A soft mewling noise came from Mama's throat. Her hard head rubbed my calf. I was glad now that she'd been changed; gulos couldn't weep. I could, but I blinked back the tears the admission provoked. I waited for instructions. None came.

"Blessings on your undertaking," the old woman said, jamming her pipe stem in her mouth and chewing it into the right alignment.

Again, I knew of no traditional response. I stood with an effort under the weight of my rope. We left the porch and the Guardian behind. The thread strung out behind me as we set out across the desert.

I looked back once. A monster, large as the cabin, coiled where the cabin had stood a moment ago. It shimmered in the desert heat as if its existence were divided between this place and another. The pointed head of a viper swayed above a thick body with four taloned wings folded around long, thin legs, shiny and lithe like a widow-maker spider's legs. I couldn't see and couldn't guess the hind end of the creature.

My rope weighed me down as much as it had since I'd first picked it up. The thread pulling from the raveled end lightened the weight so minutely, step-by-step, that I noticed no difference. The rope and the deep sand made each step an effort. Mama fared little better with her heavy coat, lifting her stubby legs high with every stride so her long nails didn't drag.

"Look there," I said. I pointed and she followed my arm and finger to a hazy, purple outline at the horizon. I'd heard tales of mountains, and wondered if that might be them. If so, they were smaller than I'd been led to believe.

The desert must not have been as flat as it looked, for a short while later we topped a small dune and discovered a hidden depression over the crest. At the bottom of the depression lay a man. I'd seen no sign of tracks, but perhaps shifting sand had covered them. I wondered how long he'd been here. I squatted at his back and touched his shoulder, thinking him dead until he moaned.

His shoulders were as wide as my own, his upper arms and chest larger. From there he tapered to a narrow waist, as I did, but below that he shriveled to hips that could never have born weight, and legs no larger around than my forearms. Over his left shoulder was an enormous coil of rope, equaling my own. He must've crawled here from wherever he started, but it was certain he'd go no farther.

I pulled the flask that Mama and I shared from my pocket and offered him a drink. Mama growled, but I held it to his lips. He drank, but only a sip. The urge to take more must've been mighty, but with lindel juice a little was enough.

I pulled his legs toward me and supported his back, working him into a sitting position against the dune.

"I thank you for your kindness." His voice was hoarse even after the juice. "May I have your name to keep while I yet live?"

"Cinder," I said.

"Fulgere," he said.

"You're headed for the mountains?"

"I was. I got farther than I thought I would."

I wondered if all from his land were physically challenged, the same as him, or if his family had been chosen despite one person's challenges.

"How many have gone before you?" he asked me.

"Four from my line. I'm the youngest."

He nodded, understanding all that implied. "And your companion?"

"My mother."

"Ah," was his only response.

I offered the flask again, but he shook his head. "You'll need it more."

I looked toward the distant mountains. They had grown perhaps a finger since I first saw them. Even if he abandoned his rope, he couldn't crawl home. Daddy had told us there was no going back. And in this state, he'd never make it to his goal, not even if I left him the whole flask.

Mama growled, a low rumble starting deep in her chest. She'd always been able to guess what I was thinking.

"We'd better get going," I said to him. "Sorry this won't be more comfortable for you." I leaned my right shoulder into his midsection. The weight of my rope nearly unbalanced me when my hands sank into the soft sand. Mama nipped at my fingers.

"You can't," he protested. "You'll only die too."

"Your rope will slide down once I lift you. You'll have to hold it with your hands. Can you do it?"

"Yes."

He didn't have a chance to say more as I pushed my shoulder into him. His broad torso fell across my back. I straightened, still on my knees, balancing his weight with the weight of my rope. That was only the half of it, I knew. His rope still rested on the ground. Mama growled again, a long, angry rumbling.

There was no way to use my hands to push to my feet without my rope slipping from my shoulder. I braced one hand on the coil and one on his deformed hips, dragging my left knee up until my foot was under me. My weight, the weight of my rope, the weight of the man and his rope—my thigh took it all. Or so I thought until I looked down and saw Mama on her hind legs at my side, pushing up on Fulgere's rope with all her muscular animal strength. My thigh shook and strained as I lifted high enough to get my right foot flat on the ground. If something in my leg tore, we were all lost. If I fell, I didn't know if I'd have it in me to start over.

I stood. My feet sunk to the ankles in the sand. Mama's bushy tail lashed in anger. I took a step, then another.

"What were your siblings' names?" Fulgere's voice drifted up from the area of my low back. Breathless. It must've been hard for him to talk in that position.

I was breathless too, but the little air I spent on words made no difference; the distraction did—as he must've known it would.

"Clay was oldest." The words came haltingly, every few steps when I paused for breath. "Mama went through," a few steps more, "about a dozen… other names first… When she reached that one… Daddy agreed." Slowly we left the dune behind as I told our history. I kept my eyes fixed on the mountains as I told him that Coal was next. That was okay by Daddy, too, but she had to change the spelling from C-o-l-e to C-o-a-l. My name was all Daddy, though he more often called me "Little Bit." Little bit of trouble, little bit of sunshine, little bit of mischief."

Those few sentences took me more than a hundred strides. Sweat dripped from my face and ran down my back. I looked up and the mountains were half again as high, as if they rushed to meet us like the cabin had done. I wondered how far I'd actually walked.

The hot desert turned cool and blue. I glanced up at the sun. It stood directly overhead still, but it receded from us, as if it flew up and away from this mid-world.

"Fulgere," I panted, "day's ending and I have to rest. Can you drop your rope and still hold one end?" Daddy had told me I must never put my rope down once I'd picked it up. Hopefully this would count close enough for Fulgere, as I couldn't kneel under the full weight with my strained thigh.

Without question he did as I asked. Mama skittered to the side as it fell with a thump. Muscles in my back that had been in spasm from the first step, lengthened. The compression on my spine lightened and my left thigh ached a little less. I dropped to my knees, bent forward, and eased Fulgere to the sand. Falling next to him, I rolled to my back, my rope still on my shoulder. Mama licked my face.

I opened my eyes feeling certain I hadn't slept, yet it was full dark. Mama lay curled against my free shoulder with her nose tucked beneath her tail. Fulgere snored lightly on my other side. I closed my eyes.

I sat with my back to the great tree, my rope at my feet. Mama was her old self. I was dreaming, and yet I knew I wasn't.

"Why, Cinder?" she said. "If you were afraid of this all along, why didn't you stay with me? Bind your palm to Appleonia and live out your days?"

I gave her the only answer I had. "I had to try."

"Then why help Fulgere? It'll kill you both before you ever reach the mountains." She shook her head in frustration. "Your logic is as full of holes as your name."

I gave a small shrug. It felt good not to have the weight of the rope on my shoulder. "Why bind ourselves to the core and join other lands if all we care about is ourselves?"

"Why, indeed?" she said with a bite to her words. "Many of us argued against it."

"*Some* did," I corrected with a smile.

"We might have been fine breaking off. Maybe it's joining the core that will be our undoing, tying ourselves to lands with strange ways."

I shrugged again. "Maybe, but not according to Umber. We've

had two generations since that first prophesy to see all his others come true. The lands beyond ours that didn't tie on broke off one by one. Nothing left anymore between us and the void. And now the earthquakes have started." I leaned my head back against the bark of the great tree. "He also said the lands that drifted away would shrivel and die."

"He said so, but we have no way to know for sure."

I tipped my head and met her eyes. "Do you really disbelieve, Mama?" I'd never thought she did. I always thought it was just that losing her family one by one was more hurtful to her than losing the whole world.

She didn't reply. She planted her hand in the grass and clenched at the soil beneath, as if she still had the long nails of a gulo.

I woke in the morning to the sun overhead approaching incrementally, like a burning hand reaching down toward me. My muscles felt stiff, my skin cool everywhere except where my mother lay against my shoulder. I looked to my other side and Fulgere was gone. There were no hand prints or drag marks in the sand. His rope was nowhere to be seen. The thread of my own rope remained unchanged, trailing back the way we'd come.

I took a quick sip from the flask and handed it to Mama. She held it for herself as she drank, sitting on her haunches and gripping it between the pads of her paws.

We walked on until the thud-hiss of trudging through sand filled my world. My left thigh burned like fire with every step, my rope dragged at my left shoulder and never seemed to lighten. Mama panted and sometimes took a drunkard's weaving step. I finally took another drink from the flask, but Mama refused.

In what might've been afternoon there, partway between us and the mountains that now seemed as tall as my head, another figure shuffled. Even with the distance, I guessed their stature small, bowed under the weight of their rope. Their greater struggle slowed them, and Mama and I soon came even. The other person's path had angled away to my left, where before they had looked to be straight ahead of us. The person stopped on seeing us. We halted as well.

I could see now it was a woman. She looked older than me, perhaps in her prime or a little past. Her hair, orange as an attastick flower, had frazzled, despite the braid holding the rest. Framed against the sky, it formed a hazy nimbus around her head.

"Do you seek to reach the mountains?" she shouted.

"I do," I called back.

"You had best come this way then," she said. She panted her words, much as I had yesterday under the weight of Fulgere and the two ropes.

"Straight to the center peak is the way I was taught," I replied. Mama bumped my calf. I looked down but she was staring straight ahead, as if to tell me to mind my own business.

"No," the woman shouted. "If you approach the goddess to her face, it's an act of hubris. You'll be struck down for it."

Umber had told my daddy's mama that we had to pass the Guardian and survive the journey. There had been no talk of a deity. He'd seen no more, but said if one lived to reach the mountains, they would see then how to tether our land.

"Perhaps we're both right," I said, thinking that maybe each land had a different protocol to follow. I looked down at Mama. She stared somewhere off to our right now; ignoring me, I suspected, for continuing the discourse.

"There is one way only," the woman said, sounding more exhausted with each exchange. "Learn it or die."

As with the Guardian's questions, I looked for my own truth and found it. "I need to follow my heart. My heart believes what my father told us, that the direct path offers the surest chance of success. If you wish to travel with us, I'll do what I can to help you." Mama rumbled, though it was soft and resigned.

"Your father was wrong," the woman replied without hesitation. "You must approach from the side or you will die."

"Have your people tried before?" If they had tried and failed, I had had no reason to believe her.

"I'm the first," she said. She looked ready to fall where she stood.

I scanned the expanse of the mountain range, the untold days extra she would need to reach the left-most point where the peaks dwindled to low foothills. "I'll follow my heart," I said again, "as you must. I hope we're both right and that I'll see you at the mountains."

"What you'll see is that I spoke the truth," she said. "You'll wish you'd listened."

With that, she trudged onward and leftward. Her arguments seemed to have drained her. She stumbled twice before I looked away.

That night, as I dreamed, I asked Mama what she thought. "Are they real, the people we're seeing?"

"I don't know," she said. She lay back on one elbow under the tree. Her hair hung loose, brushing the grass. "I know no more about this place than you do."

"I'm not sure about Fulgere," I said, "but the woman felt real."

I wondered if anyone had encountered my family out here; had seen them vanish when they failed some oblique test. I'd always thought myself the weakest. Full of holes, as Mama said. I'd thought it a flaw that I didn't have the stubbornness and independence of the rest of the family, or most of the folks I knew. As strong as they were, though, it hadn't been enough.

"Don't worry, Cinder," she said, as if her thoughts ran along similar lines. "All you can do is your best. Your daddy gave the three of you the best chance he could, in case he failed." Her face tightened at his memory, even all these years later. "He said Clay could be both hard and soft, malleable and unyielding. Coal was strong and could withstand pressure. Cinder, he said, was porous. It could both withstand and absorb. A rock that could float."

"I'm sorry you came with me," I said. "But I'm glad for your company."

She reached out and touched my forearm. It felt real.

I woke the next morning and sensed two bodies near me. Mama lay near my shoulder again, her thick fur tickling my neck. Looking to my right, a man slept on his side, facing away from me. The arm not against the ground rested atop his coiled rope, the other pillowed his head. Each breath cost him effort against the weight of the rope on his ribs.

Mama's beady black eyes widened when I sat up and she saw him. She must have been as surprised as I that she hadn't heard his coming. Our stirring woke the man. Like my own effort a moment before, he struggled to sit, but managed to keep his rope centered on his shoulder.

The skin below his light purple eyes were limned with black shadows of exhaustion. "I'd hoped to pass you as you slept." He spoke with the rough voice of one who had been deeply asleep. "It seems my feet wouldn't take me one step farther."

"If you prefer solitude to company, we'll be on our way soon, friend."

He studied me as if I mocked him. His face relaxed only a little when he saw I didn't. "I nearly drove myself into the ground trying to pass you yesterday. I prefer solitude, yes, you could say that. Because I plan to be in front." He rocked onto his knees and pushed to his feet. "You'd do best not to hinder me."

He wore a yellow tunic nearly to his knees over a long brown skirt. As he tried to rise, he stumbled forward, stepping onto the hem of the skirt and nearly tripping. I reached out and grabbed his hand. My purpose was to steady him, but stopping his momentum helped pull me to my feet on my sore thigh. I grabbed him by both shoulders until he was stable.

"I'll not hinder you, friend," I said, "but no reason we can't work together, seeing as we have a common goal."

"Isn't there now?" He pulled away from me. "So you can get in the lead, you mean? We both know there's only room for so many." He adjusted the rope on his shoulder and winced as it dragged back to center. "Me and mine aren't going to miss out so that you and yours can have a spot." He trudged forward, his steps heavy. I didn't know how well he'd moved before, but I guessed the extra effort of catching up to us had cost him.

I'd never heard of any limit, but if there were no more room when I got there, then I would fail. I doubted things would end that easy for me. I pulled the flask from my pocket, watching his thread spool out behind him as he weaved away from us. Mama nipped at my calf, but she couldn't make me hurry to catch him, and there was no point in her going faster than me.

The flask felt light and I handed it to Mama before drinking myself. I could tell she took next to nothing, but when I tipped it to my lips there were only drops left. I sucked every one and tossed the empty flask to the sand. We started ahead, Mama and me, side by side.

The fellow's thread disappeared over another of the short dunes that contoured the deceptively flat expanse. When we reached the crest of the dune, I could see he'd vanished; so had his footprints and his thread. Looking back to check, I saw my own thread and my deep prints shadowed by Mama's smaller ones near them. They stretched back until the heat haze erased them.

That night we were both silent a long while, absorbing the peace of the great tree over our heads.

"Are you still afraid?" she asked.

"More than ever."

"I'd hoped when we came here I could talk you out of this. That maybe we could live our lives out here if not at home. But I see now it isn't a real land, just an in-between place. I don't think either of us would live a single day if you stopped." She looked away, toward the border we'd irrevocably crossed. "I wish I could take this burden from you, but I don't know how."

"It's mine to bear, Mama."

I only hoped I could.

I woke to the mountains right in front of us, as if they'd marched up on us in the night. They rose out of the ground, rock and earth of weight and substance beyond anything I'd ever imagined. Solid, like nothing I'd ever seen. Their weight would've punched a hole in our land and fallen right through the other side.

I stood easily and stared in amazement at my rope. The coil on my shoulder was maybe a quarter of what it had been the day before. The pressure on my bruised shoulder felt like a feather in comparison. I saw no sign of my earlier companions. No one standing before the mountains except Mama and me.

Mama stood on her hind legs, her short front legs hanging down, long claws resting against her belly fur. She stared at the mountains like they might jump forward and devour us. My hands trembled as I took the coil from my shoulder. Mama and I looked at each other a long moment.

The center peak came to a hook at the top. I had no doubt that was the place to tether. I found the free end of the rope and fashioned an immense loop. I wondered if any of the others in my family had come this far. I doubted it. They'd been braver than me; if they'd made it this far, they would have made it the rest of the way. I tried not to imagine what it would feel like if I succeeded. What it would be like to become the rope, tied at one end to the tree and the other to the mountain. The strain of the world on my limbs. Forever.

Daddy said he believed it was *intent* that would get the rope wherever it needed to go. The one thing I didn't have. Maybe Daddy had named me wrong, left me *too* full of holes. If I stood here until tomorrow, perhaps come morning I'd be gone, like the others. I wouldn't have to quit, I could just do nothing. If I didn't disappear, then without the lindel juice I'd be dead before long. So would Mama. It might not be quick, but it wouldn't be eternity, either.

I dropped my hands, but I didn't drop my rope. "I don't think I can do it, Mama." I didn't look at her as I said it. "There were too many that went before me. It made you mad, but it made me scared, more with each one."

She stood on her hind legs and pawed softly at my thigh. Her claws caught in my pants and pricked the skin beneath. I shifted the rope to my left hand and bent to scoop her up, finding her dense body heavier than I expected. Lifting her to my face, I kissed her triangular head at the soft spot between her eyes. She licked the stubble on my cheek. I didn't know if she encouraged me onward or begged me to stop, but I couldn't ask her and she couldn't tell. I set her down.

She looked up, waiting on my decision, her whiskers vibrating. To her, I'd been more important than everyone in our land put together. I thought I was different from her, that I'd come here to do this thing for them, but perhaps I wasn't different at all. All those people counting on me couldn't conquer my fears; not even duty to the family that had gone before me. I looked down at Mama, prepared to confirm what we both already knew, that I wasn't brave enough.

Her eyes, black pupils in dark irises so wide that no whites showed, shone with the intensity of the words she couldn't share. My own eyes filled with tears that she'd followed me here. She might have been able to live out her natural days at home, even when the land broke free, but here my inaction would condemn her to death. She'd been willing to sacrifice a whole world to save me, and maybe that was my answer. Maybe I didn't need to find enough courage to save a whole world, maybe I just needed to find enough to save one.

Mama couldn't go back over the border, but if I could tether us to the core, then she might be able to walk out of this middle world and into a new life.

I looked up at the peak, at the hook. Moving before fear could grip me again, I twirled the lasso above my head. I'd only have one throw. Daddy told me so. Thinking of Mama, I threw with intent. My loop soared upward as if it had no weight, no drag of rope behind it. It flew like a bird, up and up and up, and we stood there watching it. It flew so high it passed from sight, but I felt it when it hooked. It pulled taut as it caught our land and anchored it. My body jerked taut with it, becoming the rope I'd carried. Without even time for a goodbye, I sprang up into the sky.

No tension or strain pulled at me. I didn't feel like a tether; I felt like a ray of light. I shined all the way from the tree to the mountaintop, and everywhere in between. The joining felt like a song in my heart.

I could see the other lands tied to this place. Beyond them were the ones that had tried and failed—or failed to try—drifting alone in the void. I could see Mama below me. She grew tall again. Her fur fell away to smooth, bronze skin. She must have heard my song of joy because she waved and laughed and cried. She stared at my brightness a long time. Finally, she started toward the mountains. I watched her as she progressed up and then over them, into the new lands.

"The Weight of Mountains" was a 2020
WSFA Small Press Award Finalist

From DreamForge #2, June 2019

Liz Colter has followed her heart through a wide variety of careers, including farming, field paramedic, Outward Bound instructor, athletic trainer, and roller-skating waitress. She writes contemporary fantasy under the name L. D. Colter and epic fantasy as L. Deni Colter. She's an active SFWA member with multiple short story publications. Her debut novel *A Borrowed Hell* was the winner of the 2018 Colorado Book Award for Science Fiction/Fantasy.

Sapiens

by Davide Mana

It's easy, for the guys in the Artifact Recovery Branch. They just need to find a dead spot along the Line and pick up the stuff, and that's it. Nobody sees, nobody knows. Time Raiders, they call themselves, and are so smug about it.

Oral Tradition is quite another story. You have to actually get there and interact, talk to the actual people. Time Raiders, my foot. What's a vase, a piece of hardware, an old book, without the cultural milieu? And that's what we do. We collect stories, ideas, and beliefs, then weave them together to re-create the milieu. We flirt with the Paradox and the Shift every day, up and down the Line. And there's been no Shift yet. We *are* good.

And yes, we do call the subjects "zombies," sometimes, and there's old hands in OT that will tell unlikely tales of bopping their grand-grandmother or what else, but it's all an act, to keep emotions at arm's length. Oral Tradition work is hard. Because they are people. They are our ancestors. Poor relations, maybe, country bumpkins that live in the wooded hills of the past, but you can't but feel a sense of kinship. It's so hard because it is so personal.

And yet you can't do away with emotions.

I was in Shanghai in 2137. Side-job, pick up local color. Filler, basically. Autumn of '37. The evening air was hot and wet. You can tell you're in the Thirties by the warmth and the humidity. We were on top of Oriental Pearl Tower, Three Degrees' latest song in the background, drinks on the house. Waves made the pylons of the tower tremble as we observed the sinking skyline of the Bund. The proud Paris of the East was going Venice, had been for a while, ever since the River Flood Discharge system had failed. Chongming Island was gone, Pudong Airport was gone. The floating islands had been scared away by the freak monsoon weather and now the Bund was about to go. About one hundred high-profile digerati milled about, drones trailing, socials aflame with updates. Meme-fying and live-feeding the catastrophe.

Then the Custom House tower disappeared. It was not the waves, not really. The acidic waters of the Pacific had eaten at the foundations of the building for a decade, weakening the concrete, oxidizing the iron. The waves just tipped the balance, and the Custom House folded like a house of cards, disappearing under the water. It was fast. Definitive.

I knew it would, of course.

That was the reason I was here, to pick up the heat-of-the-moment reminiscences. But that didn't make it any easier. What struck me was the silence. Because, for a long moment, that I measured in ten heartbeats, nobody spoke, nobody breathed. Only the electronic voice of the girl in Three Degrees, and the bass, pounding. Distant. Forgotten.

Then the columns in the front of the Bank of Taiwan snapped like matchsticks. There was a collective intake of breath as the facade of the building collapsed, gray spray flying. Then everybody was talking at the same time.

But we already had a number of those social and live streams. I was here for the personal stuff.

"We'll never make it," a young woman said.

She was tall, slender, in a simple black cheongsam. Timeless, in a way. Beautiful, maybe. She was holding an empty flute glass in her fingers. Blue nails, matching makeup.

"I beg your pardon?" I said, coming closer. It's rare to have a zombie start a conversation. Rare and precious.

She looked at me like I was an apparition, and for a moment I had this wild, impossible idea she could see through me like she had X-ray eyes and know me for what I was: an interloper, a gatecrasher.

"I was talking to myself," she said.

I waited, leaving her room to speak.

"You ever heard about Cyanobacteria?" she asked.

"I think I have."

It was part of the *weltanschauung*. The belief the climate catastrophe would be terminal for our species, because it had been so for the bacteria in the Proterozoic, two-and-a-half billion years before. A toxic meme, if ever there had been one, an enduring gift of the previous century's passive guilt mindset.

"The Cyanobacteria poisoned their world, committed species suicide," she said in a soft voice. "Species can be too successful, see?"

We moved aside, making room for a couple trying to drive their drone over the collapsing buildings.

"You think we have been too successful?" I asked her.

"We, like them, poisoned our world," she said. She placed her glass on a passing tray, folded her arms. "Beyond recovery."

"But we are no bacteria," I said.

She shrugged. "You think that makes a difference?"

"Yes," I said.

Yes, I wanted to say, such was the emptiness in her eyes, *it will be hard and it will be horrible and millions will die, but we will survive. And adapt, and then thrive once more. We will still be going in five hundred years. We'll embrace change and promote diversity, ditching the old self-destructive idols we once worshiped, those that led us astray.*

"It makes a difference," I said. *Damn the rules.* "We have been focusing so much on how we adapted our world to ourselves, that we forgot how much we adapted ourselves to our world."

"This is different." She looked at me. She was so alone, and lost, and resigned.

"This is not the first time," I said. "You—we belong to a species that survived two glaciations. A species that was born in the grasslands of Africa and expanded to the Arctic circle, to the Mongolian steppe. To the ocean's shelf. To Mars. Ours is a species that survives. A species that thrives on change. That learns and passes its knowledge on."

"This is different," she said again. As to underscore her words, the pyramid of Sassoon House, black in the advancing twilight, leaned to one side, pouring tiles in the sea before being engulfed in a tall wave. "Sic transit gloria mundi," she whispered.

"Why is it different this time?" I asked. I could justify my Flirting with the need to collect first-hand insight on the Collapse mindset that had almost extinguished us.

"There's eight billion of us," she said. "And we keep pouring poison into the system."

I looked at her. "If you know what's wrong, why don't you change it?"

She turned away and looked at the sea, black water under black sky, the lights of the drones like distant fireflies. She shrugged. "You can't change people," she said.

"Three hundred thousand years of history disprove that belief. Change is the only constant in the history of our species. We should embrace it, not try and stave it off."

She clicked her tongue and shook her head. "You have too much faith in humanity," she said.

"What if it's you that do not have enough? We are Homo sapiens, not politicians."

She chuckled, and her cheeks acquired a hint of color.

"My friend," she said, nodding, "would not like such talk."

I looked at the guy surrounded by a bunch of hanger-ons. Some *politico* I was supposed to know. I would have liked to tell her we had lost the memory of such individuals, that she should not waste her time. "What if he doesn't?" I asked.

She stared at me. There was no longer fear there, but curiosity.

"Are you preaching anarchy?" she asked with an impish smile.

"I am not a preacher," I replied. "And I'd rather preach survival, if I were."

"You can't change people," she repeated. It was the core of her belief. Her faith.

"People can change," I replied. "We were cannibals far longer than we were fire-builders. But we have a big brain, and science, and art."

"The economic system would collapse."

It was my time to shrug. "We built it, we can build another, a better one."

"That's the spirit!"

I turned. My friend's companion was standing too close, smiling the aggressive smile of one who's in control. He gestured toward the darkness, where the drone lights illuminated a chunk of the Gutzlaff Signal Tower, like a broken finger pointed at the sky, rising from the waters.

"We will rebuild the Bund better than before," he said. He squinted at me. "Are you an engineer? A designer?"

I shook my head. "A historian."

He snorted. "Fascinating subject. Useless, but fascinating."

Another wave crashed at the base of the tower. The structure creaked, people screamed. But I knew it would be all right.

I smiled at the young woman in the black cheongsam. "Remember," I said, "We don't have to be cannibals."

She smiled back. Her man frowned. I kissed her hand, and I went down to the jetties, taking the stairs. I had all the time in the world. Oriental Pearl Tower would not collapse. Not today.

Born in Turin, Italy, Davide Mana is a former environmental scientist currently paying his bills as a writer and translator. His stories have been translated both traditionally and independently, both in Italian and English. Davide writes mostly genre fiction—science fiction, fantasy, and historical adventure.

The Dead Don't Dream

by Gordon Linzner

Tamotsu Hirokei's aide—a short, thin, ageless, almost sexless woman in an elegant, wine-colored kimono—slid aside a rice paper panel at the far end of the waiting room. I grew increasingly self-conscious in my ill-fitting suit jacket and mismatched turtleneck.

"Mr. Hirokei will see you now." She bowed, then stood to one side so I could pass.

I walked forward gingerly, partly in awe at my proximity to so much wealth, but mostly because the polished mahogany floor offered little traction for my socks. None of the visitors' slippers lined up in the foyer fit my oversized feet.

Entering Mr. Hirokei's private quarters, I failed at first to make eye contact with my client. My attention was riveted by the panoramic view of Central Park from his penthouse window. Under clear, almost cloudless skies, I could see north to the 110th Street end and beyond. The once verdant rectangle looked nostalgically restful in the early morning glow, despite large scruffy patches of wasteland. Over the past few months, this gem of Manhattan had become a no man's land, causing real estate values to plummet along Fifth Avenue and Central Park West... and, to a lesser degree, here on Central Park South.

Tamotsu Hirokei cleared his throat.

My potential client sat cross-legged on a raised platform in the middle of the room. His kimono, adorned in a subdued floral pattern, flowed gracefully as he bowed his head in greeting. The billionaire looked about my age, early thirties, in decent shape considering his sedentary occupation. His weary, coal black eyes were those of a man much older.

Three elegant lacquer chests lined the walls, along with a handful of delicate framed pen-and-ink sketches. Directly behind the man, a trio of swords occupied their display stand, short tanto on top, katana lowermost, blades well polished and no doubt razor-sharp. Otherwise, the room was unfurnished.

The vast space, coupled with the height of the penthouse, made me dizzy. I gladly accepted Hirokei's silent invitation to sit at the platform's edge.

"May I offer you some refreshment, Mr. James?" His English was impeccable; barely a trace of accent. "Tea? Sake?"

I shook my head.

"No," he observed. "Like most Americans, you wish to get down to business immediately. Very well." He waved at his assistant. "Azumi, you may go."

The woman bowed and left us.

"The task is a simple one," Hirokei explained. "I need you to find my father Osamu."

I wet my lips, worried where this was heading. "The police still have a missing persons bureau."

"The police aren't interested, Mr. James. They don't waste time looking for dead people."

I was afraid he'd say that.

"I will pay you ten thousand U.S. dollars just to look," the businessman continued. "Another ten thousand if you find him. A further eighty thousand if you can deliver him to me intact. Here is a thousand on account."

He slid a thick red envelope from his left kimono sleeve and placed it on the platform before me. I stared at it, fingers quivering. The retainer alone was ten times more than I'd made to date this year, tracking stolen property and cheating spouses.

But money would be useless if I did not survive to spend. Despite the efforts of scientists and researchers worldwide, they had yet to discover why, over the past year, across the entire planet, after people's life functions ceased, their bodies continued to wander as mindless threats to the living.

I took a deep breath, fighting temptation. "My professional advice," I replied, "is for you to simply accept your father's death. The state issued a certificate, didn't they?"

"And the *Times* ran his obituary." Hirokei nodded agreement. "My father was ill a long time. His death was not unexpected. I am his only son. I must honor his memory. He would wish me to make every effort to do so."

"You could hold a ceremony without the presence of a body. It's done all the time these days. People want to move on."

Hirokei's lips thinned. "While my father's shell shambles through the streets of your city, impelled by a mindless cannibalism, such a memorial would be a travesty."

"He might have already been, ah, stopped." Nearly a year after the plague's arrival, no one had yet devised a proper word for killing a corpse. The world couldn't even agree on a better description for what was happening than *plague*. "The police sniper squads…"

"I would have been informed. Osamu Hirokei is not your ordinary plague victim. The police might not bother actively looking, but they are legally required to identify any, ah, truly dead." The red envelope was gently nudged closer to me. The move's lack of subtlety obviously pained the younger Hirokei. "Will you accept the job?"

My hands itched. With the amount he offered, I could move into a live-in office in one of the new high-security building complexes. Clients could come to me, rather than my chasing after them.

"Why me?"

Hirokei looked past me, toward his view of Central Park. "I only arrived from Tokyo a few days ago. My time has been spent entirely tending to my father's business affairs. Despite having a car and driver at my disposal, I have not been able to step outside this building since my company's private helicopter brought me from the airport. This kind of search is best undertaken by someone more familiar with the byways of Manhattan."

That wasn't what I meant, and Hirokei knew it. I'd become a private investigator by default, two months earlier, when the man for whom I'd been doing part-time legwork died. I had no illusions about my reputation in the field.

"Why *me*?" I repeated.

Hirokei sighed. "Your tone is correct; you were not my first choice, Mr. James. A score of other investigators turned me down. A couple mentioned your name."

"I can mention others."

The fathomless eyes grew harsh. "Too much time has been lost already, Mr. James. If you, too, turn down this job, I will have no other choice but to undertake the search personally."

I scanned him again. His appearance was definitely not that of a man of action. And, despite his outer stoicism, Hirokei was emotionally involved. A sure formula for mistakes.

"You'd get killed. Or worse."

Hirokei shrugged. His right hand snaked free of the kimono sleeve, toward the red envelope.

I reached it first. "I need more details," I said.

Like every other façade that faced Central Park along Fifth Avenue, the former main entrance to Mt. Sinai Hospital had been bricked over. As had the first and second floor windows. I entered the maze from the Madison Avenue side. Rifle-bearing guards allowed me to pass without a flicker. The armed National Guardsmen stationed outside critical condition wards and operating rooms were understandably more on edge.

Dr. Marilyn Sandstone had been the resident in charge of the elder Hirokei's case. I found her in the cafeteria, where she wallowed in garrulous self-pity.

"Look at me!" she whined. "I've gained forty pounds. On hospital food! I used to jog around the reservoir every morning before my shift. Now my only recreation is eating." She waved a half-eaten hoagie in my face.

Ignoring the spray of mayonnaise and drawing on my brief off-off-Broadway acting experience, I nodded in faux sympathy. How anyone could cultivate an appetite these days baffled me, but we all deal with tragedy in our own way.

"About the Hirokei case…" I prodded.

She looked at her hoagie as if assessing a new patient, then lowered it to her tray. "Osamu Hirokei was dying. Melanoma spread throughout his body. Even the new vaccine could only slow his cancer's progress marginally. We—I—didn't expect his heart to give out first." Her voice dropped to a whisper. "We used every means possible to resuscitate him. *Every* means."

"I thought extraordinary methods no longer permissible."

Sandstone glared at her sandwich, then pushed the tray aside. "I know, Mr. James. I was present at the incident responsible for that policy, voted for it myself. An intern, a very promising surgeon, tried to revive a woman whose heart had stopped. Her recovery seemed miraculous, so much so that no one noticed the monitors still flatlining. Not until she bit off three of the intern's fingers.

"He was lucky. That young man is now in our pharmacology department."

I didn't have to fake sympathy now. My former employer died trying to save a badly injured client. I was a block away when a sniper squad took them both down.

I was also present when he came back to our office. The snipers had missed his brain.

"What changed with Mr. Hirokei?"

"Money, Mr. James. The Hirokei family has holdings throughout the world, including a good chunk of midtown Manhattan real estate. In exchange for a generous contribution to the hospital, Tamotsu Hirokei insisted we exhaust every means before pronouncing his father dead." She snorted. "I thought the Japanese were supposed to be fatalists."

Aren't we all, in these times? But I kept that observation to myself. "And Osamu Hirokei's corpse escaped before the guards could be summoned?"

She nodded. "Through a second-floor window on the Fifth Avenue side. Since bricked up. Fortunately, none of my staff was seriously injured. Two of them resigned on the spot." Her fingers drummed against the cafeteria table, then reached out to retrieve her hoagie.

"Did anyone see where he went?"

The surgeon frowned. "Into the park, of course. That's where they usually go."

My heart sank, but I needed the first-hand confirmation. "The park itself or the transverse at 97th Street?"

"Straight in, at 99th Street."

I stifled a curse.

"Your details checked out," I told my client. "If he'd wandered onto the transverse road, your father could have passed all the way through to the West Side. Access from that roadway is sealed off." I'd grabbed my theatrical makeup kit from my apartment and now sat on the edge of Hirokei's raised platform, applying white face paint as I spoke.

"If he had, the snipers stationed there would have taken him down." Hirokei grimaced. "I remind you, Mr. James, in that event I would have been informed. I have several very well paid sources."

I squinted into my mirror. "More likely, he'd have been struck by a steel-plated bus and left in place until the plows came through. Since he entered the park itself, though, and as you say your informants are reliable, he must still be within its boundaries."

I took a deep breath. The greasepaint odor brought back fond memories. I was almost grateful for this opportunity to dust off my old kit.

Almost.

Hirokei turned to gaze out his panoramic window. "A large territory. Eight hundred and forty-odd acres."

"My guess is he's still wandering the north end. The former reservoir acts as a natural barrier, especially since the west wall was dynamited to flood the former swampland. The dead are more likely to stray back onto the streets than go around the barricades on the East Drive. In addition, the south end is swept regularly by helicopter snipers, while the north remains too heavily wooded for them to be effective. Too many places to hide."

"We handle such things more efficiently in Tokyo."

"New York's police force was understaffed even before the plague struck."

"Why not simply defoliate the area?"

"They did, with the Ramble. See that ugly scar mid-park? The community protested. Walking corpses or not, many of the influential people living nearby want the view they paid for."

Hirokei nodded. "You know Central Park well."

"I spent two summers as an Urban Park Ranger. Actors do a lot of odd jobs. It's how I stumbled into private investigation." I frowned at a sudden realization. "You already knew that, Mr. Hirokei. That's why you hired me. I was your first resort, not your last. You already knew where your father was."

He offered a thin smile with no hint of apology. "I'd guessed."

No, *I* should have guessed.

But I was already committed. "Your limo driver can drop me by the north end, right? I'd rather not be seen wandering the streets looking like a dead man."

"I can arrange to have the company helicopter leave you inside the park."

"That would attract unwanted attention from the dead." I didn't add that I'd rather not deal with the angst of flying until I had to. "I'll need your pilot on standby, though. Among other resources."

"You will have whatever is needed."

I burrowed through my kit for the tube of green paste at the bottom. It felt grainy between my fingers. When the plague ended live theater, I thought I'd never get to use it up.

Now I hoped I had enough.

Tamotsu Hirokei's limousine left me at the corner of West 110th Street and Seventh Avenue. The wide entryway to the park provided ample open space for reconnaissance in all directions and still permitted nearby access to the unmanicured north woods.

This entrance was officially named Warriors' Gate. I could hardly have felt less like a warrior. Beneath a disguise of ragged, stinking clothing, my late employer's .22 revolver pressed coldly against my stomach. The weapon would have felt more reassuring had I been sure I could bring myself to use it. I'd only had the opportunity to do so once before, and failed, with grisly results.

I'd shuffled but a few paces into the park when a middle-aged woman stepped clear of the brush to halt in front of me. She was naked save for a wisp of cotton at her crotch. There was nothing remotely sensuous about her slack jaw, her hunched gait, or the white bone protruding from the blackened flesh of her left arm. I froze as her yellowed eyes fixed on me. Had she sensed something off about the hump on my back, the bulge beneath my stained cliché of a trench coat? My palms grew moist. I stuffed my hands deep into the coat's pockets. Did dead people sweat?

Her yellowed eyes turned away as she slid away and past me. I barely noticed her sour, rotting odor. The whole city stank of death these days.

She shambled toward the gap by which I'd entered.

The hollow metal frame covering my chest, concealing my breathing, didn't allow for a sigh of relief. My makeup passed its first test.

A thin whine made me look back. The woman dropped onto the broken sidewalk along 110th Street, just outside the park. No blood spilled from the hole in her forehead.

Had I tried to withdraw at this stage, I would surely have joined her.

Atop a rise to my right stood the blockhouse, a remnant of the War of 1812 and the source of the gate's name. It stood, as it had for decades, a roofless, four-walled shell of rough-hewn stone. A single unadorned flagpole jutted up from its center. Were I a dead man, I thought, that's where I would go—the site had originally been chosen two centuries earlier for its strategic location and all-encompassing views.

Fortunately, as I discovered after climbing the steep, crumbling path, the dead think differently. If at all. The structure's single entrance was low and narrow and off to the side. Few corpses were likely to stumble in by accident.

I slipped off my concealed knapsack, with its day's worth of food and water, and hid it near the flagpole base. With luck, I would complete my search and be done by nightfall, but it was best to be prepared.

Without luck, I *really* wouldn't need it.

A quick check, using my mobile phone as a hand mirror, told me to touch up a spot near my hairline. The remaining makeup supplies were transferred to a jacket pocket. I patted the .22 for the umpteenth time, checked the compact flare in my hip pocket, and started back down a steep dirt path. That remnant of the original Victorian trail was at some points barely wide enough for one person. I dreaded every blind corner.

A crash in the underbrush to my left made my hand reflexively reach for the gun. The ruckus turned out to be a pair of justifiably wary squirrels. Bones of more trusting rodents littered the woods.

The fact that only humans were affected by the dead/alive plague was another mystery the world's scientists had yet to resolve.

Farther in from the park's perimeter, a broad asphalt drive proved a popular gathering place. An obvious choice, in retrospect. Decaying muscles, rotting flesh, and deteriorating ligaments make one's balance unstable on the steeper slopes. Clinging to tree trunks and shrubs for support was unreliable. Best to keep to flat surfaces.

Half a dozen corpses shambled toward me. I tensed, channeling my will power to resist sprinting across the road. A display of agility would immediately betray my status as alive. I might be able to outrun one group and even dodge the next. I could never escape them all.

Five dead humans shuffled past, ignoring me. The sixth, an older black woman with a bloated stomach, paused to display her burden. A ragged strip of leather dangled from what looked like a terrier with its belly torn open. Little more than half a jaw remained above the scrap of collar.

Even in these uncertain times, some idiots refused understand the purpose of leash laws.

The dead woman ripped off a foreleg and thrust it toward me.

I felt my face go gray beneath my greenish tint. Such horrors had become commonplace for New Yorkers, for the world, in recent months, but still...!

She pressed the leg into my left hand, curling what remained of her lips into a charitable smile.

I grunted what I hoped sounded like gratitude, then turned away, pretending to gnaw on the canine limb, struggling to ignore the maggots crawling over my fingers. The dead Samaritan nodded and moved on.

At the edge of the woods, I tossed the rotting leg as far as possible. I had one more spot to reconnoiter before my search began in earnest.

The Great Hill, with its relatively easy slopes leading to a high area of green oval lawn on the park's west side, also turned out to be popular. Unfortunately, none of the assembled corpses resembled my client's father.

The planned pick-up would be trickier than I'd hoped.

I turned back toward the Drive.

And found myself face to maggot-ridden chest with a towering revenant I instantly named Big Guy.

His right eye-socket was an empty hole. A dislocated jaw canted to that side as well. Bare bone showed behind his right ear. Someone had tried to stove in Big Guy's brain. It hadn't worked.

Unlike when I'd had to smash in the skull of my late friend and employer with a heavy socket wrench because I'd been too chicken-shit to use his gun, because I thought he might remember me, because I desperately wanted to believe that, despite the absence of blood from the stump of his right arm, he might still be alive.

All of this ran through my mind as I stared at Big Guy. The emotions must have showed on my face.

Big Guy's mouth twisted in something resembling a grin. He knew I wasn't one of them.

He *knew*.

I stumbled backwards, barely eluding the swing of his massive arm.

Thin strands of lips curled back, exposing rust-colored broken teeth. Big Guy moaned his disappointment.

I reluctantly reached beneath my coat, still unsure if I could bring myself to use the gun.

Something crunched behind me. I turned.

Two more corpses staggered forward, alerted by Big Guy's moaning.

Other heads, in various stages of decomposition, turned my way.

Fuck the gun. I ran, not looking back, not even when I tripped and tumbled down steep, bone-littered hillsides, crumpling my wire chest-frame.

A small man-made grotto concealed a waterfall that fed the 100th Street pool from the east. I took cover there, listening as Big Guy and a dozen others rumbled by. Sounds of rushing water covered my panting.

When things quieted, I reached for my mobile to check my makeup in the mirror function again. Between the chase, the fall, and the waterfall's spray, I knew most of my corpse makeup was gone. Worse, I'd suffered several cuts and scratches, including a nasty gash above one eyebrow that still bled. Fresh, leaking wounds were—I couldn't help thinking—a dead giveaway.

My hand froze.

The phone was gone.

I cursed myself for not tucking it in an inside pocket.

I slapped a handful of moss over the bleeding gash, then peered out from my hiding place. Big Guy's group, long out of sight, had probably forgotten about me, assuming they had anything resembling a memory. A handful of disinterested stragglers waded through the muddy shoreline between myself and Central Park West.

A hundred thousand dollars wasn't enough compensation for this job—not in American currency, not in silver or gold. I wanted out. Now.

I also needed to see what, if anything, might be coming my way. Rather than retreat through the north woods or follow the obvious, crumbling porous asphalt path along the loch, where every turn might conceal another moving corpse, I veered southeast. Collar up to conceal my features, I aimed for the open ballfields built during the Depression, replacing the original North Meadow.

And abruptly found what I was looking for: the late Osamu Hirokei.

Tall wire-mesh fences partially enclosed the ballfields. A handful of the dead shambled about those dusty patches, seemingly unable to find the breaks in the fences by which they'd entered.

Wandering idly, except for a single unmoving corpse that sat cross-legged on the pitcher's mound of the easternmost ballfield.

Perhaps his lack of movement was a remnant of that cliched inbred Japanese fatalism referenced by Dr. Sandstone. Maybe Hirokei's corpse lost its spirit in its final living hours. More likely I was projecting; the dead moved by pure reflex, unable to think beyond basic motor skills, or emote, or even dream about what being alive felt like. Whatever the reason, the old man now rested as if in serene mediation. Shreds of his blue hospital gown wavered in the breeze. After leaving the hospital, he must have walked due west, across the East Meadow, settling here in confusion.

I resisted an urge to rush to his side. After my close call with Big Guy, I did not need further attention. Instead, I slowly shuffled nearer to confirm his identity, and to check if he was dead or truly dead.

Hirokei did not blink. He barely moved, save for a nervous twitch of his fingers. That told me enough. The handful of meandering mobile dead bodies about us seemed as oblivious to him as to my own presence.

I hoped they stayed that way.

South of the ballfields stood the stone Recreation Center, which once also housed a communications center for the city's parks department. I shambled toward it as quickly as I dared without betraying my live status. With luck, their radio equipment would still be functional. I'd even settle for a landline. My client's pilot had to be advised of this change of plan, and quickly.

The phone lines had been disconnected but the radio still worked, with a little cajoling. Handy post-it notes next to the transmitter made coding easy. Aside from official broadcasts, there was little shortwave activity, and I soon made my report. With my last supplies, I refreshed my makeup and shambled back to the ballfield. By then, I could clearly hear the echoing chuk-chuk-chuk of helicopter blades approaching from the south.

Unfortunately, so could every corpse in the north end. Even the ones whose inner ears had completely rotted away could sense the vibrations. The sound drew them like a magnet—any change in the environment might mean fresh meat, even though their bodies were incapable of processing food.

Even old Hirokei rose to start rambling about. I breathed a curse. If he wandered too close to a fence or a thicket of trees, the chopper's net would be useless.

I ran toward him, screaming and waving my arms in the most undead manner possible.

Hirokei stopped. I'd gotten his attention.

Along with that of every other starving corpse on the playing field.

The helicopter swooped so low I imagined seeing my reflection in the pilot's mirrored glasses. I pointed toward his target. He released the net, and clouds of yellow dust billowed as sturdy, steel-reinforced hemp struck the earth between the elder Hirokei and myself. I coughed.

Another very not dead thing to do.

The old man flexed his thin fingers, hesitant, turning in my direction. I waved, shouting wildly again. He stumbled toward me.

A soon as he was in position, in the center of the net, I raised my right thumb high enough for the pilot to see.

The chopper rose suddenly. The net closed around Osamu Hirokei, jerking him off the ground. My right hand shaded my eyes to watch as the helicopter turned east, then south. The net twisted and spun beneath the craft as Hirokei thrashed within. They needed to reach the penthouse and the cell his son had prepared before the old man chewed through the reinforced hemp.

After which, the copter would presumably come back for me. I knew the risk. It could not have swooped down again for me now without risking the dead man's escape. Given my discomfort with heights, I did not relish its return, but a few minutes of angst was better than the alternative. I only had to stay visible.

And alive.

As the mob closed in, I raced east, toward the nearest chain link fence. There, I clambered to the top. The dead can climb—some of them, anyway—but not well. I hoped to find safer haven on the other side.

Before I could drop to the ground, however, a half dozen more corpses shambled toward me from the East Drive. Lifeless fingers gripped the mesh on either side of the fence, rattling it, almost causing me to lose my balance.

I glanced down. A pale, three-fingered hand wavered an arm's length from my foot.

I didn't realize I'd drawn the gun until the bullet struck that hand's owner between the eyes. That close, I couldn't miss. In eerie silence, the dead man fell backwards to lay unmoving on the hard-packed dirt below.

I had no time to reflect on my reaction. Another corpse was already crawling up the fence. I fired again, in panic. She lost her grip, struck the ground, but quickly recovered and began to climb again.

I'd missed the brain.

After that, I forced myself to wait until each corpse came within a hand's-breadth before firing. The tricky part was reloading as I balanced awkwardly atop the fence. At one point, after nervously dropping a handful of bullets, I wished my late boss had owned an automatic. I'd have gladly exchanged a slight chance of it jamming for the convenience of a quick-loading magazine.

The sky above remained empty of aircraft.

Fifteen minutes later, down to my last six bullets, I decided to wait no longer. Two of the corpses started piling up their brain-dead brethren to facilitate their climb. The choice was to escape now or be pulled down into the mob.

I pocketed the .22 and reached for my miniature flare. Originally, it was to signal the helicopter from the Great Hill once I'd lured Hirokei there.

I discharged the flare downwards, into the group. Its sizzle was unexpectedly subdued.

Ragged clothing burst into flame. The stench of burning meat filled the air. Thick smoke drifted upward. Outlying corpses collapsed atop their smoldering brethren. The ones on the western side of the fence pressed against the wire mesh, as if they could squeeze through.

Everyone likes a barbecue.

I inched along the top of the fence, ignoring cuts from the jagged metal. Once clear of the crowd, I dropped to the ground. More of the dead, attracted by smoke and smell, shuffled down the drive. I forced myself to shuffle as well, fighting my body's instinct to run as I angled toward the cover of thick brush. There, I crouched in its shadows, heart racing, watching the sky grow dusky.

Still no chuk-chuk-chuk.

Maybe my client had second thoughts about that hundred thousand.

As twilight deepened, I eased toward the stone eastern perimeter wall of the park. There I scrubbed off what remained of my makeup and hunkered down again, awaiting the all-enveloping night.

A park entrance lay one block south of me, another two blocks north. Police snipers would have both covered. In full darkness, though, they might not notice me slipping over the wall between.

I spent the time amusing myself with ever more impossible thoughts of revenge.

Fifth Avenue looked black as pitch. Since the onset of the plague, streetlights had burnt out or been shattered by sniper bullets, perhaps ricocheting, perhaps intentionally. Ground-floor entrances and windows facing the park had been sealed off for months; upper floors had thick shades drawn or lights turned off. No sensible person wished to attract attention from either armed vigilantes or their non-living prey.

I'd already discarded my clunky metal framework, along with the outer trench coat, which had gotten entangled in the frame. Now I clung to the top of the eastern wall, partially sheltered by a tall elm tree just outside the park. One leg dangled on either side; my fingers clutched the barrier's capstone. The near-empty gun dug into my ribs. I paused, lying as flat and still as possible, checking I had not been detected, planning my next move.

A disturbance came from the shrubs on the park side. I slowly turned my head.

Big Guy's cold dead hand was inches from my leg. Apparently, some dead did remember.

I stifled a panicked yelp and half-jumped, half-fell onto the cobblestones lining the outside of the wall. Too anxious, I landed awkwardly, twisting my ankle. I collapsed onto one knee. Broken glass slashed my calf. My left hand stifled my moan. A trigger-happy sniper could easily fix on a sound.

Mount Sinai hospital loomed before me. Shouting Dr. Sandstone's name might dissuade the guards from picking me off on my approach, but the entrance was a long block away. Fifth Avenue only provided a handful of derelict cars along the curb for cover. I'd counted on speed to make my break; snipers, both official and vigilante, would expect the plodding pace of a dead man. Now I could barely limp.

Using the stone wall for support, I started pulling myself erect. Bits of grit pattered against my skull and shoulders. I looked up.

The dent in Big Guy's skull as he leaned over the wall gave the appearance of a gibbous moon.

The dead don't bother climbing over barriers without a reason.

I was Big Guy's reason.

One rotting leg swung over the wall.

I half-crawled, half-scrambled toward the shelter of a nearby abandoned vehicle. If I didn't make it, at least a sniper's high-velocity bullet would end things quickly.

Because its headlights were off, I failed to notice the limousine until it screeched to a halt a foot in front of me. Momentum caused me to bounce off its right front fender. I managed to break my backwards fall by clutching at the trunk of another curbside elm.

The front passenger side window lowered and a rifle barrel snaked out in my direction.

I shut my eyes. I didn't need to see my end.

The discharge was deafening.

I felt nothing.

Was this how those corpses transitioned from life to death? Without sensation? Had the shooter missed my brain despite my being only a few feet away?

I forced myself to look.

The vehicle's rear door opened. I blinked at the dim interior light. Tamotsu Hirokei's aide, Azumi, leaned out, one hand beckoning me.

With the rifle blast echoing in my ears, I couldn't make out her words, but I was able to read her lips.

Speak, Mr. James, she urged. *Speak now.*

"Azumi?"

She nodded with obvious relief, then signaled to her driver. The rifle retracted.

I rolled onto my stomach, looking back. Big Guy lay sprawled face up on the sidewalk, mere paces behind me. A dark bloodless hole marked the center of his forehead.

"Get in. Hurry." Her words, still muffled, as from a distance, slowly grew clearer. In any case, her tone made their meaning unmistakable. I gripped her extended hand, let her help me climb inside.

"Azumi," I repeated gratefully as she pulled the car door closed behind me. "I was afraid your boss had abandoned me."

She signaled the rifle-wielding driver to move on. Sudden acceleration pressed me back against the plush seat.

"That could not be. Mr. Hirokei is a man of honor." The servant retrieved a medical kit from beneath her seat.

"I had a hard time remembering that when the helicopter didn't return."

"The craft suffered structural damage after landing."

"Pilot error? I'd be shaken, too, if I were him."

"Not the pilot's fault. Lie back, please." Azumi sorted through her kit.

It wasn't difficult to read between the lines. "Mr. Hirokei's father escaped the net. I'm sorry."

"Briefly, but long enough to damage a rotor. No one was hurt." Scissors sliced open my blood-soaked pants leg, allowing the aide to bandage my wound. "He was soon tamed, but the helicopter could not lift off. My driver and I have been circling the north end for hours, in hopes you would make your way out. Bend over to your right, please."

Paper-dry fingers pushed aside my jacket and shirt. I caught a glimpse of the hypodermic needle in the servant's other hand.

"What's that?" I pulled back out of reflex.

"For tetanus, Mr. James. Please contain your paranoia. If Mr. Hirokei wished you dead, why would he have sent us to retrieve you?"

"To make—ow!—sure?"

She took a thick red envelope from her bag and stuffed it in my jacket pocket. "Your payment, Mr. James. With a ten-percent bonus to compensate for the additional stress of the past few hours. Also, Mr. Hirokei wishes to invite you to a private ceremony—although, by this time, it may have already taken place. Given the circumstances, there is no shame should you wish to decline. We are instructed to deliver you wherever you request."

Ashamed of my suspicions and convinced I would be more comfortable recovering in my client's penthouse than my own windowless hotel room, I nodded.

"I am honored to accept Mr. Hirokei's invitation," I murmured.

. . .

Once I'd changed back into my regular clothes, transferring my weapon and other essentials, Azumi presented me with a handsome cane of polished ebony, topped with an ivory badger's head. I was hesitant to use such a fine work of art for the mundane purpose of easing my limp, but the assistant acted perfectly natural about it, even blasé.

"Where is Mr. Hirokei?" I asked, leaning on the cane.

Azumi lowered her eyes. "You are about to become privy to a secret known to few. In the heart of this apartment is a tiny window-less room so cunningly concealed that, without a blueprint, one would not even suspect its existence. The elder Mr. Hirokei had it constructed as a precaution—great wealth often attracts dangerous criminals."

"Are you certain you should be revealing this secret to me?"

She looked up at me and shrugged. "It does not matter. Mr. Hirokei is shutting down his New York operations over the coming week. As part of his memorial."

So much for mutual trust.

Azumi led me to the room in which I'd first met Hirokei. In the bleakness of night, the panoramic view of the park resembled a gaping, hungry black hole, one that had nearly swallowed me. The dimly lit room otherwise looked as I remembered, with two exceptions: Tamotsu Hirokei was not present, and both the tanto and katana swords were missing from their display stand.

I didn't like that. At all.

Noticing my discomfort, Azumi said, "It would appear the ritual has already…"

She was interrupted by a piercing scream.

Azumi rushed past me to press her hand against a nearly invisible wall panel, shoving it aside.

In a small, windowless version of the main room, Osamu Hirokei's headless body lay sprawled across a bamboo mat. Decaying, putrid gray intestines spilled from his abdomen. One twitching hand still clutched the tanto.

The head itself was attached to my client's arm, gnawing away.

Tamotsu Hirokei screamed again. Blood pooled about his kneeling form.

"No!" Azumi screamed. She rushed toward her employer, only to trip over the decapitated body when its dead hand grasped her ankle.

I brought the cane's ivory badger head down on the groping hand, knocking it aside, then moved forward to tackle the attacking skull.

The teeth would not pry loose.

I stepped back, pressed the muzzle of my .22 against its forehead, and fired.

The head dropped like a deflated soccer ball.

I kicked it aside as Azumi, recovering her balance, came forward to help. Hirokei waved her away.

"But…" she started, then held back. She knew her place.

"You can do nothing more, Azumi," Hirokei told her. "Go! I would have private words with this man."

She hesitated.

"I said go!"

Azumi bowed and hastily exited. From my angle, I could tell she had not fully closed the door. Good for her.

I could hold my tongue no longer. "What the hell were you thinking, giving a weapon to a dead man?"

Hirokei sniffed, tightening the grip of his left hand across his abdomen. "An ancient ritual," he gasped. "Seppuku. I was acting as my father's second. It was my duty to remove his head at the critical moment."

I shook my head in disbelief. "What does a mindless corpse care about ritual?"

"He did it, Mr. James. I did not force him. My father followed my pantomimed instructions. But when I gave the final blow, beheading him, he pulled the tanto from his abdomen and stabbed me as well. And I forgot the head would still be... I suppose alive is the wrong word." He coughed. Fresh blood and viscera oozed from between his fingers.

"I'll call Azumi back."

"No," he ordered, scraping together what dignity he could. "I know when a wound is fatal. I was careless. I now pay for that carelessness with my own life."

"Nonsense," I lied. "You can afford the best doctors in the city. They'll fix you up."

Hirokei raised his free hand. "One last service, Mr. James." He nodded at the .22 in my hand.

I shook my head. "I just used my last bullet."

Hirokei was too clever not to see through that clumsy lie. He stared at me, eyes wide and pleading, saying nothing.

"I... I can't," I finally managed. "I could barely defend myself against those corpses in the park. To kill a living man..."

Tamotsu Hirokei's free hand fumbled for the katana with which he'd severed his father's head. Wordlessly, before I realized what he was doing, he thrust its blade deeper into the wound his father made. Holding my gaze, he twisted it violently to the right.

Pain hissed from between his lips. "Now!" he whispered, his fresh blood spurting over my feet. "Before I die and become a monster, too."

Shambling forward like one of the dead, I pressed the gun to his forehead and closed my eyes. My finger tightened on the trigger.

The gunshot echoed through the tiny room.

Shooting dead people was far less messy.

I turned to leave. Azumi stood wide-eyed in the open doorway.

"You knew he would do this!" I accused her. "You knew the minute you realized what happened! Why didn't you try to stop him?"

"Mr. Hirokei," Azumi answered softly, eyes moist, "is a man of honor."

"Was." I could not keep the bitterness from my tone.

She pointed to the cane I'd dropped beside the father's body. "In the legends of our ancestors, Mr. James, the badger is a master of change and disguise. Please, keep the cane. Mr. Hirokei wished you to. Even before..." Her voice trailed off as she focused on her employer's bloody corpse.

My anger drained. I nodded acceptance. What else could I do? How could I refuse a posthumous gift from a man of honor?

And it might come in handy if I ever again had to hunt for the missing dead.

From Space & Time #138, Autumn 2020

Gordon Linzner is founder and former editor
of *Space & Time* magazine, and author of three
published novels and dozens of short stories in *F&SF*,
Twilight Zone, and numerous other magazines and
anthologies. He is a member of HWA
and a lifetime member of SFWA.

Collecting Violet

By Austin Gragg

"More orders already?" Morrígu asks.

Skeleton glares at the bird for rummaging around in her mind again. Morrígu perches atop the scythe's silver blade, which leans against the far wall of the Garden's basement. Skeleton closes her leather notebook. She keeps names in it. She began collecting them when she realized the world wouldn't use names much longer, being a human invention.

As always, their orders are to collect. The name to gather is "Violet."

Collections are ramping up these days because all of Mother's children are sick. Dying.

Violet is a beautiful name. Well crafted, too; the way it evokes colors and images when spoken.

Skeletons do not have names and cannot have names. Their cosmic role is clerical, and like many things, predestined. But throughout time, humans had given the skeletons names. They described the cosmic clericus with strange notions and bestowed them with mythologies. But Anubis or Nergal had "died" long ago. Now, almost all the skeletons' names have passed into fabular or devolved into shallow concepts like "reapers."

Sadly, most humans just called them Death.

"It's a shame everything's changed," Morrígu says. "You'll live to see it happen."

It feels like Morrígu's rubbing it in. He isn't. Eternity only gives cynical stoicism or madness. Thankfully, her steersman has the former; the bar being high for the latter. Skeleton just envies him. The crows are allowed names because of their mortal-variety cousins on Earth.

Morrígu is ancient. His sight, his literal flesh and blood vision, is aligned with the cosmos. Particles of him pulse with the ebb and flow of reality. His silver irises sputter in and out of existence. Often, he uses his sight to read orders from Skeleton's mind. He's seen more change than she can imagine and keeps saying these changes on Earth are the biggest yet. He's looking ahead, so he can try to help.

Recently created, Skeleton is a child in this world—a babe, to all of this. In Eternity, centuries are nothing. But hers had been centuries of purpose. Now, with humanity at an end, her purpose was in flux.

Maybe Morrígu is right. Maybe it's best to feel it, then move on. But how? Skeleton would feel this damned saudade forever. For a world she barely knew. What a way to close her second century in Eternity.

Only advanced age could make the loss hurt more. Morrígu is evidence of this. At night, curled under his wing, the crow weeps in his dreams.

Skeleton goes to the door, robes herself, and takes up her scythe. Morrígu balances on the thick of the blade and shifts closer to the vibrant ash wood as Skeleton gives a routine look over her tool.

"Come, Morrígu," Skeleton says. "Let's be off."

• • •

Dead, dry, brown matter covers everything outside. It paints once-suburbia with a forever-sepia. Skeleton and Morrígu move along the road. Skeleton's white robes gleam and her bones blaze bright in the sun. Morrígu is invisible in the sandy winds overhead.

The air is putrid.

Skeleton knows how exquisite the air once was. Morrígu knows what it was like when the air was new. But Mother's *eldest* children, they knew the Earth before any creature breathed out of necessity. Anything older predates Mother—if one can imagine.

They arrive at a colonial with a large Greek revival porch. It's clear the house was once a lofty sight. Now it blends in with everything else it overlooks from its premium Orange County hilltop. Its roof is melted and blackened, scorched by long days in the sun. The porch's wood stairs are as dry as the piles of fallen brush strewn about the yard, each waiting its turn to combust.

Skeleton's navigator lands on her blade and ruffles his sun-bleached wings. A coat of dust falls from his feathers and joins the gentle sand current underfoot, then drags up on the wind toward an open front door.

Drystan sat in the marble-floored foyer of his luxury home and thought about dying. He stared out the open front door and dared the universe to send his death through it. An armed scavenger or wild animal—he'd take anything. His stomach had stopped wanting for food long ago. But he always thirsted.

He couldn't end it himself. Not that he was religious, but offing yourself was considered bad news by many who believed in an upstairs with pearly gates. It was *death* for Christ's sake, why risk it?

Perhaps Drystan's fear had grown into a religion of sorts. He'd been praying to the devil lately, after all. He proudly begged God and prayed to the devil in the same breath. He just wanted this to end.

These last few years, *his* world had been perfection, but *the* world had burned.

Photos of the globe's current affairs had been top dollar, and he had been one of the last photojournalists selling them. This house, the cars, the sex, and notoriety these last years... He knew his fun would run out. So he had a lot of it while he watched the world waste away.

Then everything had run out.

He ran out of hydroponic nutrients for his indoor grow areas months ago. His water purification system was no good in total drought. And he emptied his lounge's koi pond of water and fish weeks ago. The air still tasted like their habitat.

Money had bought time, but now it was spent. Drystan wanted to die.

Then Death came.

It stood picturesque in the doorway.

Death's robes were angelic, its weapon classic. Its crow screamed, then flew from the scythe and vanished, as if leading the eyeless carcass to him was its only purpose.

Drystan could only stare and shake and sweat as Death sailed swiftly to him. Death leaned over him. Its bones creaked like ancient wood. Drystan closed his eyes and cried. "Please," he begged. "Do it quickly."

Cold, thin fingers brushed aside his hair.

How would it take him? The scythe? A kiss? If this unapologetic image of the Grim Reaper were real, what else could be? Would there be Judgment?

Death spoke in a voice of horrendous beauty and finality.

"What is your name?"

It was finally here. Drystan's guts knotted, and he trembled. If he could piss himself, he would. Somehow, he knew that to get what he wanted, all he had to do was answer the question.

But, knowing what an answer brought, would it be suicide? Death had given the choice...

Drystan ached as he leaned forward and bowed before Death. No, he couldn't starve or thirst any longer.

"Drystan," he answered. He squeezed his eyes tight and waited.

The floor creaked, the bird squawked, and Drystan waited for the bliss of ending. But it never came. Eventually, he opened his eyes.

Death and its friend were gone.

Death denied him; it had left him to suffer.

Was this Judgment?

Morrígu returns with one of Mother's eldest in hand, gives the plant to Skeleton and they leave.

On the way back to the Garden, Skeleton adds new names to her journal. Disappointed, because she already has a Drystan in her notebook, she asks Morrígu what humans call the plant, other than a violet.

Saintpaulia ionantha sounds like poetry when each syllable is enunciated. Skeleton sees more names inside of it, too. Paulia, Ona, Liaion, and Nantha were some of her favorites. A few score from now, would she still be able to imagine their sounds? What about a millennium? Would her notebook scrawlings mean nothing?

One of the last of its kind, the violet is weak and losing color.

"Will it make it?" Morrígu asks.

Skeleton nods. They're almost there, but Morrígu's concern is just. She turns her scythe around and touches the snath's lively ash to the plant. Color returns to the flower's withered paddle hands. It isn't true life, but it's a chance at it.

When they arrive at the Garden, Skeleton walks Violet through rows of weary flora. The greenhouse temperature is marginally lower than outside, and the beds are guarded from the raining ash of wildfires and the rest of Earth's harsh surface.

Yet, the Garden doesn't look well at all. It's worse than yesterday or the day before. Skeleton doesn't know why. She hopes Mother can heal this child. Or maybe this violet will bring some new life to Mother's last attempt to save Herself.

Skeleton finds an open patch, sits, and digs. This is what Mother had in mind when She made humanoid fingers small, dexterous, and sensitive. They're perfect for digging in the dirt. Even without flesh, Skeleton enjoys this connection to Mother as best she can.

After Skeleton places Violet, she bows her head and listens.

Mother doesn't speak words of health or comfort.

She weeps.

Shrill ancient cries surge through the soil and root themselves in Skeleton's mind. She knows what she must do. Mother's soil is loamy. It's desperate for fertilizer—organic material—something as rare as clear spring water. Skeleton feels how disgusted Mother is with Her own order.

But skeletons collect.

When Skeleton returns to the colonial home, Drystan begs. It's strange how humans now beg for death as her purpose shifts slowly away from it.

Normally, she would ask for his name before taking his life. But she already has it. And this could be the last human she sees. So she asks: "What do you call me?"

Drystan answers.

But there's no satisfaction in the name: Death.

If names ever return to Earth, Skeleton would rather be called something beautiful, like Violet.

From Space & Time #138, Autumn 2020

Austin Gragg lives in Independence, Missouri, is a member of HWA, and was a 2019 finalist in the Writers of the Future Contest. He is an associate editor at *Space & Time* magazine. When not writing or gardening, he can be found playing D&D with his partner, friends, and a pride of small domestic lions.

Humani

By John Palisano

Blue strips of Caalrit gas wove in front of Pioneer's bow, shading the entire bridge in its hue. The color reminded Shin of the blue sky from one of his favorite childhood memories. He remembered his father lifting him and tossing him in the waves at Sunset Beach. He smelled the salty water and the lemon cake his mother had made, its scent filling the air as she'd opened the plastic bin.

The scene flooded over him in a blink. He tasted the sea in his throat. Tasted the dry lemon drops. Felt his father's stubble on his neck as he'd been carried back onto the sand, too tired to make it back on his own.

Shin remembered how the oiled swing set chains felt creaking under his bony fingers. He looked down at his hands, surprised at how they looked just like his father's had all those years ago.

It'd all led to this moment, he thought. His life distilled inside a collage of memories. If he could only replay that day once more. If he could just… see his father one more time.

The Pioneer tilted, pushing everything inside. He held on to his chair, his heart racing, the ring on his finger buzzing, alarming him his own biological system had been jarred by fear—if the Caalrit gas got inside, they'd all be doomed.

A second hit tilted the Pioneer more.

Shin took note of who was with him. All the Vi were off. Of course. He'd been operating the ship manually to save power. He thought about the Vi and they turned on. Their names and launch announcements appeared on his screen.

Virtual Intelligence 2072

Virtual Intelligence 2072-B

Virtual Intelligence 2082

The Pioneer kept seven Vi, each chosen by Shin to look like his own breed.

So comforting. Surrounded by Humani. His own voice in his head, then his father's.

You need me to carry you, kiddo?

The gases were close to encompassing the ship and stretched toward the top.

He had to maneuver the ship to evade the breach. Shin rolled the Pioneer. "You want to spin, I'll spin."

He rolled it fast enough that the world outside the large screen blurred.

A loud, rumbling sound overtook the bridge. The propulsion had maximized.

Shin nodded. *Yes. We'll make it.*

He thought the next move.

Fore.

The Pioneer spun and went forth. Fast as possible. The Vi knew what to do. Evasive action. Culled from the best minds back home, the Vi quickly created a route, an alternate, and a destination. Shin registered their plan in half a blink.

The displays showed him the breakdown. Coordinates slipped across one another in near-impossible combinations.

He looked across the bridge of the Pioneer and saw the Vi in several dimensions at once. Shin could see through them—see from every angle at once. He tasted the organic electricity that'd projected the Vi. Felt the small protons that made the beams.

Shin felt numb from it all, as was normal, but couldn't help but look down to make sure his hands were still there.

His.

Hands.

That day in the water at Sunset Beach, with his dad. Flashed back. More details. More memories Shin tried to forget, pushed down, down, deep. No one noticed. Not at first. Even he hadn't. Not at first.

Playing in the surf. Close to shore. Blue. Clear water and clear sky. He dug for the little clear-bodied shrimp things. They swam. He laughed. They were so panicked and scared. They gave off little pink clouds of ink, like squid. They burrowed inside the sand, and Shin reached in. He only had to put his hand down into the soft sand a bit, cup his fingers, and pull them out. They'd then shoot out their ink, and he could run his hands and fingers through it, making cloudy patterns in the water that'd soon dissipate with the endless tides.

Endless tides. Just like those of the stars. The solar winds. Like waves. Dissipating the Caalrit gases. Patterns swirling, organic shapes ever changing, hosted by oceans, hosted by space.

His father lifted him from the water, a large strong arm wrapped around his middle. He could still feel the soft hair of his father's arm against his belly. Comforting. Swaddling. Safe.

Rising from the water, his arms lifted from the sand. Pinkish clouds swirled and made huge, majestic patterns. How many clear-bodied shrimp had he grabbed? It had to have been dozens to have released so much ink.

Shin did not see them… did not see his hands. Where were they? Hidden by the pinkish ink? So dark at the middle of the cloud bursts, filling the water.

He thought, *Not pink at all. Bright red, actually.* He could not feel. Could not sense anything at all.

His father hoisted him over his shoulder. "Come on, kiddo," he said, laughing, playing. "Your mother says it's time to go, and I'm starved."

Shin looked at the surface of the water below them.

He could barely see the pinkish pools—they'd already dissipated— but the red ink still dripped from his hands. He still couldn't see them. What happened to them? He tried to move his fingers, but they didn't move. Flexing his wrists didn't work, either.

He called his father, but wasn't heard. They walked to the shore, toward his mother. She smiled. *Her boys.*

As they got closer, her expression changed. Her voice went high-pitched, and she called his Dad's real name. "John. John. John," she said, then said his name, "Shin. Shin. Look. My God. What happened to Shin?"

There were others near them, hovering, and caught in the pull. Shin sensed them. Felt their magnetics, their auras, their electricity. Just like he always did. The Vi alerted him.

He projected his thoughts to the Vi, telling them he was aware.

I'm still faster than the machines, he thought. *Flesh is still better. Even if it's a nanosecond. It makes a difference. Sometimes that's all the time it takes.*

Solar wind rushed them, traveling a four hundred kilometers a second.

We'll need to hit light speed to escape this now.

The Vi knew his thought and told him they'd have less than a three-percent chance. If that. The Humani never sugar-coated things for him.

Got to try.

That's what his father always said.

Aim directly into the heart of the matter. Don't falter. Don't think twice. Don't second-guess. Just do it. No ifs, ands, or buts.

He put his hands down, looked dead ahead. "We need to go right in," he said, even though he didn't have to speak. It felt good. Solid. More real.

His hands. So much like his father's, even more so after that day at the beach, and even more so after the Humani hands were attached. They grew inside, their electrical cables and pulses programmed to meld with his own, and to wire into his brain. He could feel with them, and grab with them, and use them. There was no pain, only they weren't quite the same. How could they be?

Echoes of words his father spoke. "Kiddo, I lost mine, too. The damn Techniche machine took them. You know." His job: Installing Hypernetworks in skyscrapers. Something slipped, and his father tried to catch it, but it took his hands. Clean off, then spiraling down a shaft hundreds of feet, crushed under the weight of the mainframe that'd come loose. "Nearly bled to death. No one knew what to do. No one had a bandage. Only that damn Healthcorder. Thing was dead. Probably useless, anyway. The only thing it was good for was little scrapes and such. About it."

Now I'm like Dad.

He remembered his mom racing them to the hospital. His Dad was asleep when they got there. The worst of it was hidden behind two puffy gauze wraps. Then, when his father came home, he had the Humani hands. They looked real, except when he moved them; you could see little gears pushing up on the skin. They even detailed them with minute wrinkles, hair, and their own fingerprints. Those weren't like people's prints, though. Instead, they were patterns of intersecting circles. That's how you knew they were Humani and not human.

Shin spotted his own fingertips. Clamped his hand around the till. "Stronger than they were before," he said, repeating what his father had said when he'd come home. Shin remembered his smile. He'd marveled at the hands. Then life went on, just like before. Until the day at the beach.

Remembered his father's last words to him, much, much later in life.

If you ever want to see me, look at the stars.
I'll be there.

Shin knew in that moment he'd become a traveler. A way to still somehow be with his father, if only through wishing.

The Caalrit gas surrounded them. They couldn't see, but the threat was hidden inside the gas. If the ship went inside, the things inside could get in. Just like when he put his hands in the sand and there was something unseen.

"Ahead," he said. "Take the Pioneer at mid-speed."

Vi 2082 said, "You know we have a small chance, and that we should probably hit top speed?"

"Trust me," Shin said. "We're going to confuse them. Do what they don't expect."

"I don't…"

One of the Caalrit things was inside the Pioneer. Shin didn't know how he knew, but he sensed it. Felt it. Saw it in his mind's eye.

Limbless and dark, the thing moved through the lower level of the Pioneer at alarming speed. Shin knew how it worked instinctively. It'd been able to travel through the Pioneer, as its many countless parts could come apart and then reassemble. They knew where the other parts were, somehow. They communicated. It reminded him of a cloud, or a vapor, with parts smaller than he could imagine.

How will I get rid of it? he thought. *This dark cloud?*
What takes clouds away?
What does it want?

If it got inside his body… if it were able to touch him… the cloud could reassemble… he'd be torn apart. His essence would be released, if only for a moment... and the cloud would drink it... and all his thoughts would be gone forever... food in the cloud's millions of little starving bellies. His father. His mother. His life. Turned into nothing.

Take the clouds away. Bring back that sunny day.

Shin knew what he had to do.

Vi 2072? Go to corridor B.

But there is something there. It will take me. I saw what it does, playing inside your mind. How do you know what it does?

Intuition.

Shin froze. The transporter. Couldn't send organic living things through space back home. It reassembled them wrong. The distance was too great, believed its engineers. So they installed it hoping there'd be a software fix. They might upload it later in the decades-long mission to the Casanova cluster.

The cloud things disassembled life. If they got to the transport, and if they got back home... it'd be beyond anything imaginable.

Vi 2072 was gone by the time Shin snapped out of his thought. He brought up the monitors. Vi 2072 struggled in the corridor, its form shaking and struggling to stay coherent.

Now, Shin thought. *Directive zero. I direct you to directive zero.*

Vi 2072 folded in on itself. The cloud had been trying to swallow the Humani. It picked up on the faint organic signature, but failed to sense the pinhead-sized cold fusion unit. That fired up. In a nano-second, the corridor lit. Then went immeasurably dark. Nothing replaced what'd been there.

Warnings sounded. The hull had been breached. Of course. Vi 2072 had ripped a hole in it.

Seal the surrounding corridors. Equalize. We'll be fine. Time to step up.

More clouds appeared in the corridor. Shin sensed them before he saw them on the screens. They were worse than he believed. Their hunger brought them, he knew. They'd be unstoppable.

The three making their way toward them would only be the

beginning. Soon the Pioneer would be overrun, and overtaken. Shin and the Humani would be overtaken. They'd find the transport. They'd go home. The world would fall to them. Memories would be devoured. History would be changed from being lost. There'd be no life. They'd not only take Human and Humani, but also, they'd travel through the forests and take everything there. When they grew hungry again, they'd comb the oceans and seas, disappearing everything they'd find, no depth or hiding place enough to stop the Caalrit.

When the life was gone and their hunger returned, they'd take the seas themselves, finding the smallest building blocks of life barely enough to satisfy. They'd take it, nonetheless. Then, they'd take the trees, the plants, the green. Last, they'd take the air, and they'd go, leaving a dead world behind. Home would be pummeled, its protections gone. Home would be a dead world, turned to dust.

You will not take me. Not us. Not this way.

"We are not going to use the regular way to go through," he said. "It's too late. They know. They've seen."

The Caalrit moved through the Pioneer.

Aim for the flare to the side of the star: the one going toward the black hole—the one being sucked away.

"Sir? That is suicide. We will not escape once we enter the singularity. The Pioneer will be crushed. It is not designed to travel through. Nothing can."

Yes. Nothing can. Not us. Not them. Make our course irreversible. Break the console if you must.

Shin focused his mind and showed the Humani what he knew would happen to Home.

Life extinguished.

We can stop it but we will be lost.

The Caalrit approached the bridge. Soon, they'd know about the transport.

Get us there quickly.

The Humani knew.

"It's been a pleasure, Sir."

Likewise.

"I wish it didn't have to end this way."

Me, as well. Me, as well. The fastest. Now. Eighth-Light.

It only took a moment for the Pioneer to reach speed. One eighth as fast as light speed.

The Pioneer headed toward the point of no returning back; toward the singularity.

Shin looked at his hands. They'd somehow changed. They were his own. His flesh and the machine were one, they, too, singular. *Maybe just an illusion. Maybe just in my head.*

Their approach toward the dark star was very real.

"You will not turn me into nothing. You will not have my memories. You will not have my home."

Shin called the Caalrit, broadcasting to them, showing them his life.

"You are nothing but eaters, so come eat. Come destroy."

They found the Pioneer. Found the Humani.

The flare of Caalrit fast approached, and they spun around, helpless, their back toward the great pull of the dark, unimaginable hole.

Shin looked out at the stars.

Heard his father.

If you ever want to see me, look at the stars.
I'll be there.

Shin closed his eyes and sensed his father nearby. Then, he felt his touch. Remembered his strong embrace and his sweet cologne. Heard his gentle laugh. Smelled the hot sand and sea once more.

You cannot have this, he said to the Caalrit. *You can't have us.*

The Caalrit plagued the ship.

They'd read the Humani and knew where they were headed— into a trap, to die within a black sun.

Go on. Try to escape.

They tried, but the pull was too strong. Even their little particles could not flee. The Caalrit bounced backwards, like flies caught on flypaper.

Hope I got all of you, Shin thought. *Each awful, soulless bit of you.*

The Pioneer went dark.

Soon the life support systems would run out and there would be nothing.

As the oxygen thinned, Shin stared at the stars.

He was not in the Pioneer.

Shin had made one last trip. He stood back on the beach with his father, laughing, the sky and water so blue.

Everything is perfect. I'll be here forever.

On the Pioneer, had Shin had opened his eyes one last time, he'd have seen black. Then, there'd be nothing.

The warm water felt like heaven. The sun warmed him and spotlighted him. His parents smiled and waved, and Shin knew he could do anything in the world. He could do anything at all.

Shin looked down.

With these hands, my past.

With these hands, my future.

Then dark.

Then nothing.

Then blinding light. He blinked. The Sun. From home. Sea water. His father's laugh. His father's arms, lifting him, up, up and away. In the clear blue sky, ever so faintly, Shin saw the stars. They were still there. Home was safe. Everything he knew before faded, except that there were new memories to be lived, and so with that known, Shin shut his eyes to the sky one last time, and his laughs, and his father's laughs, were all he heard.

If you ever want to see me, look at the stars.

I'll be there.

From Space & Time #134, Fall 2019

John Palisano's nonfiction, short fiction, poetry, and novels have appeared in literary anthologies and magazines such as *Cemetery Dance, Fangoria, Shmoop University,* and many more. He won the Bram Stoker Award© for excellence in short fiction in 2016.

JOY OF LIFE

by Alessandro Manzetti

Out there, in Calcutta, there's nothing but snow, and something has bitten one of Kali's bronze arms. Outside, the ice reflects the diamonds of motionless white snakes: the heartbeat hunters.

They call them that way because they are the ones who rule the Cold Earth—the frozen East, the glass eye of the planet. They just came out of nowhere at fifty-five degrees below zero, and nobody saw a pied piper or a reptilian queen bee. No music, no mother or egg pandemic.

It's as if they have always been, like the air, death, and the Hooghly River which now stands solid with a belly full of torpedoes of corpses. Men, women, and animals, shrouds of divers and kidnappers, down to the Gulf of Bengal. Sculptures buried under the water surface. When it was… liquid.

Those monsters have biological radar always listening, a network of coils connected by the spirit of a Bodhisattva constrictor, a magic lizard saliva, or the glue of chaos of Vṛtra poured out thousands of years ago. They are always alert. Night and day, continuously counting the heartbeats of the living. They feel them on their skin from a great distance, fading or becoming fast, too fast.

That's the right time to crawl, to start hunting, when humans fail to control their emotions it sounds like electrical impulses planted like needles in the dermis of the colorless coils of the white snakes, awakening their stomachs, turning on alarms of hunger.

At that moment, hundreds of watertight eyes roll back into ancient sockets, thousands of brains armored inside triangular skulls light up, and millions of tongues start to moisten with ammonia.

Out there, in Calcutta, there's nothing but snow, and something has strangled the statue Indra's plaster neck. Outside, the ice reflects the face of a girl and, surprised, it breaks apart, creating a crack with long, thin ends. Surya's eyes, which weep like wet cracks under the fifty-five degrees below zero rigid equipment, now look like blue and green kaleidoscopes and appear to have become ten, maybe twenty.

A heartbeat hunter begins to crawl faster, raising its spearhead, confused by the vibrations that have barely grazed its coils, its catatonic albino instruments.

A human heart still beats, despite everything.

But that muscle, which seems so small, almost new, is not afraid— it doesn't feel anything. The petals of its valves move like metronomes, and the blood runs slowly, even in the tight corners of arteries.

The snake considers a faulty skin which feels ghosts. Does it need to shed?

No, it's not yet time to change. The heartbeat hunter is not mistaken. The thing that is moving is a human female, alive. The reptile senses her ovaries rotating inside the estrogen broth.

Warm blood, tides.

Surya is well aware of how things work in the Cold Land; she watches the snake slowly crawling on the snow, moving towards her, salivating. She doesn't move. She knows that her heart beats too slowly. It's tasteless as long as she controls thoughts and reactions of her so-imperfect biology.

An endangered species, the human one.

But it is not so easy to control the heart, which suddenly wakes up images, frozen memories that hurt, and stirs up stupid hopes that can shake the kettle of the human mind.

She cannot resist long, but in Calcutta there is no longer anyone but the heartbeat hunters, gnawed gods, statues of flesh and frost, dead nerves, tough as whips. She's alone.

She closes her eyes and her mind flies back in time: five years ago, during the last Olympic Games. Now she can see the green, red, and blue City of Delhi again, and breathe the obsidian air of those sharp moments: The Warm World, which was just starting to freeze. Her heart almost stops beating, she hears an invisible audience shouting all around her. A Seventh Cavalry of ghosts.

The snake stops ten feet from its prey and curls up again, listening, saving energies, waiting for new proof of something alive. It's hoping for a progression of fear to sound like a gong in an empty cathedral. The heart of the human female doesn't ring.

Surya breathes in the freezing air, which smells of chrysanthemum crystals and crumbs of garlands.

She holds in her mind the spicy flavors of the alleys of Chitpur Road and Bara Bazar, the bamboo paint of Jorasanko, the screaming engines of the rickshaws in Sonagachi which fight in traffic like roosters, the ripe fruit on the belly of the Kalighat, the incense of the kiosks of the tea, the buzz and the coconut pastries of the colonial quarter, the hissing of the banks in Diamond Harbor when the river was still liquid.

The Warm World, Calcutta Warm. *Joy of Life*, which no longer exists.

It's time to jump. She takes off her fifty-five degrees below zero equipment, wearing only a purple and orange competition suit, barefoot, like a Tahitian muse.

She puts her skates on, tightens the laces, controlling trembles. There's still time to die.

She straightens back and soul, and picks up speed, spreads her arms, forming an elegant winged figure, a living spot shot in that so persistent white. A punch of dance.

Fast, bronzy, sensual like an exotic goddess the winter has never seen, a shot of revolution that shakes the rigid striped curtains of the shops, frozen by that Pompeii of frost.

Pieces of ice are falling all over. Calcutta feels the life running on its old streets again.

Surya looks left and right, smiles toward the stands of an imaginary Olympic Stadium, crowded by colorful specters. When she's ready, she loads the muscles and takes a backflip, landing gracefully on the ice and then following a wavy line between Stalingrad's corpses, coils of snakes, and an infinite row of empty taxis which can take you to Heaven or Hell.

Joy of Life. While her heart stops beating.

From Space & Time #137, Summer 2020

Alessandro Manzetti of Rome, Italy, is a two-time
Bram Stoker Award®-winning author, editor, and translator
of horror fiction and dark poetry whose work has been published
extensively in Italian and English, including novels, short and
long fiction, poetry, essays, graphic novels, and collections.

Artifact

A Joe Ledger Story

by Jonathan Maberry

-1-

I hung upside down inside the laser network of a bioweapons lab. Tripping the laser would trigger a hard containment, which would effectively turn the small subterranean lab on the picturesque little island in the south Pacific into my tomb.

I wish I could say this was the first time I'd been in this kind of situation.

Wish I could say—with real honesty—that it would be my last.

I was, as we say in the super spy business, resource light.

All I had was a bug in me ear, a Snellig Model A19 gas dart pistol in a nylon shoulder rig, and the few prayers I still remembered from Sunday school. Sweat ran in vertical lines from chin to hairline, and one fat drop hung pendulously from the tip of my nose. The watch on my wrist told me that there was nineteen minutes left on the mission clock. I needed fifteen of those to do this job.

I needed another twenty to get out. It wasn't the heat that was making me sweat.

The earbud in my ear buzzed.

"The laser grid is off," said a voice. Male, slightly nasal, young.

I composed myself before I replied. Barking at my support team like a cross dog would probably not yield useful results. So I said, very calmly, "Actually, Bug, the laser grid is *still* on."

"It's off, Cowboy. All of the systems mark it as in shutdown mode."

The network of red lasers suddenly throbbed. The crosshatch pattern, once comfortably large enough for my body to slip through, abruptly narrowed to a grid with only scant inches to spare on all sides.

"It's on and it's getting cranky."

"What did you do?"

"I didn't *do* anything, Bug. I'm still hanging here like a frigging bat. The floor is thirty feet below me and the laser net is getting smaller. So... really, anything you could do to shut it down would be super. Very much appreciated. Might be a bonus in it for you."

"Um. Okay. Maybe there's a redundancy system..."

"And, Bug...?"

"Yeah, Cowboy?"

"If you don't stop humming the fucking *Mission: Impossible* theme song while you're working... I *will* kill you."

"But—"

"My whole body is a weapon."

"I know... you could kill me more ways than I know how to die, blah, blah, blah."

The laser grid throbbed again.

I knew that the lasers couldn't hurt me. This wasn't a science-fiction movie. Passing through them wouldn't result in an arm falling off or my body being neatly diced into bloody cubes. However, they would trigger the alarms; and for the last hour and sixteen minutes, I'd been very, very careful not to let that happen.

Very bad things would occur if that happened.

Our best intel gave a conservative estimate of sixty security personnel on site, not one of whom was bound by international treaties, human rights agreements, or basic human decency. This place recruited from groups like Blackwater and Blue Diamond Security. The kind of contractors who give mercenaries a bad name.

They would shoot me. A lot.

Bug knew there was no reset button on the mission. It was a matter of getting it right the first time, which made the learning curve more like a straight line.

"Oh, wait," said Bug. "Looks like they have a ghost program hiding the real operations menu. You need to input a set of false commands—which work as a faux password—in order to reach the—"

"Bug…"

"Long story short," he said, *"voila."*

The laser grid switched off.

I exhaled a breath I think I'd been holding for an hour and dropped the rest of the way down the main venting shaft to the concrete floor sixty yards below.

No alarms went off. No bells, no whistles.

No army of guards storming through the hatch to do bad things to Mama Ledger's firstborn son.

"Down," I said. I unclipped from the drop harness and stood back as the cables whipped up out of sight.

"Lasers are going back on in three, two…"

The burning grid reappeared above me.

"Good job, Bug."

"Sorry for the delay," he said. "These guys are pretty tricky."

"Be trickier."

"Copy that. Sending the floor plan to Karnak."

Karnak was the nickname of the portable MindReader computer tablet strapped to my left forearm. It's a couple of generations snazzier than anything currently on the market, but my boss, Mr. Church, always makes sure his people have the best toys. It's dual hardwired and wireless connected to a whole series of geegaws and doodads built into my combat suit. I had everything in the James Bond catalog, from miniature explosives to a small EDS—explosive detection system—and even a miniature BAMS—bio-aerosol mass spectrometer, which sniffed the air for dangerous particles like viruses and bacteria. Dr. Hu, the head of our science division, has several times told me that the collective value of those gadgets was worth ten of me. Considering that the rig I wore had a three-million-dollar price tag, it was tough to build a convincing argument.

One-man army is the idea. Or, in this case, one-man high-tech infiltration team.

The thing that really tickled Hu is that if I happened to be killed during the mission, the suit would continue to transmit useful information. So... the next guy would know what killed me and maybe not get killed himself. And then, when all useful info had been uploaded, small thermal charges built into the fabric would detonate and turn all of the electronics—and the body inside the suit—into so much carbon dust.

Hu thinks that's hilarious.

He and I have not worked up much of a sweat trying to be nice to one another. If he stepped in front of a bullet train and got smeared along half a mile of tracks, I would—believe me—find some way to struggle on with my life. Sadly, he doesn't play on the train tracks as much as I'd like.

So, there I was, a mile below the April sunshine, wearing my science-fiction getup, all alone, looking for something that none of us understood.

This was not an unusual day for me.

-2-

It might be an unusual day for the world, though.

Hence the reason for my being here.

Hence the reason why our best intel suggested that I might not be the only cockroach in the walls. A lot of teams were scrambling around looking for the same thing. Good guys, bad guys, some unaffiliated guys, and maybe some nutjobs guys. Last time there was this much of a scramble was when a set of four man-portable mini-nukes went missing from the inventory of former Soviet play toys supposedly under guard in Kazakhstan. I'd been hunting for those, too, but they were scooped up by Colonel Samson Riggs. He's the most senior of the DMS field team leaders. Kind of an action-figure demi-superhero. Even has a lantern jaw, crinkles around his piercing blue eyes, and an inflexible moral compass. We all geek out around Colonel Riggs. He's the closest this planet will probably ever get to a real-life Captain America.

Riggs was gone, now, though. Swept away by recent events the way so many other top operatives are who maybe spend one day too long in the path of the storm. Leaving guys like me to take the next job. And the next.

This was the next job.

So far, there had been fourteen separate attempts to recover the package.

Those fourteen attempts had resulted in sixty-three deaths and over a hundred severe injuries. That butcher's bill is shared pretty evenly between all of the teams in this game. There are six DMS agents in the morgue. Five more who will never stand in the line of battle.

And all for something that nobody really understands.

We call it the package or the football when we're on an open mike.

Between ourselves, off the radio, we call it "that thing" or maybe "that fucking thing."

Its designation in all official documents is simpler.

The artifact. Just that. It's as precise a label as is possible to give, at least for now.

Why? Simple. No one—no-fucking-body—knows what it is. Or what it does. Or where it came from. Or who made it. Or why.

All we know is that twenty-nine days ago a team in Egypt ran the thing through an X-ray machine at what was the Egypt-Japan University of Science and Technology in Alexandria.

Yeah. You read about Alexandria.

The news services said that it was a terrorist device. Some new kind of nuke. The authorities and the U.N. aid teams keep adding more numbers to the count. So far it stands at seven thousand and four. Everyone who was at the University. Everyone who lived within a two-block radius. Not that the aid workers are counting bodies. There aren't any. All that's there is a big, round hole. Everything— every brick, every pane of glass, every mote of dust and every person—is simply gone.

Yeah, gone.

And the ballbuster is that there is no dust, no blast debris, and no radiation.

There's just a hole in the world where all those people worked, studied, and lived.

All that was left, sitting there at the bottom of the crater, was the artifact.

One meter long. Silver and green. Probably made of metal. Nearly weightless.

Unscratched and untouched.

We saw it on a satellite photo and in photos by helicopters doing flyovers.

The Egyptian government sent in a team.

The artifact was collected.

Then their team was hit by another team. Mercs this time. Multinational badasses. They hit the Egyptians like the wrath of God and wiped them out.

The artifact was taken.

And the games began. The multinational hunt. The accusations. The political pissing contests. The media shitstorm.

Seventeen days later, everyone is still yelling. Everyone's pointing fingers. But nobody's really sure who was responsible for the blast. Not that it mattered. Something like that makes a great excuse for settling old debts, starting new fights, and generally proving to the world that you swing a big dick. Even if you don't. If there hadn't been such a price tag on it in terms of human life and suffering, it would be funny.

We left funny behind a long way back.

From about one millisecond after the team of mercs hit the Egyptians, every police agency and intelligence service in the world was looking for the package. Everyone wanted it. Even though nobody understood what it was, everyone wanted it.

The official stance—the one they gave to budget committees—was that the device was clearly some kind of renewable energy source. A super battery. Something like that. Analysis of the blast suggested that the X-ray machine triggered some kind of energetic discharge. What kind was unknown and, for the purposes of the budget discussions, irrelevant. The thing blew the Egypt-Japan University of Science and Technology off the world and didn't destroy itself in the process.

If there were even the slightest chance the process could be duplicated, then it *had* to be obtained. Had to. No question.

That was real power.

That was world-changing power.

For two really big reasons.

The first was obvious. Any energetic discharge, once studied, could be quantified and captured. You just need to build a battery capable of absorbing and storing the charge. Conservative estimates by guys like Dr. Hu tell me that such a storage battery would be, give or take a few square feet, the size of Detroit. There were already physicists and engineers working out how to relay that captured energy into a new power grid that could, if the explosion could be endlessly repeated under controlled circumstances, power... everything.

Everything that needed power.

People have killed each other over a gallon of gas.

What would they do to obtain perfect, endlessly renewable, and absolutely clean energy?

Yeah. They'd kill a lot of people. They'd wipe whole countries off the map. Don't believe it, go read a book about the history of the Middle East oil wars.

Then there was the second reason teams were scrambled from six of the seven continents.

Something like that was the world's only perfect weapon.

Who would dare go to war with anyone who owned and could deploy such a weapon?

For seven and a half days, no one knew where it was. Everyone held their breath. The U.S. military went to its highest state of alert and parked itself there. Everyone else did, too. We all expected something important to go *boom*. Like New York City. Or Washington, DC.

When that didn't happen, no one breathed any sighs of relief.

It meant that someone was keeping it. Studying it. Getting to *know* it.

That is very, very scary.

Sure as hell scared me.

Scared my boss, Mr. Church, too, and he does not spook easily.

Halfway through the eighth day, there was a mass slaughter at a research facility in Turkey. Less than a day later, a Russian freighter was attacked with a total loss of life.

And on and on.

Now it was twenty-nine days later, and a very shaky network of spies, paid informants, and traitors had provided enough reliable intel to have me sliding down a wire into a deep, deep hole in North Korea.

If the artifact were here, then any action I took could be justified because even his allies know that Kim Jong-un is a fucking psycho. Basically, you don't let your idiot nephew play with hand grenades. Not when the rest of the family is in the potential blast radius.

On the other hand, if the North Koreans *didn't* have it, then I was committing an act of war and espionage. Being shot would be the very least—and probably best—I could expect.

Which is why I had no I.D. on me. Nothing I wore or carried could be traced to an American manufacturer. My fingerprints and DNA had been erased from all searchable databases. Ditto for my photos. I didn't exist. I was a ghost.

A ghost can't be used as a lever against the American government.

I even had a suicide pill in a molar in case the North Koreans captured me and proved how creative they were in their domestic version of enhanced interrogation. I tried not to think about how far I'd let things go before I decided that was a good option.

I ran down a featureless concrete tunnel that was badly lit with small bulbs in wire cages. All alone. Too much risk and too little mission confidence to send in the whole team.

Just me.

Alone. Racing the clock. Scared out of my mind. Hurrying as fast as I could into the unknown.

My life kind of sucks.

-3-

"I'm losing your signal," Bug said. "Some kind of interference from—"

That was all he said. After that, all I had in my ear was a dead piece of plastic.

I looked at Karnak.

The small HD screen still showed a floor plan, which was good. But it wasn't updating, which was bad. The data it showed was what Bug had sent me when I'd detached from the spider cable. We had an eye-in-the-sky using ground-penetrating radar to build a map, but that was a slow process and suddenly I was behind the curve. The corridor ran for forty more yards past blank walls and ended at a big red steel door. Very shiny and imposing, with a single keycard device mounted on the wall beside it. Knowing what was on the other side of that steel door was the whole point of the satellite. Pretty much no chance it was a broom closet. Before I tried to bypass the security, I'd like to know that it was my target. Intel suggested that it was, but a suggestion was all it was. That's a long, long way from certain knowledge or even high confidence.

"Balls," I said, though I said it very quietly.

Our timetable was based on the fact that two things were about to happen at the same time. A motorcade of official cars and trucks was headed here. We'd tracked it all the way from the Strategic Rocket Forces divisional headquarters in Kusŏng. Infrared on the satellites counted eighty men.

The second incoming problem was a two-truck mini convoy coming in hot and fast from the east. Six men and a driver in each truck. We almost didn't spot them because their trucks were shielded with the latest in stealth tech—radar-repelling scales that also contained thousands of tiny cameras and screens so that it took real-time images from its surroundings and painted them all over its shell. The effect was that you could look at it and look right through it. Only a very focused thermal scan can peek inside, but it has to be a tight beam. We were able to do that because of the one flaw in that kind of technology—human eyes. One of our spotters saw the thing roll past. Video camouflage works great at a distance. Up close, not so much, which is why it's mostly used on planes or ships. The science is cutting edge, but it's not Harry Potter's cloak of invisibility. Not yet, anyway.

If I wasn't out of here real damn fast, I was going to get caught between three hostile forces—the guards here, the incoming military convoy, and whoever was in those two trucks. I did not think this was going to be a matter of embarrassed smiles, handshakes, and a trip to the local bar for a couple of beers.

I'd wasted too much time with the laser grid, and now I could feel each wasted second being carved off of my skin.

I quickly knelt by the door and fished several devices from my pockets. The first was a signal counter, which is a nifty piece of intrusion technology that essentially hacked into the command programs of something like—say—a keycard scanner. It's proprietary MindReader tech, so it used the super computer's software to ninja its way in and rewrite the target software so that it believed the new programs were part of its normal operating system. In the right hands, it's saved millions, possibly billions, of lives by helping the Department of Military Sciences stop the world's most dangerous terrorists. If it ever fell into the wrong hands, MindReader and her children could become as devastating a weapon as the device I was here to steal.

Which is why each of the devices I carried had a self-destruct subroutine. If I died, they blew up. If they were too far away from me for too long, they blew up. If Bug, Dr. Hu, or Mr. Church hit the right button, they blew up.

Such a comfort to know that all the devices hanging from my belt near all my own proprietary materials were poised to go boom.

I placed the device on the side of the keycard housing and pressed a button. A little red light flickered, flickered, and then turned green. I then plugged a USB cable into it and attacked the other end to second device I had, which was flat gray and the size of a deck of playing cards. After too many seconds, a green light appeared on it as well and a slim plastic card slid from one end.

I removed it, took a breath, and then swiped it through the keycard slot.

And prayed.

Nothing happened. My balls tried to climb up inside my body. I swiped it again. Nothing.

"Shit," I said.

And tried one more time. Slower.

There was a faint *click*, and then the big red door shifted inward by almost an inch.

I let out the air that was going stale in my chest. My balls stayed where they were. They didn't trust happy endings.

When I bent my ear close to the doorframe, all I could hear was machine noise. A faint hum and something else that went ka-chug, ka-chung. Could have been anything from a centrifuge refining plutonium to a Kenmore dishwasher. I didn't know and didn't much care. All I wanted was the package.

No voices, though. That was key.

I nudged the door so that it swung inward very slowly and only slightly. Light spilled out. Fluorescent. Bright. The machine sounds intensified.

No one shouted. No voice spoke at all.

I pushed the door open enough to let me take a look inside. Not one of those dart-in, dart-out looks you use in combat situations. When there's no action, then the speed of that kind of movement was noticeable in an otherwise still room. I moved slowly and tried not to embrace any expectations of what I'd see. Expectations can slow you, and if this got weird, then even losing a half-step could get me killed.

The room was very large and, as far as I could see, very empty.

I held another breath as I stepped inside.

The ceiling soared upward into shadows at least fifty yards above me. Banks of fluorescent lights hung down on long cables. Bright light gleamed on the surfaces and screens and display panels of rank after rank of machines. Computers of some kind, though what they were being used for or why they were even here was unknown. I've seen a lot of industrial computer setups and there had to be eighty-, ninety-million-dollars' worth of stuff here. Then, I spotted a glass wall beyond which were rows upon rows of very modern mainframe supercomputers, and I rounded my estimate up to a quarter-billion dollars. The floor was polished to mirror brightness.

I tapped my earbud, hoping to get Bug back on the line.

Nothing.

I faded over to the closest wall and ghosted along it, taking a lot of small, quick steps. There was a second door at the far end of the big room. If any of my intel was reliable, then the artifact had to be in there, or near there.

Fifty feet to go, and I was already reaching for another of the bypass doohickeys when a man stepped out from between two rows of computers. A security guard. Young, maybe twenty-two. With a gun.

He stared at me.

I stared at him.

His eyes bugged wide and he opened his mouth to let out a scream of warning.

-4-

There are times in a combat situation where you have options. You can take someone prisoner. You can use some hand-to-hand stuff and subdue him, leave him bound and gagged. Or you overpower him and juice him with some animal tranquilizers.

Those are options that let the moment become an anecdote for both of you, allow it to be a story—however painful or embarrassing—to tell later on. Maybe over beers with your buddies, maybe at your court martial, maybe to your wife as she holds you to her breast in the dark of night.

Those are moments when mercy and a regard for human life are allowable elements in the equation. They're moments where even if blood is spilled, it's merely a price to be paid. A small price. No one dies. The price doesn't pay the ferryman's fee.

This wasn't one of those moments.

This was the kind of moment where there is no allowance for human life, for compassion, for choice.

The guard opened his mouth to scream and I killed him.

That's the only way the moment could end because there wasn't time for anything else. If he screamed, I'd die. If he screamed, then the artifact would slip beyond the reach of people who wanted it stored and studied rather than used.

So he had to die. This young man. This peasant soldier working for people who had no regard at all for his life.

Nor, in that terrible moment, did I.

As his mouth opened, I moved into him, intruding inside his personal envelope of mental and physical safety. My left hand cupped the back of his neck and I struck him under the Adam's apple with the open Y of the space between thumb and index finger. The blow slams the side of the primary knuckle of the index finger against the eggshell-fragile hyoid bone. He stopped breathing right there and then. His face instantly turned a violent red and seemed to expand as he tried to drag air in through an impossible route. I swung him around, turning him so that his panicked face was pointed to the ceiling as I dropped to my right knee and broke his back over my left.

It all took one second.

One bad second that changed his world and broke a hole in the lives of everyone he knew and everyone who loved him, and slammed the door on every experience he would ever have. Bang. That fast.

And it chipped off a big piece of my soul.

I knew, with absolute certainty, that I would see his young face watching me from the shadows of my deathbed when it was finally my time to go. He would be waiting for me, along with too many others whose lives had ended because of the necessities of my job.

Yeah, I'm a good guy. Tell anyone.

Fuck.

-5-

Tick-tock.

I laid him down on the floor and moved on. Grief and regrets are for after the war. I raced to the far end of the chamber, pulled the keycard scanner, reprogrammed my master key, and slid it through the slot.

It went green on the first try. No, I wasn't going to suddenly start believing in good luck. The door opened and I stepped through.

The room was a lot smaller. Maybe twenty by twenty. There was a big steel table set in the exact middle of the room. A whole lot of weird-looking equipment was grouped around the table. Scanners and other stuff that looked like they came from a Star Trek movie were arranged to point at the thing that squatted under a glass dome on the table.

The artifact.

Right there. Closer than I could have hoped. Not hidden beyond an airlock, not wired up to fifty kinds of alarms.

I could have taken four paces and touched it.

Except.

The whole damn room was filled with people.

Three little guys in white lab coats. Not a problem.

Six bigger guys in uniforms.

Problem.

-6-

We all went for our guns at the same time.

I was already totally wired, so I was maybe one heartbeat faster than the others.

The Snellig gas pistol fires tiny thin-walled glass darts filled with a fast-acting, non-lethal nerve agent. A new synthetic version of tetrodotoxin. Granted you fall down and shit your pants, but you do not die, so put it in the win column.

I was firing while I moved, rushing to put one of the lab coat guys between me and the guards, hoping they wouldn't want to risk shooting them. That bought me another heartbeat.

Two of the guards spun away, their eyes rolling high and white within a microsecond of the darts bursting on their skin. They went down hard. One of them collapsed against a third guard, dragging him down, too. The other three clawed at their sidearms. I shoved my human shield against one, fired over the scientist's shoulder and took another guard in the cheek. He dropped and I closed on the one soldier left standing and pistol-whipped him across the chops. Teeth flew and he spun around so hard I thought he was going to screw himself into the floor.

Four guards down.

I pivoted toward the one who'd been accidentally dragged down and kicked him in the face. Twice. Real damn hard.

That left the one who was trying to push away the scientist I'd shoved at him. I shot the scientist in the back, and when he crumpled, I shot the sixth guard.

It was all over in the space of those salvaged heartbeats.

Bang, bang, bang.

That left me standing with the gun in my hand and the remaining lab coat guys with their dicks in theirs. Metaphorically speaking.

They spent a couple of seconds being shocked, which is fine. I wanted them to fully appreciate the situation.

But all I could spare was a couple of seconds.

Then I said, in reasonably passable Korean, "Give me the device."

The two scientists looked blankly at me. Shock or training or good poker faces, it was all the same to me.

I pointed the gun at the closest guy's face.

"Now."

In this situation, you'd think they'd say fuck it, we lost. All their security guys on the floor, snoring and shitting their pants. Them, looking like book nerds. Me, looking like the big hulking thug I am. Gun, looking like a gun. You'd think this would be easy math. A no-win situation so clear that it was almost no-fault. They couldn't be expected to do anything here but acquiesce and hand it over.

That's what you'd think.

That was what logic and sanity dictated in no uncertain terms.

It didn't play out that way, and I knew it when one of them smiled at me.

This was not a smiling situation. Not even for me and I had the gun.

The guy farther from me—he was a half-step behind the other scientist—smiled. A small, ugly little smile.

Then he shoved his buddy right at me. It was so damn quick that it caught us both off-guard. The closer man fell right against me and I shot him more by reflex than intention. But his body was already falling and it was a crowded room with bodies on the floor.

We both went down in a tangle.

Even little guys are a bastard when it comes to dead weight, and the dart made him totally slack.

I fell with him on top of me.

The other guy hit two buttons. One popped the glass dome over the artifact, which he scooped up and tucked under his arm like a wide receiver.

The other was the central alarm button.

Fuck.

Klaxons began blaring with an ear-crushing loudness. Red lights slid out from slots in the walls and flashed with hysterical pulses. If I'd had epilepsy, this would have triggered a fit.

I heard the hiss of a hydraulic door, and just as I shoved the unconscious scientist off of me, I saw the other guy vanish through the doorway. The door began to slide shut.

I flung the guy off of me and shot to my feet, ran over several bodies—stepping on chests and faces and crotches as I fought to beat the close of that door. I leapt through a gap that didn't look anywhere near big enough, tucked to make sure I didn't lose a foot, hit the ground in a roll, felt the jolt as the concrete floor found every goddamn exposed piece of bone in my body, came up onto my feet, and pelted after the scientist. He was heading for another security door at the other end, and he was running faster than I ever saw Calvin Johnson run when there was nothing on the clock and the entire defensive squad on his ass.

He was already halfway down the hall, and I capped off three rounds. Two hit the flaps of his lap coat and burst harmlessly. The third grazed him. He jerked sideways but didn't go down.

I fired again and got nothing. The magazine was out.

I dropped it, fished for a spare, slapped it in place, and emptied the whole thing as I tore up the hallway. The Snellig has a twelve-shot capacity. I think I hit him with number eleven, because he dropped and my last shot passed right over his head.

The artifact dropped, too.

It hit the ground and bounced.

I think my heart stopped.

It landed and rolled awkwardly against the wall while I skidded to a stop. Until now, it had been a lumpy chunk of silver metal with no discernable seams or openings, no lights, no switches or dials. In every photo I'd seen of it, the device looked like it had been molded rather than assembled.

Now it looked different. Now it had lights. When it hit the floor, something happened. As I bent over it, a series of small green lights suddenly flicked on all along its sides. The lights were intensely bright; the colors more striking than LED Christmas lights.

I hesitated before touching it. I mean… of *course* I did. Who wouldn't? After all, no one knows where this thing is from.

And right then, I swear to God I heard a voice say, "Don't touch it."

I whirled, reaching for my last magazine, swapping out the old one with the speed born of constant practice. But I brought the gun up and pointed it at nothing.

The hallway was empty except for the scientist who'd dropped the package.

The room on the other side of the closed door was filled with his colleagues and their guards and everyone was sleeping.

The alarms blared and the red lights flashed, but there was no one around to speak those words.

The voice repeated the warning.

"Don't touch it."

Here's the thing. The voice I heard sounded like my own.

-7-

Granted, I make no claims about being sane. Or even in the same ZIP Code as sane. On my best day, I have three different people living inside my head. The Civilized Man—who is the innocent and optimistic part of me. The one who wasn't destroyed during the childhood trauma that otherwise turned me into a psychological basket of hamsters. Then there's the Killer, that rough, crude, and dangerous part of my mind that was always looking to take it to the bad guys in very ugly ways. And there was the Cop, the closest thing I have to a sane and sober central self.

Each of them spoke in a particular voice inside my thoughts.

This wasn't any of those voices.

The voice I heard was the one I use in normal conversation. My regular voice.

Clear as day.

I spun around, bringing the gun up in a two-hand grip. There was an empty hall in front of me and an empty hall behind me. Just the sleeping scientist on the floor. Red flashing lights on the walls. Nothing else.

No one else.

That voice, though… it had been real.

There's nothing in the playbook on how to react to that kind of situation. I didn't feel like I'd suddenly gone crazier than I already was. There was no way on earth the North Koreans had somehow sampled my voice and rigged a playback just to screw with me. It was too improbable and there was no point. So, that wasn't it.

The voice, though.

I *had* heard it.

I switched the gun to one hand and slowly knelt beside the artifact. The little green lights were pulsing now. Steady. Like a slow heartbeat.

I swallowed what felt like a throatful of dust.

"Fuck it," I said, and gently scooped up the object.

It weighed almost nothing. It felt like metal, but there was no heft to it at all. Lighter than aluminum or magnesium. Lighter than Styrofoam. I had to press my fingers against its planes and angles to assure myself that it was actually there.

That alone was strange. If this was some new alloy, then someone had broken through the ceiling of superlight design. If it was durable— and given the thing's history, I had to believe it was—then that alone would be worth billions to the aeronautics industry. Durable super- light materials are the dream, the holy grail of metallurgy. If it could be studied and reproduced, it would totally revolutionize military aircraft. Maybe space travel as well.

And yet that was, as far as my team was concerned, a secondary benefit. An unknown benefit. It added another element of mystery to this thing. Science, as it's known by the teams working with the Department of Military Sciences—including the uber-geeks at DARPA—couldn't do this. The energy discharge alone was freakish. Now this.

The artifact was warm to the touch.

Creepy warm.

Not warm like metal.

Touching it was like touching flesh. If I closed my eyes, that's what it would have been like. Skin, at normal body temperature.

Not metal.

"Jesus," I said, and I wished I could have dropped it right there and then. I wanted to. It was repulsive.

"Do it," said the voice. My voice. "Drop it and get out."

I whirled around again.

The hall was still empty.

"Fuck me," I told the emptiness.

The clock was ticking. I needed to be at the extraction point in ten minutes.

So I clutched the package to me, and I ran.

The corridors fed one into another. I ran up flights of stairs. I ran down. I burned seconds I couldn't spare bypassing locks on security doors.

Twice, I encountered security personnel.

Twice, I put them down before they could get off a shot.

After I dropped the last one, I passed through another door that took me out of the lab complex and into what was clearly an administrative wing. There were vault-style doors on that level, and the place was entirely deserted. Not sure if it was because of the hour—local time here was three in the morning—or because of the alarms. North Korean military protocols sent workers into secure bunkers during emergencies. I'd passed several locked chambers. Any staff working this late was probably squirrelled away in there. Good. Better for everyone concerned. Besides, I was down to three rounds in the Snellig. If I met any real resistance, I'd have to switch to something more lethal. I'd already killed one poor dumb son of a bitch; I'd didn't want to compound my crimes.

I hurried through the offices. At most of the desks, the chairs were neatly snugged into the footwells, computers were off or on screen-saver, and the desk lamps were dark. A few were less tidy, and those probably belonged to the workers hiding in the bunkers.

There were no security guards in this wing. That concerned me. Not that I wanted to meet any, but it seemed odd.

Everything, in fact, seemed odd.

Then I rounded a corner and found something even odder.

Three uniformed guards lay sprawled on the floor.

There was no blood. No marks of violence.

For all the world, they appeared to be… *sleeping.*

I think I actually said, "What the fuck?"

Beneath my arm, the artifact throbbed.

Actually throbbed. It was a feeling of heat that pulsed so quickly and abated so immediately that the effect was like the device had expanded and contracted. Like something taking a breath.

I almost flung the thing away from me.

Instead, I held it out at arm's length –despite its size, I could easily hold it with one hand, it was that light—and looked at it.

Metal. Green lights. Same as before. But not exactly the same. That pulse or throb or whatever it was… I didn't like it. No, sir. Not one bit. It felt wrong. Like the surface temperature and texture of it were wrong. For all the world, I was reacting to it as if it were not a machine at all. It felt to me like something…

The word is "alive," but I can't really use it because that's stupid. It's metal. It can't *be* alive.

The thing pulsed again.

The green lights went from a neutral intensity on a par with traffic "go" lights to a glare that, for a split second, was eye-hurtingly intense. I winced and cried out and…

And, yes, I dropped the thing. Or maybe I flung it away. Hard to say. Hard to actually think about.

The artifact hit the ground and rolled bumpity-bumpity across the floor.

And stopped when someone placed the sole of his foot against it.

Someone who, I swear to God, was not there a moment ago.

-8-

The man was dressed all in black.

All.

Head to toe. Black pants and pullover. Black socks and shoes.

Black gloves. A black balaclava and black goggles. I couldn't see a single square inch of his skin. He could have been white, Asian, or, yeah, black.

He was big, though. About my height. Not as bulky in the arms and chest, but close enough.

And he was just there.

Standing where he shouldn't have been standing, within arm's reach, and I hadn't seen or heard him approach.

So, fuck it, I shot him. Point blank.

In the script in my head that I was writing for this scene, he should have folded up like a deck chair and that should have been that.

That wasn't how it played out.

I fired the dart gun and he moved out of the line of fire.

It was weird. He was fast but not the Flash. It wasn't like he dodged a bullet, so to speak. He wasn't that fast. No, it was like he had such perfect timing that as I fired, he was already moving—as if knowing exactly the timing and angle of my shot.

Then he pivoted and slapped the gun out of my hand.

There's a way to do that if you know what you're doing. You hit the gun at one angle and the back of the wrist at another. Do it fast and simultaneously, and the gun goes flying.

My gun went flying. I have been disarmed exactly once in my adult life. That time. If anyone had wanted to wager on whether someone could do that to me, I'd have bet my whole pension on that answer being "no." My gun went flying anyway.

I wasted no time goggling at it. I kicked him right in the knee. Which he blocked with a raised-leg hoof kick.

I hooked a left at his short ribs, but he chop-blocked with his elbow and counter-punched me in the biceps, numbing my arm. Growling in pain and anger, I faked once, twice, and hit him with a jab in the nose.

Except that he turned his head two inches to the left so that my jab hit the point of his cheekbone.

Then he switched from defense to offense, throwing a series of punches and kicks at me that hammered me all the way across the hall and against the wall. He blocked every single one of my counter-punches, parried every kick, even intruded into my attempted head-butt by head-butting me.

It was all very fast and very painful. I won't lie and I won't sugar-coat it. He beat the shit out of me. He humiliated me. I didn't land a single solid punch on him, and he hit me as often as he wanted to, and it was pretty clear that he really wanted to.

Winded, bleeding, bruised, and dazed, I sagged against the wall.

I tried to win that fight.

I've never really lost a fight. Not in years. Not any fight that's ever mattered to me. No matter how tough the other guy was, I was tougher. Or, if he was too tough, then I won because I was crazier. I don't care if I get hurt, but I will win a fight. I'll burn down a house if that's what it takes to win a fight.

Except that I lost this fight. Lost it fast, and lost it completely. This man, whoever he was, outfought me. I am a special operator. I'm a senior martial artist. I'm a warrior and I'm a killer, and he simply took me apart.

He even used some of my own favorite moves, some of the things I tried to use on him. He used them faster and he used them better and I went down.

On my knees, blood dripping from my mashed lips, I tried to change the game on him. I snagged the rapid-release folding knife from its little spring clip inside my trouser pocket. It came into my hand, and with a flick I locked the three-point-seven-five-inch blade into place. I lunged in and up and tried to castrate the fucker.

He twisted away. I heard cloth rip. I saw droplets of blood seed the air, but he moved so fast that all I did was slash him. I could tell from the resistance that the blade hadn't gone deep enough to cut muscle or tendon. Only trousers and skin.

The blood was red. The skin that showed through the torn fabric was white. Not the light brown skin of an Asian. This guy was Caucasian.

The guy twisted and hit the side of my hand with a one-knuckle punch that turned my entire hand into a useless bag of pain. The knife clattered to the floor. He bent, scooped it up, and suddenly I was pressed back against the wall with the wicked edge pressed against the flesh of my throat. He held the knife the way an expert does when he wants you to know that you're not going to take that blade away from him. Not in this lifetime.

I was done. I was cooked. Beaten, bloodied, and disarmed. With a knife to my throat and his fingers knotted in my hair to hold me still. Then he bent close and spoke with quiet urgency into my ear.

"Believe me when I tell you that neither of us want you dead," he said.

I froze. I didn't dare move a muscle.

"I need you to listen to me," he continued, "and I need you to understand. You can't ask any questions. The best and *only* thing you can do is to listen and tell me you understand and agree."

He pressed the knife more firmly against my throat to emphasize his point. A drop of warm blood ran down alongside my Adam's apple.

"You listening, sport?"

"Y—yes…"

"Good, 'cause I'm only going to say this once." He was leaning so close that even through his mask I could feel the heat of his breath on my ear. "You don't know what this device is. None of you do. You can't know and, believe me, you shouldn't. You don't want to."

"Pretty fucking sure we *do*," I growled.

He made a sound. Might have been a laugh. "No, you really don't."

"Who are you?"

For a moment, I thought he was going to move the knife away. Or cut my throat. His hand trembled.

"Let me ask you a question, chief," he said. "And you give me a straight answer. No bullshit. Can you do that?"

I said nothing. Wasn't really feeling all that chatty.

He took it as assent, regardless. "What do you think they're going to do with the device? I'm not talking about the North Koreans. What do you think *we're* going to do with it?"

I said nothing.

"Do you honestly and without reservation believe that once the U.S. government gets their hands on it that they'll hide it away and never use it? Do you think that if they *did* use it, they'd only concentrate on its potential for unlimited power? Do you think they can resist the temptation to study its potential as a weapon?"

I said nothing.

"You have good intentions, Joe," he said. I didn't ask him how he knew my name. I was pretty sure I didn't want to know that answer. "But sometimes you're naïve. You're too trusting. You think everyone has the same altruism as Mr. Church. You think that you can keep this thing from ever falling into the wrong hands. Tell me that's not true. Tell me I'm lying."

I still said nothing. My heart was hammering in my chest.

He sighed.

"I'm going to take the device out of play," he said. "Nobody gets it. Not our people, not theirs. Nobody."

"Bullshit," I said finally.

"No," he replied. "No bullshit. I know where it comes from. I know what it is. And I know what will absolutely happen if anyone— *anyone*–fucks with it. And they will. You know it, sport. They'll fuck with it and fuck around with it and then it'll all go to hell."

"You can't know that."

"No," he said, "*you* can't. I can. I do." He paused, and there was a strange quality in his voice. A kind of sadness that runs all the way down to the cellar of the soul. "I've seen it. That's why I can't let you take it."

He took the knife away and gave me a hip-check that knocked me sideways, and stepped backwards out of reach before I could recover my balance. The device lay pulsing on the floor between us. Closer to him than to me.

Very slowly and carefully, he knelt down and scooped it up with the hand not holding the knife.

"Who are you?" I demanded. "Who are you working for?"

He hesitated, studying me, then he dropped the knife on the floor and reached up to pull the goggles off. He dropped them onto the floor next to the knife. The he pulled the balaclava over his head and dropped that as well.

I stared at him. The hinges of the world seemed to snap and cracked off, and for a moment the whole room seemed to tilt.

I knew that face. I knew those blue eyes and the scuffle of blond hair. I knew that crooked nose and the scars. Some of the scars. There were more of them than when I'd seen that face last.

More than there had been when I looked into the shaving mirror that morning.

I said, "I don't…"

It was all that would come out. The face was older than mine. Harder, sadder, with deeper lines and more evidence of damage. But it was my face.

He looked down at me with my own eyes. There was such a look of deep hurt and enduring pain in those eyes.

"I'm taking it with me," he said. "Once I'm gone, you'll have six minutes to get out. You'll need four and a half."

He smiled then. There was no joy in it. Not for him. Not for me. Then he turned and walked away. Within a few steps, he was running. He rounded a corner and was gone.

I knew, with absolute certainty but with no understanding of why I knew it, that if I ran to that corner and looked around it, he wouldn't be there.

There was a brief squelch in my ear and then Bug's voice. "…to

Cowboy, do you copy?" I tapped my earbud, but I had to suck some spit into my mouth and swallow it before I could trust myself to talk.

"Cowboy here."

"Thank God! We were having kittens and—"

"Shut up, Bug. How do I get out?"

"Do you have the package?"

I hesitated, trying to construct a reply that would make sense. "Mission accomplished," I said. Or something like that, I don't really remember.

He gave me the route. I ran it.

I got out.

-9-

They grilled me for days about it. No sleep. No easing up. My boss, Mr. Church. Dr. Rudy Sanchez. Aunt Sallie. Others. They asked me hundreds of questions. Or maybe it was the same few questions hundreds of times. It blurred together after a while. They hooked me to a polygraph.

Someone—it might have been Dr. Hu—slipped me a pentothal cocktail and then grilled me through the haze. They kept asking the same questions. And I gave them the same story every single fucking time. After a while, they stopped asking. They let me sleep.

Eventually they even let me go home.

Tomorrow the interviews or interrogations may start up again. I'm not sure. All I know for certain is that the artifact is gone. No one has seen it. I suspect no one ever will.

Where has it gone to? I have no idea. I really don't. What happened in the lab remains the biggest mystery of my life and that is saying a whole lot.

I know what I saw. I know what I heard.

It's just that I am absolutely certain, without any margin for error, that I will never understand it. Not, at least, until I'm older.

As *he* had been.

Older.

Sadder.

Stranger.

I don't believe in time travel and I'm not sure I buy any bullshit about parallel dimensions. But how else do I explain it? What else makes sense?

Nothing. Not a goddamn thing. But… the device is gone.

Nobody has the weapon.

So… yeah… there's that.

From Space & Time #137, Summer 2020

Jonathan Maberry is a New York Times best-selling and five-time Bram Stoker Award®-winning author, anthology editor, comic book writer, magazine feature writer, playwright, content creator, and writing teacher/lecturer. He was named one of the Today's Top Ten Horror Writers and his books have been sold in more than two-dozen countries.

The Feline, the Witch, and the Universe

by Jennifer Shelby

"This isn't possible, ma'am. Witches don't exist in outer space. It's all science out here, I'm afraid," said the boarding guard, a large fellow with a uniform strained at the buttons and frayed along the cuffs.

Sorscha would have turned him into a toad if she didn't need access to the message board of the biggest refueling station in this solar system. The ads she'd placed in digital spaces had yielded nothing. "Yes, well, thank you for advising me that I do not exist. I recognize that you will probably not be changing your worldview today, but if you would please post this flyer on your message board, I've a missing cat who is far too magical to leave at large in your scientific universe."

"What does a magical cat do?"

"She once batted the moon's reflection out of a puddle and caused the Great Tidal Apocalypse of Earth."

The guard snorted. "Impossible."

"I'm sure the citizens of Earth will be pleased to hear that. The flyer, sir. Please." Sorscha forced herself to smile the sort of smile men expected when women asked them for a favor.

He accepted the flyer she held out to him. *Missing cat,* it read.

Below was the photo of a black cat with squinting amber eyes, its teeth bared mid-hiss. *Answers to the name of Smudge. May display magical abilities. If found, please contact Sorscha the Sorceress, 5E567.*

"If you're a witch, why can't you magic your cat back home?"

Sorscha resisted the urge to roll her eyes. He hadn't put the poster on the board yet. "Because she's my familiar. It would be a betrayal of our sacred bond."

The guard stared, his forehead scrunching into confused wrinkles. Sorscha sniffed. "A witch's familiar is a partner in the magical arts. We cannot use our magic against each other one day and in unison the next."

"Not even if it's lost?" The guard gestured to the endless twinkle of far-flung stars outside the hangar.

"She has to want to be found first," Sorscha grumbled.

Her mood lifted as the guard unlocked the bulletin board and pinned Smudge's flyer in the center. "Thank you, kind sir."

Sorscha tucked the remaining flyers back into her bike satchel and tugged her black helmet over her dark, braided hair. She swung her leg over the seat of the old red Raleigh she'd lovingly restored years ago. A basket with a Smudge-sized satin pillow hung from the handlebars. The Raleigh was the only thing she owned that wasn't black, which filled her with a strange pride. The bike's chrome glinted in the starlight, hinting at the hours she'd spent polishing it back to its original shine. Shame she never got a chance to ride much.

"Wait," said a human-hybrid refueling his Star Cruiser. "You can't go out on that—you'll die of exposure."

"It's a magic bike," Sorscha told them with pride. "I ensorcelled it with some of the best magic you'll find these sols." She handed him a business card from her pocket and reached for another flyer. "I'm a witch."

"A witch? Shouldn't you have a broom, then?"

Sorscha glared at him. "Honestly, I don't have the energy to unpack the problems with that statement, nor is it my responsibility.

I recommend you go home, educate yourself, and please let me know if you happen across my missing cat."

She pushed one of her flyers at him in disgust and pedaled through the forcefield into deep space. Where the necromancing nebulas was that cat?

She steered her Raleigh 'round the rings of Saturn, one eye on the lightning bolts flashing on the stormy planet and the other watching for Smudge in the ring debris. "Smudge!" she called out, her voice growing hoarse over time. "Here, Smudgy, Smudgy, Smudgy. Come on Smudgebot 5000. Who's a Smudge-tastic kitty?"

The lightning grew more frantic as she cycled past Saturn's dragon storm. Sorscha read about the storm years ago when she was contemplating taking a cycling tour of these rings. The storm contained no actual dragons, which irked her. Names should mean something.

Sorscha looked behind her. No one around. She conjured a smallish yellow dragon with a puff of smoke and sent it into the storm. It swirled with delight to be alive, ate a bolt of lightning, and dove deeper into the storm cell. Sorscha stifled a snort of laughter, pedaling off to resume her search for Smudge. There was no reason she couldn't have fun searching for her naughty friend.

After a lengthy rest on an asteroid, Sorscha headed to a black hole at the edge of Andromeda. What better place for a black cat to hide than a black hole? Sorscha sighed. She was reaching and she knew it, but she had to search somewhere.

The black hole's time distortion proved hard on the Raleigh's gears, but the witch soon came up with a spell to counteract the distortion. She couldn't help but be pleased with herself on that one. The jobs she'd had of late did little to challenge her skills. She hadn't realized how stagnant she'd gotten. Her delight reminded her why she got into the business of magic in the first place.

A number of ships lay trapped in the black hole's event horizon, bored faces peering from portholes and viewing decks. Sorscha slowed her pedaling and held up Smudge's flyer. The onlookers shook their heads. They hadn't seen her cat. She pasted the flyer to a few windows of the bigger ships just in case.

She conjured a brush from the ether to apply glue as she peered through one of those windows. A small girl held up a picture of her own. A man, probably her father, smiled from the photograph. Oh, necromancing nebulas, the kid's family wasn't trapped in the event horizon with her. Her parents would be ancient by the time the girl got back to them and she'd only be a week older. Poor kid. Science wasn't going to be able to solve this problem.

Sorscha pulled her agenda from the bike satchel. She'd need at least a week magicking everything to rights so the girl could grow up with her family. She found a free week, later than she would have liked, but with the girl's temporal distortion she wouldn't be waiting long. Sorscha penciled it in and held up the agenda for the girl to see.

The girl knitted her brow and shrugged. She didn't understand, but it couldn't be helped. She'd find out soon enough, and in the meantime, Smudge was still missing.

Sorscha pedaled into the gravity well, calling Smudge's name. She stopped once to bolster her forcefields and fix a flat tire. The ride inside the black hole proved a wild race through an unexpected wormhole of twisting stars and whirling nebulas. Smudge, who didn't like fast rides, would not have enjoyed it—but she wasn't in her basket. Sorscha allowed herself to have fun, whooping through the twists and turns and unexpected drops that left her belly way up in her chest and gasping with glee.

The wormhole deposited Sorscha and the Raleigh near the ruins of an old feline temple. Early space explorers had revered the many feline species found across the universe. Some too much, turning to worship, ritualistic litter box cleansings, and sacred petting hours. Monks devoted themselves to the meditation of sitting still while cats napped on their laps. The faith lasted for a few generations before the temples were abandoned, their protective forcefields left in place out of respect for history and the feral cat colonies which developed there.

It wouldn't be the worst place for Smudge to end up. There were several animal welfare groups who made sure the feral colonies had food, fresh water, and an occasional mass-neutering to keep the population in check.

Sorscha pedaled around the wreck. Built like a stone cathedral, these temples were the closest thing to castles a witch could find in outer space. She often felt a certain kinship with the things but had never visited one until now.

A small spell allowed her through the environmental forcefield, and she leaned her Raleigh against a crumbling stone wall. The place had a decent gravity considering the castle didn't spin. Rumor had it, the original monks had trapped a small gravity well and built the temple around it. The science didn't work but the magic sure as Hecate did.

Sorscha tapped her foot on the ground. To her delight, the magic inside the old cathedral tapped back. Whoever set up the original spell had an admirable longevity to their bewitchment. What was their secret? Sorscha made a mental note to look that up later. Since science became the dominant universe view, witches and magic were rarely recorded in history. Sorscha suspected there was more to these monks than mere feline worship. Too bad Smudge wasn't with her. The cat would love this place.

She stepped around the broken masonry collecting in the corridors. "Smudge! Smudge-a-puss, where are you?" Her voice echoed off the stonework and several cats peered over the tops of broken walls, their heads cocked to listen.

A large serval plodded toward her, tail erect, body held in a straight, proud line.

"I'm looking for my missing cat," said Sorscha.

The serval said nothing.

"Necromancing nebulas," Sorscha cursed. "I suppose none of you speak people, do you?"

Twitching his whiskers, the serval sat on his haunches and tilted his head up to look down his nose at her.

"I grant you the speech of a Familiar." Sorscha let the spell do its work before holding up a flyer. "I'm looking for this cat. Have you seen her around the temple?"

The serval studied Smudge's picture. "I have not, and while I know all the felines in my domain, you are welcome to search if it will ease your worry."

Sorscha nodded and tucked the flyer away. "If you were here, where would you go?"

"In the temple? The highest wall, of course, peering down on everyone. In the whole of the universe?" The serval's eyes grew distant. "I'd choose a throne made of dark matter and demand worship from the very stars. Forget my troubles."

"Have you many troubles?" asked Sorscha.

"There is no one to worship me here." The creature sniffed into the air. "Servals are magical beasts, chosen ones. Like you, I suppose."

Sorscha shook her head. "I'm no chosen one. I trained my magical bottom off, studying every manual of magic I could lay my spells on."

The serval sneered, baring an impressive canine tooth. "But you can't find your missing cat?"

Sorscha shrugged. "She'd never forgive me the disrespect if I used magic on her without her permission."

"You're not worried about her welfare? Did you two have a fight?"

This time, Sorscha's shoulders slumped. "A big one."

The serval stood and arched its back in a long stretch. "In that case, you won't be finding your feline friend until they want you to, but you're welcome to look around."

Sorscha nodded. The ruins sparkled with interstellar fungi framed by fluorescing flecks of meteor lichens. It whispered of an undiscovered magic that should have thrilled her, but it wasn't the same without Smudge. This was a place they should explore together.

Sorscha buckled up her satchel and sat on her old Raleigh. Her spirits low, energy waning, she magicked herself to one of the few places in the universe that still served dark roast.

Flossy's was an Andromedan nostalgia diner, harking to an era of occult renaissance when self-styled Andromedan archaeologists roamed the galaxy, secretly documenting the occult practices of countless species. The revolving walls of the diner were painted with a parade of runic symbols. Sorscha discovered the place soon after she took up witchcraft. When she was stuck on a particular spell, she'd come here and stare at the revolving runes until her magical blockage eased with caffeine and a rare sense of belonging.

She waved to the owner and server, Flossy, a moth-like species of Andromedan, and settled into one of the few chairs that comfortably sat a human. The restaurant lay empty save a trio of Titans in the far gallery. They were laughing over a plate of Sparft, an Andromedan delicacy Flossy's was renowned for. Sorscha made the mistake of ordering it once. Most Andromedan food proved unpalatable by human standards, but their dark roast was to die for.

Flossy set Sorscha's coffee down without needing to take her order. The server's pink tentacles waved with concern as they turned on their universal translator. "Something's wrong. I can tell." One yellow and pink wing touched Sorscha's shoulder gently.

The kindness of the gesture almost set Sorscha to tears. She shook it off and showed Smudge's flyer to her friend. "Smudge has run away. Could you post this for me somewhere where it will be seen?"

"Sure. Did you two have a fight?" The liquid layer over the brown orbs of Flossy's eyes trembled with the vibration of the restaurant's engines, not unlike a human eye filling with tears. Sorscha knew better, but let the comforting sensation of empathy soothe her just the same.

"Yeah. I told her we couldn't take the vacation we'd hoped for. My caseload was just too heavy."

Flossy made a clucking sound with their mouth parts. "Sounds like a recipe for burnout. Maybe kitty had your best interests at heart."

Sorscha sipped her coffee. "If Smudge wanted me to relax, she wouldn't have run away."

Flossy's wings shifted in her species's version of a shrug. "And where were the two of you hoping to go for this cancelled vacation of yours?"

"We hadn't agreed on a place yet. Smudge wanted to go visit the catnip fields of the Feline Moons, while I wanted to take a cycling tour, explore somewhere I've never been before." Sorscha's voice trailed off.

"I assume you've already checked these catnip fields for your missing friend?"

Sorscha's face burned with sudden heat. "I... haven't."

Flossy's wings nodded. "Tell you what, I'll put this coffee on your tab. You go have yourself a look at those moons."

Gulping down the last of her dark roast, Sorscha raced back to her bike. She cycled under a speed spell to the Feline Moons and considered what she'd say if she found Smudge there. Should she be angry? Cats had little interest in human anger, but Sorscha just couldn't let this go, a familiar couldn't run out on their witch every time they didn't get their way. They were partners. Sure, maybe she had ignored Smudge's complaints of working too hard, but that didn't mean Sorscha considered herself "in charge." There was a shortage of witches in the wider universe, an abundance of sentient creatures getting into situations science couldn't rescue them from, and Sorscha didn't want them to suffer any longer than they had to. Still. She could have been a better witch to Smudge.

The Feline Moons loomed large on the horizon over Felinia, a small, dark planet known for the excellent naps one could have there. By contrast, its spinning moons were lush with greenery. It was the thirteenth moon Smudge wanted to visit. She always chose thirteen, given the chance.

Sorscha coasted the Raleigh down through the moon's atmosphere and landed gently on the surface. Once there, she shifted gears and cruised along an empty road through the catnip meadows, watching the green crop sway in the wind. Sorscha let it pull her into a deep state of meditative cycling. Maybe Smudge was right and the pair of them needed to take more breaks, more vacations. There must be some way to make that possible without leaving their clients twisting in the solar winds.

Small hills rose and fell, enough to make the horizon interesting but not so high as to make the cycling a struggle. Sorscha's feet pumped steadily at the pedals. What if she altered the spell she'd used in the event horizon of the black hole she'd searched? Sorscha chewed on it for a bit, taking the mechanics of the spell apart and playing with the composition. If she tweaked this, and swapped that, she could fold a temporal distortion of a few sols into an hour. Enough time to get away, recharge, and keep a better work/life balance for her and for Smudge.

Hmm. Imagine how many more clients they could take on if time wasn't a concern? No. No, no, no. She couldn't do that to Smudge. In fact, she'd put the cat in charge of making sure they only manipulated time to get away and take a break. Nothing more.

As the system's sun rotated behind Felinia's twelfth moon, the ringed moon's silhouette filled the endless sky above the fields. For a few breathless minutes, the sun's rays shone through the water droplets suspended in the moon's rings, bathing the fields in a myriad of rainbows which sent Sorscha's heart skipping with joy.

She stopped pedaling and watched them, basking in her own forgotten sense of wonder, until the rainbows faded. Re-energized, Sorscha's magic tingled and zapped in her fingertips, eager to play. How long had it been since she felt like that?

The road soon led her to the sort of intergalactic hostel that attracted customers who craved experience over luxury. The employee, a local species of sentient automatons, nodded when Sorscha showed them Smudge's flyer.

"Yeah, that cat's been around. Saw her heading into the catnip to catch the rainbows. She'll probably be back soon if you want to wait."

"I will," said Sorscha. Back outside, she walked her Raleigh over to a bench in the shade of a blue-leafed tree to wait.

As she sat down, she noticed a black cat curled in a small pool of sunlight leaking through the tree's branches. Smudge. Small snores climbed through the air, a steady rhythm gaining traction over the wind. Sorscha stood in the beam of light, blocking it from the curled-up cat.

Smudge opened a single eye, saw her there, and purred.

"Do you have any idea how worried I was?" asked Sorscha, her hands on her hips.

"Witch, please." Smudge got to her paws and stretched. "You had a blast. I bet you searched one of those black holes you've been going on about for years."

Sorscha fixed her witchiest glare on the cat.

Smudge twisted around her feet, rubbing against Sorscha's ankles. "I'm guessing you explored something wild, cleared your mind of a decade's worth of cobwebs and finally gave the old Raleigh the adventure of its lifecycle."

"Maybe." Sorscha smirked. "I *was* worried, though."

"I'm the familiar here, remember? I worry about you. And you were getting burnt out, my dear sorceress. You weren't going to take a vacation, so I ran away. I knew you'd come looking for me and I'm willing to bet the sense of purpose suited you better than one of those cycling tours where you have to do what the group wants and stick to mundane trails so you don't offend the scientists. And you didn't have to 'people,' as you like to call it."

Sorscha reached for a flyer, holding it up. "I did have to people. I had to put these up all over the galaxy."

Sniffing at the ink, Smudge preened her whiskers. "Did Flossy get one of these?"

"Yes." Sorscha could have magicked the blush creeping over her face away, but Smudge would have known.

"Any chance there's a few on the rings of Saturn?"

"How'd you know that?"

Smudge purred and said nothing.

"I also stopped at the ruins of a feline temple."

"Without me?"

Sorscha patted Smudge's cushion in the Raleigh's basket. "We can go back together. There's a serval there you would adore."

"A serval!" The cat leapt into the basket. "Did it demand you worship it at once?"

The witch smiled and swung her leg over the bike seat while Smudge purred and kneaded her cushion. "Shall we magic ourselves there or take the long way?"

"The long way, please. I'm in no hurry to get back to work."

From Space & Time #135, Winter 2019

Jennifer Shelby hunts for stories in the beetled undergrowth of fairy-infested forests. She fishes for them in the dark spaces between the stars. As part of her ongoing catch-and-release, you can read these stories in *Space & Time*, Vivian Caethe's *Unlocking the Magic*, *Flights from the Rock*, and others.

Hands of a Toolmaker

by Eric Del Carlo

It used to get nervous giggles, Silas remembered. That was mostly because of the vague—and usually misunderstood—sexual connotations of the word. You could make a dumb kid's joke by saying "tool" loud enough that it would force a laugh out of your playmates because they didn't want to look like they didn't get it.

But that was past. Silas was now old enough to feel he truly had a *past*. Fifteen was a significant age. It had that cool, squared-off feel to it as a number; fives were halfway between tens in math, and were almost as important in equations and calculations. But fifteen meant more than that, of course.

It was the age when he would have to decide whether or not he would get Tooled.

He could feel the pressures. Society was tilted a certain way. He was invested with enough adolescent cynicism to see that now. The persuasions came by way of social media, the entertainment industry, even politics, which he was just starting to pay a little attention to. The bias toward getting oneself Tooled was encoded in the social fabric, in ways subtle and—increasingly—more overt.

But it was Silas's decision. All his. Every fifteen year old got to make up her or his own mind on the matter. At least, that was the letter of the law.

The reality, Silas thought as he got on the school shuttle, was something else. Adults he barely knew would come right out and ask if he was going to get Tooled. How rude was *that*? He shook his head, looking gloomily out of the vehicle's window at the passing cityscape. His mom kept tagging him in boring articles and pompous webclips preaching the gospel of the Tooled. She wished she had gotten Tooled. Well, that was her damn privilege. But when she started in about how Dad should have... that was when full-throttle teenage anger blazed in him, and he would be on the perilous brink of actually cussing out his mother. *My decision, Mom! My fucking decision. And Dad didn't die 'cause he wasn't Tooled! He was just in the wrong goddamn place at the wrong–*

A body thumped onto the seat next to him. "So, we got another zittin' assembly speaker today."

Silas groaned as he turned. Coco was dressed in her hodgepodge—winter camou cargo shorts, Hawaiian shirt, biker vest, Neolithic Doc Martens, and was that a tutu? He had no idea how she decided what to put on, or how she never seemed to wear the same item twice.

She took his sound of exasperation as conversation, continuing, "Yeppers. Gonna be a military shill. Wanna bet this one'll be... oh, I don't know... Tooled?"

"Nobody's taking that bet, Coco." He couldn't help but smile a little at her. Friends did that to you, the good ones. He'd known Coco since they were five. Now they were fifteen, facing the same life-defining moment, and both equally annoyed with the influences neither of them had fully appreciated were present before they'd reached this age.

It had been a tense school year. Hell, being a high school sophomore was anxiety-inducing enough, he figured. But then to have this Tooling madness thrust upon you...

"Y'know," he said, gazing into the middle distance, "we're fifteen years old. We can't decide to drive. Can't decide to liq or nark. Can't decide to have sex. But this thing—this we've got make up our minds about. And all those grown-ups and authority figures and talking heads on the streams, they have to live with whatever we decide. No matter what, half the people will be disappointed." He shook his head again, still glum. "I wish there was a third option."

"A third?"

"Yeah. One that would piss everybody off."

Coco laughed, a genuine full-throated bray, and it dragged him along in its mirthful wake. They made banter-y talk the rest of the way to the school. Just before the driver-less shuttle let them off, Coco turned and asked, seriously, "Half? You really think it's half for and half against? The media streams and stuff always make it seem like most people are in favor of getting Tooled."

"Propaganda," he said with juvenile world-weariness as they shuffled off the vehicle. But he wondered where the sentiment had come from. It almost sounded political.

The assembly was worse than he'd braced himself for. The army zomb made her case for schoolkids signing up for early-privilege military service. It was a monstrous practice, but one, unlike Tooling, that required parental/guardian approval. You could practically hear the eye-rolling in the assembly hall, along with murmurs of "Zittin' bullshit," but here and there a student was listening raptly, enthralled by the idea of going overseas to meet new people and slaughter them.

Silas tried not to think about his father.

But when the recruitment spiel ended, there were still twenty minutes left, and the soldier—or, actually, Soldier—used that time to laud the virtues of getting Tooled. She recited her success percentages on the gun range, in sim hand-to-hand, on parachute drops. That last, it seemed to Silas, was probably an all-or-nothing proposition. You won the parachute contest or you splatted.

"I was able to initiate my military career as a fully formed unit," she said, her face holo'ed and embiggened behind her. "I already possessed valuable skill sets. Adjustment was minimal. When I became a Soldier, I knew I was realizing my total potential." She managed to make the assemblage hear the capital S. "Whatever calling captures your imagination, whatever vocation touches your soul, Tooling will allow you to eventually be successful at it. I would be very pleased if you all chose the military, but I recognize that is unlikely." Jesus, did she just pause for laughter she must have known wouldn't come? "But the first step in your professional lives to come, is to opt to be Tooled. There's really... really no other respectable choice."

Silas blinked. That last bit had chilled him. It had an off-script tenor, like she'd been moved to say it, which contrasted her previous androidic manner. Respectable? Was that what Tooling was now?

Few kids applauded, but those who did did it vociferously. Silas shook his head. Didn't they see that this Soldier clown was the same as the Engineer zomb and the Firefighter one and the Tooled Maglev Pilot who'd all spoken at these assemblies just in the past couple of months? They weren't selling their professions. They were carnival barking for Tooling. Stoned-crow doubtless. How could all his class-mates not realize that?

It was because some had already made up their minds to be Tooled. Or had had their minds made up for them. A lifetime of family indoctrination could do that.

But couldn't they at least hear how these representatives spoke? Again and again, Silas caught the same phrases, too many for any comfort. Different speakers, same presentation. Like they were stamped off a conveyor belt. Like Tooling had endowed them with a boilerplate vocabulary, or worse—lots, lots worse—a commonized mentality.

Get Tooled. Get regimented. Get fucking hive-minded.

Ancient creepy movie he'd streamed once when he was too young; the freaks chanting: "One of us! One of us!"

It played in his head, louder than the military woman's words, as he exited the hall.

Of course, there were intelligent arguments in favor of Tooling. And some criticism of anti-Tooling sentiment came off as quite rational. Silas acknowledged all that.

Getting Tooled didn't change you. It was only a process which prepared you to accept professional skill sets when you reached adulthood. Thing was, fifteen was the age when the human brain could accommodate Tooling. Neural activity was where it needed to be. The chemical growth was at just the right level of fermentation, before it aged into a non-receptive state.

So, for a fifteen year old, it was now or never.

Once Tooled, you basically had a guaranteed future. All you had to do was pick your profession. Do like the army zomb had said: go with what captured your imagination, what zinged your soul. Wanted to fly planes since you were a kid? Okay. As a Tooled person, you were eligible to enroll in the course of coded chemical instruction, get your education practically overnight. As an outpatient, you'd suddenly find yourself inscribed with the necessary abilities to get a three-hundred-ton jetliner smoothly up in the air. All you would require from there was confirmation that the neurological engraving had taken (it always did, stoned-crow guaranteed), final certification, and you were set for the proverbial friendly skies.

Silas had met plenty of Tooled people. His mom knew lots. Hell, there were juniors and seniors at his school who'd had it done, though they had yet to receive any of the chemical inscriptions that would make them instant experts at their chosen livelihoods. You had to be an adult before that could happen. As a fifteen year old, you could only decide whether or not you would modify your brain to one day be receptive to the preprogrammed skill sets.

Tooled adults, the ones succeeding in their dream jobs, didn't come off as zombies. Silas knew that, even if it was fun to call them zombs. They demonstrated emotions, got married, had children, voiced opinions. They weren't—what was the term from that other old movie that had once scared him pissless?—weren't pod people.

And yet... and yet... if you watched closely, if you listened carefully, there was a vague sameness to them. It was subtler than the cultural pressure brought to bear on those of Tooling age. The Tooled seemed to have a slight surfeit of common points of emotional reference. A little too often, Tooled adults reasoned the same way, responded in too similar a fashion to outside stimuli. Silas had observed it. When he'd pointed it out to his mother, she dismissed it in that teens-aren't-sensible way which so pissed him off.

But it was the practicality of getting Tooled which was really the most persuasive argument. The high-profile, profitable vocations all had preset inscriptions just waiting for recipients. The chemical supply would never run out. On day one of legal adulthood, a person could step right into an expert field, be making decent money, have a settled future.

And if you didn't get Tooled and you still wanted one of those platinum gigs? Sure, you could still become, say, a cop the hard way. Enlist, train, train some more, study, start as a rookie, learn the ropes bit by bit, gain some competency, then some confidence. In four years, you might be a reliable, capable police officer. You might have a natural flair for the work. You could even make a worthy detective in another five years. Or ten.

Or—you get chem-etched and you wake up a Cop.

And what about the other side of the whole social equation, the part most people didn't like to talk about? What were the likely jobs for the unTooled? None of the scientific magicians who had invented Tooling had concocted a miraculous inscription for being a dishwasher or a mop jockey or convenience store cashier. So those opportunities were readily available. So was the work Silas's mom did, which was data-scut. A mindless grind, repetitive to the point of madness, so she never failed to tell him as prelude to her implorations that he not make the mistake she had. Get Tooled, Si. For God's sake, give yourself a better life than what I got, what your father—

No. Don't bring up Dad. He signed for a four-year hot hitch, mechanized amphibious unit, combat pay all the way so he could support us. And he was good, he made noncom, earned medals. Him being Tooled wouldn't have put him anywhere but in that same swampy bomb crater. So shut up about him, Mom. Just shut the fuck up!

These mental arguments continued to play in Silas's head as the weeks passed, including his macho outbursts to his mother, which made it all the more painful when she was pulled off her job and put on suicide watch and he was sent off to stay with a relative outside the city.

Another shuttle ride. This one wasn't taking him to school. He'd been granted a leave of absence. *What did school matter anymore anyway, in the larger picture?* he asked himself scornfully. Only the unTooled went to college, miring themselves in student loans as they accumulated their Luddite knowledge with excruciating slowness. Then again, was it really a good idea to slot eighteen year olds with no real life experience into critical jobs where the lives of others were on the line?

Silas could do both sides of the debate quite skillfully by now. (Maybe he could get a gig doing that.) It pointed up to the stark fact that he had not yet made up his mind.

The shuttle—a solar coach, with an actual driver—had collected passengers at the maglev station. Silas was being ferried through the chipbelt countryside, past acres of frankenwheat and junkyards swaying with towers of discarded metaplastic.

At least he had Coco for company, albeit only on his vhone. But good friends could be company that way. The fly-eye screen could see in virtually every direction, but he pointed out the apocalyptic landscape to her anyway. It was how the future had used to look, all hardware and mechanicals.

He liked the mordant flair of that last observation and was about to say it out loud when Coco asked, "Whozit relation, again? Granddad?"

"Nopers," he grunted. "My mom's great uncle. So whatever that is to me. I don't think I've ever met him."

Coco had on a hockey jersey, with a pink bowtie about her neck. On her head was what appeared to be a Homburg. "What's he doing in the chipbelt?"

"Being old. Though… I guess it's pretty snazz of him to take me in. Like this." Suddenly, his throat was tight.

"Yeah," Coco said solemnly, as if touched by the same emotion. He hadn't had much detail about his mother, but he'd told it all to Coco. The routine psych eval at her job, the red flags that had gone up. There was a high suicide rate among data-scuts. Silas had known that for some while; but the fact had never quite connected to Mom, in his mind, even when she'd seemed most nerve-taut and ground under.

He could always try to get word to her that he'd opted to get Tooled. That would help her mental state, wouldn't it? Wouldn't it?

Coco was apparently still reading his face. She said, with a faux brightness meant to cheer him up or at least distract him, "Hey! You want me to flash my tits at you?"

"Did they get bigger?"

"You tell me." She went to shuck up the front of her jersey. But they fell into a shared bout of laughter before it went any further. Silas had never really swung that way, anyway. He wondered if she was any closer than he was to making her decision about Tooling. But she would have told him.

The shuttle let him off at the foot of a dirt road, after having dropped other passengers at similarly dubious destinations. He stepped out into eerie silence that wasn't silence at all. A wind was up, and it rustled every natural and humanmade object within sight—arthritic tree branches, sun-bleached fenceposts, weeds, sheaves of transparencies that were probably peelings of old photovoltaic skins. One of these last rolled against his foot. He stepped on it with his other foot, and it broke apart like candle wax. Probably they'd all blown off one of the junk piles he had passed.

The rustic non-quiet was heavy. He felt it against his eardrums and on his narrow chest. Nobody was here but him.

Yora Westling was the name of the man who was going to be his—evidently—legal guardian for the foreseeable future. Great uncle. Or great-grand-whateverthehell uncle. Question was, where was this Yora?

Silas had a travel bag with him. He had his vhone, but something made him refrain from using it. The chipbelt had been an R&D hotspot, a sprawling countrified meth lab of industrial innovation. Now it was a technological badlands. He wanted his first move here to have some poise.

After twenty minutes of waiting, he started up the road. It was striped with tire tracks. It inclined a bit and it wound some, and fences were falling apart on either side. He had worn soft boots. They were comfortable, but he started to feel the road, every stone, then every pebble on it. The sun came straight down.

A structure lay ahead; more than one, a ramshackle little compound appearing. Everything had a shack-like look to it. There was more junk here, chunks of machinery lying in the open.

Silas palmed his slick forehead. He saw two vehicles and wondered if either worked. As he halted amid the small cluster of buildings, he heard something contesting the country hush. Clang, clang, clang rang on the air.

Stepping up to a broad open doorway, he peered in at a barn-ish interior. Hot metal smells came from within, along with the rhythmic poundings that had a strange primal sound to them. A figure stood over a worktable. Sparse white hair stood out like albino nettles on a dark skull.

The man didn't turn. Still hoping to maintain a certain composure, Silas knocked sharply on the nearest wall. The clanging stopped.

"I had the impression you would be waiting for me," Silas said in a flat tone.

The man was mostly silhouette in the dim interior with a light source directly behind him. But it was a big silhouette. When his voice came, it was rumbly. "I am waiting."

"At the bottom of the road, maybe. That road I walked. You didn't know when the shuttle was due?" It was difficult to stand his ground when the big man turned around and approached. Yora Westling was a head taller, shoulders like a ship's keel, and a face so weathered it might have belonged to an intelligent-looking animal. But Silas didn't let himself flinch.

The old man nodded past Silas's left shoulder. "Sleep in there. There's a list of chores on the bed."

"Chores?"

"Only do them if you want to eat." There seemed no expression whatsoever on his face.

Silas tried to give him back the same deadpan, felt the fury just under his jawline, turned and went to the shack. Great. He had walked in on a Dickens novel. He flung down his bag and snatched up the printout. His chores. He shook his head; not that the tasks looked impossible, but where was this guy's sympathy? My mom's on suicide watch, asshole! You might know her. She's related to you.

Then again, what had he expected? Maybe this whole deal was terribly inconvenient for Yora Westling. Silas sighed, looking around his new digs. Rural functionality. The single room was cluttered with motor parts, but the bed looked sturdy. He decided, then and there, that he would withstand his great-great-uncle, no matter what.

He changed into the most rugged clothes he'd brought with him and set out to complete his chores.

The dinner he ate was—well, no other word for it but hardy, though that almost sounded condescending. Still, after doing physical labor all afternoon, he felt a little like a ranch hand. The tasks set to him were mostly moving scrap objects from one part of the property to another. After the first hour, he had gone to his cabin for a drink of water. When he came back out, a pair of work gloves was lying on a hunk of farming equipment just outside the door. He had put them on.

No "thank you" from the old man as they sat at a table in what seemed to be Yora's shack. Then Silas realized that the robust meal was his thanks. No, his payment. Do chores, get fed; the chipbelt logic of the techie redneck.

It was a hell of a spread. Lots of buttery greens, a ton of carbs, the meat seared but dripping when you cut into it. Silas normally never ate this much, but he had an appetite, which surprised him considering all the emotional trauma recently.

He paused in his chewing and eyed Yora furtively. Had those chores been meant to occupy him, to distract, to put some physical hunger into him so he would get a nourishing meal? If so, it was sly. But Silas couldn't get a read on his much older relation. He still came off as a vaguely animated oak tree. They ate in silence.

Afterward, the old man surprised him, asking, "You want a drink?"

The way he said it, he could only mean liq, which seemed a comradely sort of gesture. But Silas had been saving up a smartass response for the next time Yora addressed him directly; so he said, "Sure, Westling." The old man froze in the act of rising from the table. Silas gave an extravagant shrug. "You never said what to call you."

He came back with two tumblers of something greenish and fumy.

Algawhiskey, Silas guessed. He didn't have much experience with alcohol.

"One time only for this," Yora said. He lifted his glass, and his face, instead of becoming solemn, appeared touched with emotion for the first time. "A drink to your mother's recovery."

Silas took up his glass. The stuff smelled like swamp water, which made him think of his dad, dead seven years now, and that confused the moment; but he righted himself and met Yora's gaze, and they drank. The display felt tidy and ceremonial and true at that table, for that time.

He sent vessages to his mom, without knowing if the psychtechs would let her see them. He kept the video missives brief and hopeful, saying Uncle Yora was taking good care of him and that he was enjoying himself on the farm or whatever this place was.

That was almost the truth. His chores strained his body, but already he felt his scrawny muscles hardening and a general increase in stamina. The old man pounded away in his work shack, heating metal and metaplastic with a fusion lamp, then whacking it with various implements.

"What're you making in there?" Silas asked over another heaping supper. The two of them hadn't reached a comfortable conversational stage yet (they might never), but sometimes Silas felt bold enough to pipe up.

Yora chewed. "Tools," he said, and kept chewing, except now he looked thoughtful. "That's a word probably already on your mind, yes?"

It made Silas start a little, as if he'd been asked about masturbation habits. Obviously, some social worker must have mentioned the age of Yora's new charge. The old man himself was unTooled, but that was because Tooling couldn't have existed when he was fifteen. "Sure..." Silas said, waiting for the intrusive follow-up question:

Was he going to get Tooled or not?

Instead, after a long cud-like pause, the old man asked, "Do you know what you want to do with your life?"

In school, this was more of an interrogation question. What profession are you interested in? The school counselors wanted you to name some prestige livelihood so they could say, Well, those skills can be chemically inscribed. You could be succeeding in that field a week into your adulthood, so long as you've already been Tooled, that is.

Yora's phrasing somehow gave the query a new spin. Silas seriously considered it, organizing the many, many speculations entertained throughout his puberty and adolescence around the old man's simple question. What to do with his life?

Silas's lips stretched. He wasn't sure if he was grinning or sneering, but he looked the bigger man in the eye and said, "I want to shake things up."

Yora's weather-beaten face was either empty of all expression again or so full his features couldn't convey the excess.

They ate once more in silence.

Silas felt bold again. He asked, "What did you used to do, before you were a toolmaker?"

Yora made a rumbling sound that was either a laugh or a grunt. "Your mother doesn't talk much about me. Well, I hadn't seen her since her wedding. I was a microtech designer. I helped invent Tooling."

Silas's fork slipped out of his fingers. When he automatically lunged for it, he knocked over his glass of grape juice. Finally, he just threw his napkin over the mess and gawked at his great-great-uncle.

Yora lifted a hand even more leathery than his face. He said, "I'll rephrase. I was one among ten thousand inventors. There were neuro specialists, geneticists, molecular biologists, genome cowboys, thousands of biochemists, and a phalanx of engineers who designed and built what equipment was needed to pull off this incredibly ambitious game-changing project."

"Tooling." Silas felt breathless. He was afraid he was just going to keep saying Tooling until he fainted.

"Some of it happened up here, in the chipbelt—when it was still a functioning region. Other researches were carried out elsewhere. Every government agency wanted a piece of it. Funding was thrown at the project right and left. And…"

"And?" Silas prompted.

"And we did it." The old man's tone was almost dismissive. "After, I went back to micro design until this place became a ghost town. Now I make tools. Good, sensible, hold-them-in-your-hand tools."

The silence that held sway over the remainder of the meal had a different tenor to it.

Only when Silas had laid down in his bed did it occur to him to wonder what Yora's opinion was about Tooling as the cultural phenomenon it had developed into.

Silas received unrevealing updates about his mother. She remained in the hospital, medicated but no longer on suicide watch. Still no direct communication was allowed. He couldn't demand to talk with her. A fifteen year old couldn't demand shit. He had found, more to his surprise than he cared to admit, that he truly loved his mom.

Twice now during the day, Yora had driven away in one of the farm's two vehicles. Silas was still mildly miffed that the old man hadn't bothered to pick him up the half mile down the road when he'd first arrived.

This afternoon, Yora told him he could come along. Silas hopped in the beat-up runabout, eager for any change of scenery. "Where we going?"

"Delivery." The weathered chin nodded toward a bundle on the back seat.

"Can I look?"

Yora hit the juice, and the rig started down the road. "Go ahead."

Silas unfolded the mothy wool blanket. A half-dozen objects were arrayed. Tools, yes. But more elegant than he would have suspected from the brute hammerings coming constantly from the worktable. They could have been engine or farming equipment components.

On the main road, Yora put on some speed. There were other vehicles out here. The sight thrilled Silas for some reason. Maybe proof the outside world still existed. He put his hand out the window, cupping and molding the wind.

An authoritative bloop sounded loudly behind them. Yora's expression didn't change, but by now Silas knew that didn't mean so much. He felt and shared the old man's tension as the runabout edged onto the shoulder.

The uniformed woman seemed to take her time walking up to Yora's window. There came the license and registration ritual, just like in every cop show Silas had ever streamed. She was young—like eighteen young—but she exuded a confident, even smarmy, manner, as if she'd been on the job thirty years and was wise to any trouble Yora might give her.

Yora had been speeding, she informed him. Silas blinked; must have been like one mile an hour over the limit. She had acne on her chin, he observed.

"Where are you going?" she asked.

Yora didn't answer.

She absorbed his silence, smiling wryly. "What are you doing out here?"

He looked straight ahead.

It appeared to amuse her. She plainly relished the authority of her position. She bent down farther, gazed around the interior, eyes passing over Silas before reaching the back seat. "What's under the blanket?" She was almost giggly by now. Strangely, that chilled Silas.

Yora finally looked up at her. "You are impeding my livelihood. May I go?"

Silas felt himself sweating, hoped it didn't show.

The uniformed woman took her time straightening up. Sunnily, she said, "No ticket this time, Mr. Westling." She strolled back to her cruiser.

Yora let her get on the road ahead of him, then pulled out. Silas came down with the shivers, which he also tried to hide, out of embarrassment. Some kids at school claimed to hate the police, but it was probably just so much shit-talking. Nonetheless, Silas thought vehemently: zittin' Cop. Which, in this case, was literally true.

"Why'd she stop you?" he asked, not because he felt bold but because the incident had unnerved him. "The real reason."

The old man continued staring ahead. "How old did she look to you?"

"Brand-new adult."

"They're coming out now like that one. Police officers. Pushing their authority."

Silas clamped his hands to his thighs to hold them still. But he was puzzled.

Yora said, "The inscription has been changed."

His shivering ceased abruptly, but that was somehow worse. The ominous statement seemed to spread through his entire being. The chemical inscriptions were, of course, routinely updated, so to accommodate current innovations in a given field. The skill sets always had to be the most modern. But that Cop back there… her attitude. Asking questions the law didn't allow. Subtle smug intimidation, maybe just for its own sake.

Somebody wanted the newest generation of law enforcement to be like that? It dismayed Silas.

Yora gave out another rumbly noise, but it was a sound of disgust this time. "You really want to shake things up? Then get yourself Tooled."

Silas blinked again. This little jaunt of theirs had turned into a stoned-crow harrowing freak ride. "Why?" he asked softly.

"I'll show you. When we make the delivery."

. . .

Old women and old men. The place was underground, tiered marble levels, empty fountains and koi ponds. This must have been a corporate showplace in the chipbelt's heyday. Now it was Squatter's Corner.

But what squatters they were, Silas noted, a little awed, a little annoyed he hadn't figured out yet what was going on. There was equipment everyplace, cables underfoot; most of the gear high-end but old, deteriorated, like it had been pulled out of scrap heaps, which was very possibly the case. A patina of long disuse lay underneath all the activity.

The old people were working with a crusty diligence. Silas had the sense they would all rather be somewhere else, maybe having a nap, but no one complained out loud. The site—whatever it was—was still plainly in the setting-up phase. Nothing was happening here. Yet.

Yora set his parts on the vacant corner of a table. Figures fluttered over, like pigeons when birdseed hits the ground. Appreciative and approving murmurs arose as the objects were examined. A few of the oldsters glanced at Silas. One smiled, one scowled, and one squinted as if he didn't trust his eyes.

The parts were carried off. The great general milling continued around him and Yora. "Okay, Westling. Tell me what's going on. Or at least tell me why you think I ought to be Tooled." Right now, he didn't care about how big his great-great-uncle was or the fact that he had to glare up into the man's eyes.

"I'll tell you both those things," Yora said. "We—" he indicated the several dozen people and himself— "are all manhattans. That's what we call ourselves. Never mind why. All of us had a hand in the creation of Tooling. I told you, ten thousand people were involved, across multiple fields. Some swath of that number lived and worked around here, when there were shiny research labs all over the place. Some small percentage of those individuals hung around when the 'belt dried up and the action went elsewhere. Some of us had fallen out of corporate favor or had lost the faith or were narking too hard to be hired anywhere again—lots of different reasons for staying."

Silas wondered, at a remove, what Yora's reason had been for remaining in the chipbelt.

Yora went on. "We manhattans have a long view of Tooling. All our professional lives we knew how to study, how to chart effects, whether chemical, mechanical, whatever. We saw what Tooling was doing. Slowly. Insidiously. Getting Tooled was not a popular option when it was initially introduced. But the pressure was gradually put on. Its virtues were touted, over and over. Media pushed it, subtly. A pro-Tooling bias crept into entertainment. Politicians were rather more flagrant about it. A minority conviction, that getting Tooled was the smart thing to do."

Silas didn't want to interrupt the flow of information, but something needed answering. "How could the minority push something that big that the majority didn't want?"

"They still teach about Republicans in school?"

Silas nodded. Then nodded again, getting it.

"It was when the industries got in on it that Tooling started to take off. Shadow money made sure the corporations received incentives to have hiring quotas for the Tooled. Really, it was already in their interests. Ready-made employees for the highest positions. Social media drove it harder still. Being Tooled became acceptable, then normal. Now it's being advanced as the proper choice, even the moral one. Society needs skilled professionals. Do your part. Join the ranks. Soon they'll be issuing hats!"

His voice had risen. It was the most passionate Silas had yet seen him. But even as he observed this, something clicked in his head. He looked around again at the equipment and hubbub. But when he looked again to Yora, he asked about something else.

"You said the Police are now like the woman who stopped us.

Tooling doesn't alter personality. She might've just been, y'know, a bitch. What's your proof?"

It was a grim smile Yora gave him, but, being the first one he'd gotten from the old man, Silas decided he would treasure it.

Yora said, "Anecdotal evidence. But a vast amount of it. And— Tooling doesn't alter personality? Maybe, maybe not. But it does work from the inside out. Behavior alters with actions. The Tooled receive skills. The jobs they take encourage relatively narrow bands of conduct. The skill sets can be refined, tightened. The people who have championed and financed Tooling from the start want Police like we met today. Next, they'll want Corporate Executives who will work collectively to restructure the economy further in their favor. Then, there will be Soldiers with less conscience, more ruthlessness. And on and on, as more people—more fifteen year olds—decide to get Tooled, not knowing that the chemical inscriptions they will receive will be part of a new wave, one which brings forth a whole new breed of citizenry. Obedient. Militant. Remorseless. And don't forget, there'll still be the unTooled around because you got to have serfs, don't you?"

Again, his voice rose, shaking with rage now. Other manhattans looked over, but no one tried to mollify him. They probably all felt the same, Silas guessed. They also bore an onus of guilt, same as Yora. What they were doing here, then, was a form of repentance.

Silas said, "You're doing something to counteract Tooling." That was what had clicked in his head a moment ago. "What is it?"

Yora had to calm himself first. But a glint came into his eyes when he spoke. "Can't fight Tooling. Too late. What we are doing is making a new inscription. We'll set up this lab. We have enough biochemists and gene transcribers and whatnot. We will design the expert Rebel."

"Rebel?" But the idea had already touched Silas, at a deep level.

"A perfect malcontent. The ideal dissenter. One equipped to disrupt this new society in multifarious ways. A little Rosa Parks, a dash of Tolstoy, a soupçon of Angela Davis. Kinsey, Bruce, Sitting Bull. There's a plethora of inspiration waiting to be tapped. We shall turn it all into a chemical etching. And anyone who is Tooled will be able to receive it."

It locked then for Silas. *I want to shake things up.* Well, this cabal of gray-haired scientific guerrillas could allow him to do that. And, it seemed, do it very fucking well.

He need only get Tooled.

Yora had gotten to know him. The old man trusted him. Professional stoned-crow Rebel? Was that his future?

Silas solemnly put out his hand. Yora put up his large leathered one, and the two shook, in the manner of men making a pact.

His mom was going to be released in two more days. He was finally able to speak directly to her. In clear tones, he said he had decided he would be Tooled. She seemed happy about that, but also ashamed of what she'd recently put herself through. When he got home, he would be supportive and help her in any way he could.

Then, he vhoned Coco. He'd been keeping her updated on his time in the chipbelt, but he didn't pass on this latest development. The manhattans would carry on their project, knowing now they already had a recruit waiting. No doubt they would set up a covert distribution network for their Rebel inscription. It would be an underground movement, stronger than anything which the new wave of Tooled could ever mount. So Silas told himself, anyway.

He did tell Coco about his deciding to get Tooled. It might influence her own decision. Good friends could do that to each other. And he wanted her by his side when they took the fight to the streets.

From Space & Time #135, Winter 2019

Eric Del Carlo's short fiction has appeared in
Clarkesworld, Analog, Asimov's, and many other venues.
He resides in his native California.

A Farewell to Worms

by John Linwood Grant

In the dark.
In the filthy, sweat-slick, lice infested dark...
there is the Saw.
It is rust, and blood, and spatters of other idle fluids. It is very large,
because what it cuts is even larger, and it shrieks as it bites through
something which surely can't exist. Its skewed edge tears at the grain,
making clumps of pale, disordered dust and resin from a perfect tree.
Into the quiet order of xylem and phloem,
it brings its toothy chaos...

and I am pig-sick of the bloody thing.

The Marinakis family have left a colander out, as usual. It sits on the doorstep, and already one of my more ambitious brothers squats by it, counting the holes. Others might congratulate him on being able to get to five or six (skipping the holy number three, of course) before he loses track. I slap him on the side of the head.

"It doesn't matter," I say. "It's for draining vegetables. Who cares how many holes there are? You don't even eat vegetables."

There's no point talking to him. He's a traditionalist. He whines and goes back to his obsessional counting.

"One, two, the bad word, four, five… one, two…"

He'll be at it until dawn, wasting the whole night. Which is pretty much why the colander is there, to distract idiots like him. That, and the fires kept burning in every hearth, and the wooden bowls of water which hold crosses wrapped with sprigs of basil. Let's all mess with the poor goat-legs and stop them doing their mischief.

I'm not normally interested in petty mischief, only in this particular town.

Not that it's much of a town—more of an industrial village about thirty miles from Thessalonika. Psariosta, it's called. Fishbone. It certainly sticks in my throat every time. It stinks of fertilizer from the agro-chemical plant, which replaced the shady groves of almonds a few years ago. People across Greece used to burn foul-smelling shoes in their hearths at Christmas, to keep my sort away. They don't need to do that in Psariosta.

As usual, I'd scrambled up through the sullen earth along with the others on the twenty fifth of December. It would have been nice to emerge on a cool evening and breathe in the sweet, thyme-scented air of some lonely mountainside, or stand next to the surging, wine-dark sea (as they say) and listen to the waves to relax a bit.

But I had made a vow, by Pan's dangling testicles. Things would be different this time.

So it's Psariosta again.

And I have to get it right. Me. Do you think I can rely on my shaggy brethren to contribute their cunning? There are mutton joints in Psariosta with more sense than they have. No, this requires my genius. Twelve days in which to change the world.

I knew a professor at the university in Patras, years ago. He was a jolly fellow, full of goodwill, and had made it his life's work to rehabilitate us, to distinguish between us kallikantzaroi and the bloody satyrs who get all the press. "The little tricksters in the earth," he called us, and told of how we were a myth which was symbolic of mockery and jest, more to do with drunken orgies than anything evil.

Bollocks to that, I say. Not that I mind getting drunk, but if there's one thing that keeps me going, it's being malevolent...

What was I talking about? Psariosta.

I've had my eye on Lukas Marinakis for a while. Born on a Saturday, and a very useful Saturday for my purposes—within the Twelve Days of Christmas and, thus, close to our domain. Mrs. Marinakis shouldn't have opened a second bottle of retsina on that steamy March night.

What is different about this fine specimen of Greek manhood, with his tight, curly black hair and his hazel eyes? Good question. Due to the date of his birth, not only is Lukas one of the few people able to see a kallikantzaros properly, he also has serious potential to become one.

Which makes him very special indeed.

His grandmother, whom I suspect of being a bit too smart, did the usual stuff at his birth. She tied him up in straw and rubbed him with garlic cloves, so no snatching from the crib, then. However, they hadn't thought that whilst you can keep the kallikantzaros from the man, you can't keep the man from the kallikantzaros. Lukas was always curious about the Twelve Days.

When he was ten years old, he tried to talk to one of my lot on a really cold Christmas. The boy picked someone who couldn't even count to two. A saw-monkey, the lowest of the already admittedly low. I spotted them in the alley behind a restaurant, where my dim brother had a hoof caught in a catering-size can of plum tomatoes and I watched to see how it went.

"You look funny," said the boy, as he watched the antics.

Funny was an interesting way of putting it. This five-foot, black-skinned creature with donkey ears, horns like a goat and a mass of shaggy fur from the waist down was hopping around in the alley and swearing.

The boy wasn't at all alarmed, though. I sauntered over, pulled the tomato can free and kicked my brother up the rear to send him on his way.

"Hello, little pink fellow," I said.

He stared at me, clearly noting that I was somewhat more humanoid, and certainly more handsome, than the alley's previous occupant. I pride myself that I always comb the sawdust out of my fur and keep my horns in good condition. My tail has a stylish swish and I'm considered a bit of a looker down below. Of course, that's not entirely an advantage when you're surrounded by thousands of desperate kallikantzaroi, but my smarts keep me mostly "off the prong," thank Pan. Not that I'm prejudiced, mind you, but have you seen my brothers? They make the most flea-bitten satyr look like Apollo's chosen.

"Hello." He pushed his right forefinger up a dripping nostril. "What are you?"

"I'm not a what, I'm a who. Philodoxos." We kallikantzaroi don't often have names, so I do, just to be different. I chose it myself.

"Oh. Got any sweets?"

I rummaged in the fur on my left leg and tugged out a few lemon-drops I remembered sitting on by accident whilst trying to burn down a local sweets shop earlier that evening. He picked some of the hair off and sucked on one.

I smiled. "You have a gift, dear child."

"What, lemon-drops?"

"No, I mean a real gift. You can see me and my brothers. You were marked by your birth, which makes you very special."

"Oh. Thanks."

At which point he simply turned 'round and wandered off. I couldn't believe it. I nearly shouted after the snotty little bugger, but already the old brain cells were churning.

The boy had potential.

. . .

In the dark.

An ax bites deep, it is true, but after six, seven blows, it sticks within the fleshy wood, a mess of iron and ooze. The tree is dotted with abandoned axes, offerings to futility.

So the Saw is our God.

Five hundred or more on this end; five hundred or less on the other. All hauling, pulling or pushing, until the fleas in our fur have drowned in our sweat. Our shoulders pop and our sinews tear from their bony anchors. Blind eyes, bulging eyes. Hands like crude clay accidents; fingers that are slender and goat-nail tipped. Bodies that loom, and those barely more substantial than a dryad's spittle. The Brothers-in-the-Earth are not easy on the eye.

We are not a happy people.

That, I think, is why we were given stupidity.

You can do a lot of planning when you have to spend fifty weeks of the year trying to cut down an enormous, mythical tree. I say mythical, but it feels real enough when you ride the Saw. The storytellers call it the Tree of Life, and claim that it holds the world up to keep everything in its place. It certainly keeps the kallikantzaroi in their place. It binds us to a task which is utterly futile down there in the squalid depths around its trunk.

Only for the Twelve Days of Christmas are we released from the dark—and to do what? To be a minor nuisance and a cautionary story which children don't believe any more. We can't go out in the daylight, even then. And when we trudge back down into the dark, what has happened? Oh look, the Tree has healed itself and we have to start all over again.

Makes you think that Sisyphos has it easy.

Makes you sick.

As does the sight of a Greek town at Christmas. Apart from the colanders and the blazing hearths, the place looks like an Orthodox Church driving a donkey cart has crashed into an American shopping mall. A neon Santa vies with icons of St. Basileios and St. Nikolaos, the patron of sailors, for pre-eminence, and half the angels are jammed next to Coca-Cola ads. No one knows what the fuck to believe.

I mean, look down that street. A troop of children in procession. Their faces gleam as they hold out little painted wooden boats to show passers-by. Some have toy drums, which they beat with the enthusiasm of the tone-deaf; others hammer on triangles and sing. Yes, they sing as well—the kalanta, seasonal carols whose main value is to increase the share price of paracetamol manufacturers.

These boys wear trainers and have been shoved out of the house to get them off their Grand Maim/Slaughter video games. They want to know if they're getting film merchandise for Christmas. The only thing that they like about the church is the funny black hats, which make good targets for their air-rifles.

Peh!

Lukas Marinakis was born with a twisted foot—nothing serious, but enough that he has to wear corrective footwear to stop him limping like a drunken fisherman fresh from a night on the cuttlefish boats. It's a typical mark of one touched by the Twelve Days. I didn't notice it when I first saw him, so maybe I'm not as smart as I think I am.

I like to think ahead. You never know what might come in handy years, even centuries, down the line. After I spotted the foot, every Christmas I whispered in the local children's ears at night. "Hopfoot, Goat-boy, Reject," I whispered. "That Marinakis kid, he's not like you."

It worked quite well, and by the time he was fifteen, most of the kids were well-versed in the art of picking on the odd one out. They didn't need a lot of encouragement, frankly. I had sown the seeds of Discord (or Eris, as we know her).

On Lukas's sixteenth birthday, I stole a half bottle of ouzo and left it by the back door of that same restaurant where I'd first met him. He was working there as a pot-washer outside of school hours and occasionally inside them. He found it when he came out for a smoke later that night. He looked around; seeing no one in the alley, he picked up the bottle and took a swig.

Three more swigs and I slipped into sight.

"Oh, it's you." He sounded morose. "Philo-wotsit."

"Philodoxos."

He offered me the bottle and I joined him. The smell of fried fish wafted from inside the restaurant and made my stomach rumble. You don't get much choice down below, clustered around the Tree. We don't exactly have spice racks or cupboards full of delicacies. We have a lot of damp things which crawl around your hooves and go squish. Earthworms are prized. If you find a rotting frog, you keep it to yourself and eat very quickly.

"Not busy?" I asked.

"Pretty dead in there."

"So you're having it easy. What's the problem?"

A subtle blend of ouzo and my charm brought out his tale of woe. Neither girlfriend nor boyfriend—no one to admire his swelling manhood—and a lot of hassle from the other kids. He was bright enough to be hurt by their jibes, but not quite bright enough to have any crushing rejoinders immediately to hand.

I flicked my tail. "Maybe some of them should be taught a lesson…"

"What do you mean?"

"Well…"

It was that easy to drag him in.

I had nine nights left in which to play. That Christmas, a number of teenagers in Psariosta had unfortunate accidents.

Funny, that.

Eleni, a pretty blonde from Lukas's street, had a revulsion to my friend's bare foot, which she'd seen at a swimming competition. On the twenty-eighth of December, she awoke from a heavily drugged sleep to find some of her toenails missing. Pulled out, to be more precise. She was quite a screamer.

The same night, Niko, a boy who prided himself on his physique, found himself being taken for a canter by kin of mine—a suitably massive and lumpen-brained kallikantzaros only too happy to cause trouble. Astride the boy's shoulders, the fellow rode him almost to cock's crow. Niko wouldn't be competing in anything physical for a year or two.

Or for variety, there was… but we won't dwell on Ioannis, a particularly obnoxious boy. He left Psariosta quite quickly the next day, not even waiting for St. Basileios to knock on his door.

Shame.

"I'll be around again," I said to Lukas before I went back down into the dark. "Next year."

He smiled.

He knew what I'd been up to, and he smiled.

I liked him.

When Lukas was eighteen, I dropped a reproduction statue of Pallas Athena, bless Her, on one man's head and helped another to appear drunk and naked in the town square with a sign saying, "Stavros Lykopodes sleeps with goats."

There was talk and some remembered the number of Christmas incidents two years before. There was also an increase in the number of locals professing renewed faith in the church, but these things happen.

The following February, Mr. Stavros Lykopodes, the hiring manager for Psariosta Agro-Chemicals, selected Lukas for a trainee management position rather than the other two young men who would have been candidates, had the first not been in a head trauma ward in a Thessaloniki hospital and the second in disgrace following that drunken incident with the sign.

I kept myself under control for a while after that. I made cheese go moldy, froze washbasins, and almost bored my own tail off but it would be worth it. For twelve nights every year, I talked to Lukas Marinakis. I suggested things; I listened. I told him of the dark, and he filled me in on certain aspects of the modern world. When he got bored, I told him tales of the Old Gods and drew him in deeper. Last Christmas, all my ideas came together, and I was ready.

I had only to leave Lukas to set things up.

In the dark.
In the ordure-filled, endless dark.
We work the Saw.
Crooked figures huddle, gasp for breath and claw at their own hides, frantic with vermin. Leaping figures laugh, their sanity gone after centuries at the Saw, lost in dreams of a falling Tree and warm oblivion. No longer can they tell when one year ends, another begins.
I do my part, but my dreams are different.
Counting out the days on my blisters, I look forward to the Twelve Days, and the plan...

Lukas Marinakis is twenty-one years old today. His family have half-memories—the colander proves that. And there is that irritating grandmother who keeps fragments of the old stories alive and insists on precautions. She gets some of them wrong, and her dentures, when she has them in, make it hard to work out what she is saying. Greek is not a good language for the dentally challenged. I have the feeling that she knows about us, somehow.

"Ochi!" she snaps when Lukas's father accidentally tips over a bowl of basil and holy water. "No, no, no..." I thought about dropping a roof tile on her head last Christmas but I got distracted by a chance to curdle all the milk next door. I said earlier that I wasn't interested in minor mischief, but it must be genetic. None of us can resist an opening like that.

The old woman's not important, though. This is my moment and here I am outside Psariosta with snow tickling the land. The snow has softened some of the stink from the factory and makes the place look almost seasonal.

There are no sleighs or jolly fat men in sight. Nor beaming Orthodox saints. Instead, I have gathered those Brothers-in-the-Earth who retain a semblance of sense. They know enough not to shove themselves down hot chimneys or give in to the siren song of the colander. They realize, in some blurred manner, that by every seventh of January, the Tree of Life has had time to recover, and there's a whole year of pointless work ahead of them.

At the bloody Saw.

They crowd around me, interested in this fresh form of trickery— which is what they think it is. The snowflakes make them look like they have sudden, uncontrollable dandruff.

"You don't have to kill," I tell them. "If you come across humans and have to sort them out, give them a mischievous blow to the head."

"Pink ones," says a monster of a kallikantzaros, lurking at the back. A long tongue the color of a burst spleen lolls from his mouth and his huge horns weigh his chin down on his breast.

"Humanthhh," says another. We have a lot of lispers, for some reason.

"Yes, quite." I bare my yellow teeth. "Knock them out and get what we need. My friend will let you in."

I lead them south to the gates by the factory warehouses. Lukas Marinakis is waiting there. He's abandoned his socks and shoes and his normal foot has begun to match the other. His toenails have grown, as well.

I hesitate.

His grandmother is by his side, which wasn't part of the deal. There is a strong moon and she peers over her reading glasses at the mob of black, distorted shapes I call my brethren. I urge my people back, waiting for a shower of holy water or imprecations and saints' names. To my surprise, she laughs.

"Nai, nai," she says. *Yes, yes* (forgive me throwing the Greek in occasionally—it makes me feel at home).

I'm a bit puzzled, which amuses her even more. Lukas looks embarrassed as the old woman hobbles over to me.

"Your idea, all this, kallikantzaros?"

"Uh, yes."

"Entaxei. Okay."

I scratch my left horn. "Really?"

She pokes my rounded belly with her stick. "I am ninety-two years old, little monster. I'm sick of all this shit, sick of sitting there with aching bones, watching television until I die."

"I... I imagine so."

"Philodoxis, eh?" She looks down at my member, which is decidedly un-priapic in her presence. "And you have a plan, my grandson tells me, to put an end to the cycle of misery. Tell me, what happens after this end of yours?"

That's a good question.

"No one is sure, giagia." I feel oddly respectful toward her. "A drunken centaur once told me that if the Tree of Life falls, the world will reshape itself. After that... maybe everything will start again. Or maybe nothing will happen except we finally get a proper holiday."

I am standing outside an agro-chemical plant, at the head of a small horde of monstrously misshapen creatures from the bowels of the earth, and an old woman is interrogating me.

It's different.

"We can only hope," I say, my voice close to cracking. "Anything is better than... the Saw."

Her head bobs in understanding, shawl fluttering in the breeze. She smells of camphor, piss, and lemon-drops. Her left eye glints at me.

"Maybe, kallikantzaros, the Old Gods will come back to us. Ochi?"

"We can only hope," I repeat.

"Good. Get on with it, then."

Glad that I hadn't thrown that roof tile at her in the end, I turn to the troops.

"You heard the lady."

The kallikantzaroi rush forward, a few of them giving polite nods to grandma, and they surge toward the open warehouses. Some miss the gates, knocking parts of the wire fencing down in their enthusiasm.

"They shouldn't meet any opposition. I managed to reduce the staff down to one night watchman," says Lukas. "And I got him drunk, in case. He's not a bad chap."

"You did very well. The feet are looking good."

His toes are hardening, the nails fusing. I see fine hooves in the making and am satisfied that I have released the kallikantzaros in him.

My kin come lisping and giggling back from the warehouses, excited. It's a nice change in routine for them. You can only curdle so much milk before the trick loses its appeal.

The large ones—and some are very large—carry great metal canisters on their shoulders. The small ones roll their prizes before them. As they head for the tunnel mouths, back into the dark, they chant a playful refrain, their own kalanta.

"Bugger the Saw; sod the Tree. Bugger the Saw; sod the Tree!"

That's not something I taught them. I feel proud, like a father whose idiot children have at least managed to stand upright.

"I told the boss it was a special order." Lukas says. "I had to call in bulk supplies from other factories, forge a lot of documents... we nearly didn't manage the quantity we agreed."

"But you did. Lukas, my boy, I couldn't be more pleased."

It's true. I have shaped a ten year old into a man who will be sung of for centuries.

A small, warped kallikantzaros stumbles past, his tail twisted round his shaggy legs. He is almost useless, but he pushes the massive canister assigned to him over rocks and hummocks all the same.

The label and the warning signs on the canister are obvious in the moonlight. A big black cross on an orange background and a skull and crossbones. It lists the actual chemicals as well, but I don't care. Lukas says they're what we need.

I expect it will take a while to work, months probably. Myths can be annoyingly persistent. But I have faith and I have a feeling that Lukas, caught between being mortal and kallikantzaros, will have got it right.

I kiss grandma on the cheek and shake Lukas's hand.

"I'll see you again," I tell them. My tail is whipping around like a dog who's been given an unexpected sheep carcass. "One way or another, next Christmas is going to be very different."

It will be. When I come above ground again, the mortals will be using colanders as helmets, to protect them from the joyful rampages of the kallikantzaroi. We'll stuff basil in their mouths and spoil their holy water. We might even disembowel a few priests, if the mood takes us. We'll dance under the sun and we'll drink deep with those who remember the Old Faith.

A grand time will be had.

I'll do what I want and I won't be going back. None of my brothers will be going back, for over five thousand gallons of concentrated herbicide are currently heading into the depths. Especially formulated for woody plants, Lukas assures me.

The Tree of Life won't know what hit it.

And if you like extra honey on your baklava, Lukas has a friend who works at an industrial smelter near Athens, just the place for melting down rusting tools that no one wants any more. I have another idea, once the Tree is dead…

In the dark.
In the thrumming dark that will belong to us.
The Saw is…
going to get a nasty surprise.

John Linwood Grant is a pro writer/editor from Yorkshire in the UK, with some 40+ stories published in a wide range of magazines and anthologies, including *Lackington's Magazine, Vastarien, Weirdbook,* and others. The second edition of his short story collection, *A Persistence of Geraniums*, came out from Ulthar Press in 2019, and his latest novel, *The Assassin's Coin*, is available from IFD. He is editor of *Occult Detective Quarterly* and various anthologies, including the recent *Hell's Empire*.

A Glass Darkly

by Ian Rogers

It was an abandoned office building in a part of the city even the homeless avoided. A wasteland of empty warehouses, crumbling factories, and acres of cracked parking lot where only rats and weeds lived. If you could call it living.

I got out of my car and stared across the bleak vista of industrial ruin and decay. Every city had a place like this. A once-thriving district of manufacturing and industry that eventually devolved into a ghost town of fallen metal castles.

I started toward the only other car in the lot, a tan Buick I recognized on sight. I recognized the man climbing out of the car, too, although I had tried for years to forget him.

"Felix," he said, flashing a nervous grin. "I wasn't sure you'd come."

"I said I would."

"Yeah, right. I forgot. The Boy Scout."

Kyle Burke's grin went from nervous to smarmy. It happened in a flash and summed him up perfectly. Kyle was a man who survived on his surface details. If people could see the person lurking within, they would lock him away in a deep dark cell or stone him to death in the city square. Like me, he was a private investigator. Unlike me, he was willing to do anything to get the job done.

"You're still pissed," he said, sounding surprised.

"I said I'd set up this meeting. That doesn't change anything between us."

"We need to stick together, Felix. We're the same, man. We just have different methods."

"That's one way of putting it," I said. "Covers a whole multitude of sins. And felonies."

Kyle made a dismissive sound. "You really want to dig all that up again?"

"No," I said. "I want to get this done so I can go home. It's late."

I glanced around. There were plenty of streetlights but no electricity to power them. The grid down here had been inactive for years. But the stars and moon were out, and the ambient glow of the city provided enough light to see by.

"Let's go," I said, and we started toward the building.

"This place is creepy," Kyle said.

"You picked it."

"I know, but I was here during the day. I didn't think about how it would look at night."

That kind of thinking summed up Kyle as adequately as his grin.

"I told you it would be easier to just go to the Toronto field office."

"Fuck that," Kyle said. "There's no way in hell I'd ever go into that pigpen."

"You realize you may have to go there eventually."

"Maybe, maybe not. But this meeting is taking place on my terms."

"That's the way you've always liked it, eh?"

Kyle turned his head and looked at me. "That's how I've managed to stay alive. What's your secret, Felix?"

"Teetotalling and prayer."

"Please." He wagged a finger at me. "You like to think we're different, but I keep telling you we're the same. You just haven't been caught yet."

"We're here," I said.

The front door didn't have a knob. I pushed it open and gestured for Kyle to enter. I followed him into darkness.

Then the darkness went supernova.

Blinding light filled my eyes, my brain, everything.

Someone shouted: "Freeze! Move and you're dead!"

Then I heard Kyle, a smile in his voice: "Felix, you fuck."

"I said I never wanted to see your face again."

I stood up and restrained the urge to take out the gun I kept in the bottom drawer of my desk.

Kyle stood in the inner office doorway, hands raised. "It's cool, Felix. You know I wouldn't be here if it wasn't serious."

"I'm not covering for your ass again."

"It's not the cops," Kyle said. "It's kind of funny, actually. This time I need them. It's…" He trailed off, shaking his head. "Okay, it's not funny at all. It's bad. Real bad, man." He lowered his hands and slumped against the doorjamb. "They're going to kill my wife."

"Ex-wife," I corrected.

"And my brother."

Then Kyle did something I'd never seen him do before: he cried. Great hitching sobs like someone was raining blows on his insides with a sledgehammer. It was horrible to watch, horrible to listen to, as genuine suffering always is. He slid down onto his haunches and hugged his knees like a child, rocking slightly.

I came around the desk and dragged over one of my client chairs. "Sit," I instructed him. He rose shakily and deposited himself in the chair. I closed my inner office door even though my secretary was off that day. Then I went back to my desk and leaned against it with my arms crossed.

"Tell me."

"I can't," Kyle said in a tired voice. "They'll come after you, too." This set off another round of sobs. I went back behind my desk and sat down. I didn't have any tissues, so I took out a shot glass and a bottle of Glen Breton. I slid them across to Kyle. He uncorked the whiskey and poured himself a slug. He slammed it back and held the empty glass in both hands, like he was praying.

"If you don't tell me, I can't help you."

"Please, Felix," he said. "They'd kill you if you knew. They could do it. They're capable." He put the shot glass on the edge of the desk and ran his hands through his thinning hair. "This is your fault, you know? That's why I came to you."

I leaned forward. "Excuse me?"

"It's true." Kyle gave me a tremulous grin. "No harm, man. I'm just saying, you started this whole thing."

"What thing?"

"Private dicks and the supernatural. Ever since you staked the vamp in that restaurant, people stopped thinking of us as Sam Spade. Now, they think we're Abraham Van Helsing. Fearless fucking vampire killers." He helped himself to another shot and drained it. "Only, it's not just vampires. They want us to kill every monster in the Black Lands. Don't get me wrong, the money's great. But the work takes its toll."

"A death toll in your case," I said.

"You really want to bring that up again?"

"Someone should."

"I've forgotten most of it," Kyle said, but his eyes drifted.

"Bullshit," I said. "Repressed, maybe. But you haven't forgotten a damn thing."

"Who cares? It's done, Felix. They're dead and there's nothing I can do about it now."

"What's that, Zen Buddhism for assholes?"

"I'm just saying I can't take it back. We're alive and all we can do is live with it."

"What's this 'we' crap? I didn't kill those people."

"Neither did I!" Kyle said indignantly.

"You may not have pulled the trigger, but you…"

"They came to me for help and I helped them."

"So you're going to speak in euphemisms now, is that it?"

"You helped, too, as I recall, Felix."

"Say that again and I will shoot you right between your fucking eyes."

Kyle held up his hands. "I didn't come here to fight with you. You're right. I made some bad calls." He frowned. "Okay, fuck it. I got people killed. People who trusted me. I can cop to that, to you. I know I can't bring them back, but I can do something to restore the balance."

"What are you talking about?"

"It's time to make them pay." Kyle's grin was thin as a razor. "Not just the ones who killed the Hardys. All of them. Every fucking creep and critter in the Black Lands. I can do it, Felix. The information I've got, when I say it's 'earth-shattering,' I'm not exaggerating or using colorful language. I mean it literally." He tapped the side of his head. "What I've got up here can close the door on every fucking portal on the planet. Good-bye, Black Lands. Forever."

"Assuming you have such information, what do you expect me to do with it?"

"Nothing," Kyle said. "I only want you to set up a meeting."

"With the Paranormal Intelligence Agency?"

Kyle nodded. "I heard you were in tight with the pigs."

"If I agree to do this, you're going to have to stop calling them that."

"Ever the Boy Scout."

"Beats the alternative," I said.

"Touché," Kyle said, and toasted me with his glass.

I leaned back in my seat, thinking. I didn't doubt that Kyle had information on the Black Lands, secrets no one else knew. He had gone deeper into the shadows than anyone I knew. Anyone still alive, that was. He even claimed to have been to the Black Lands on a few occasions. He was a liar, but I believed him on that score. He had the look of someone who had spent time in that dark dimension. But I still had doubts about his motives.

"What do you want out of this?" I asked. "A Nobel Peace Prize?"

"Protection," Kyle said. "And a shitload of money."

I nodded. That was more like it.

They had us up against the wall, arms and legs spread, while they searched us for weapons. They found my Ruger and took a Glock off Kyle. I glared at him. "Don't look at me like that," he said. "You brought one, too."

In addition to the half dozen STAR officers in full tactical armor, there were three PIA agents in standard-issue black suits. Their unimpressed expressions were also standard-issue.

The agent in charge was a tall blond with cool blue eyes who would've looked perfectly at home in a Roman amphitheater feeding Christians to hungry lions. Kyle looked over his shoulder at him. "You Enfield?"

"That's Special Agent Enfield to you, dick."

"I'm glad to see this is starting off so well," I said.

The STAR guys finished patting us down and backed off, keeping their MP5 submachine guns trained on us.

"What is this, Enfield? I said we only wanted to talk."

"We're talking," Enfield said. He and the other two suits were broad-shouldered silhouettes against the stark light from a pair of standing halogen work lamps. I wondered where the juice was coming from, then spotted the generator chugging away in the far corner.

"What's with the STAR team?" I asked.

"It's procedure to have Supernatural Threat Assessment and Response on standby," Enfield said casually. "Just covering our bases."

"Covering your asses is more like it," Kyle said. He turned to me. "I told you we couldn't trust these pigs."

Enfield stepped up close to him. "You came to us, Burke," he said. "Because you need us. Because you're afraid."

"Fuck this and fuck you," Kyle said. "I don't need this shit."

"Shut up, both of you," I snapped. I turned to Kyle. "You asked me to set this up, so you're not going anywhere." Then to Enfield: "And you said it would only be us. I told Kyle he could trust you and you lied to me."

"I'm not the only liar here," Enfield said, looking past me at Kyle. "When you told me you wanted to set up a meeting with this prick, I knew enough to bring backup."

Kyle puffed himself up, squaring his shoulders. "You need me, Enfield."

"That has yet to be determined," Enfield responded coolly.

"Then let me break it down for you," Kyle said. "You pigs have had your collective thumbs up your asses since the portals starting popping up back in '45. You've carried out experiments, investigations, even made a few excursions, and you still haven't learned enough to fill a brochure. Seventy years of research and the only thing you know is the portals lead to a sunless supernatural dimension that you creative geniuses dubbed the Black Lands. A place that's home to every nightmare we humans can think of, and even more that we can't. Hundreds of doors to this fucking place all over the planet, and for all your suits, STAR teams, and subterfuge, you haven't been able to close a single goddamn one."

"We didn't create the Dark Menace," Enfield said. "We're just trying to contain it."

"That's my point," Kyle said. "Your narrow minds are too focused on containment. Putting up fences around the portals. Running gunboats along the borders of the Bermuda Triangle. Those aren't solutions. Those are fingers in the dyke."

Enfield spread his hands. "If you've got a better solution, I'm all ears." I thought if Kyle didn't start choosing his words more carefully, Enfield would be all fists.

"You listen but you don't hear," Kyle said. "How do I know you're going to take what I know and do the right thing?"

"I'm supposed to take morality lessons from you?" Enfield said.

"The fuck is that supposed to mean? I go in with you guys and then what happens? Tell me. Do we sit down in a nice room over coffee and donuts and discuss this like civilized people? Or do you stick me in a box at some undisclosed location so one of your pet psychics can Ouija-board the info out of my skull?"

"Ouija-boarding is illegal," Enfield said.

"Oh, that makes me feel better." Kyle shook his head. "Some days I can't tell who are the real monsters. Maybe you and the rest of the PIA should be the ones living in the fucking Black Lands."

"Like I said, we didn't create this problem," Enfield said.

"That's not what I heard," Kyle fired back.

Enfield looked at me. "I didn't come here to listen to a bunch of conspiracy bullshit from a murdering sack of shit peeper."

Kyle blanched. "Fuck you, pig," he said in a voice that wavered slightly. "You don't know me."

Enfield took a step closer to him. "We know everything about you. Harold."

Kyle swallowed dryly. His forehead glowed with sweat.

Enfield turned to me. "You said he had intel on the Black Lands. Something that would help us win the war. Either he tells me what it is right now or the both of you can fuck right off."

"I'm not telling you anything until I know I'm going to be taken care of," Kyle said. "I could get killed for telling you this shit."

Enfield smiled. It was a frightening thing to watch. Like an eclipse, I thought. Staring at it for too long could be harmful.

"You've always had a knack for self-preservation, haven't you, Harold? I imagine it's the kind of skill set your clients truly appreciate. Too bad there aren't enough of them left alive to provide testimonials on your behalf. I bet the Hardys would have had some really interesting things to say. Except for Ryan Hardy, of course. He wasn't quite old enough to talk yet, was he?"

Someone might have thrown a punch at that moment, but there was a knock at the door. Everyone in the room—me, Kyle, Enfield, the other two suits, and the six STAR officers—all turned and looked in that direction. There was no need to knock. The door wasn't locked. It didn't even have a knob.

"Another surprise guest?" Enfield inquired.

I shook my head and turned to Kyle. He was looking at the door. Looking and backing away.

Kyle ran up to me the moment I came out of Toronto Police headquarters. "What did you tell them?" he asked desperately.

"What we discussed," I said curtly.

"Did they believe you?" He clenched his hands, like he wanted to grab me by the front of my jacket. If he did, I probably would've hit him.

"I think so," I said. "You know cops. They don't tell you anything, they don't show you anything."

"But you must've got some impression from them." He tried to give me his patented cool Kyle Burke grin, but it collapsed on his face. "Come on, Felix. Tell me something."

"I think you'll get away with it," I said. "Stick to your story and you should be fine."

"Yeah?" A germ of hope gleamed in his eye. "So it's cool, then? I'm clean?"

"That's the last thing you are," I said. "And that's the last thing I'm doing for you. As of now, we're done. Kaput. Finis. That's all, folks."

"Don't be like that, Felix. You're just a bit shook up. The pigs have that effect on everyone."

"You have that effect on me," I said. "You didn't always, but you do now, and I don't want to be around it anymore. I don't want to be around you anymore."

"Come on, man. Let me buy you a drink. Let me buy you a pile of drinks. I owe you, pal. Big time."

"You owe the Hardys."

Kyle tried to meet my eyes, but he couldn't. He lowered his head. "I can't do anything for them."

"Tell me something I don't know."

"I didn't know this would happen. I tried to help them. Fuck, man. I tried. You have to believe me."

"I don't have to do anything except go home and forget this ever happened."

"Sure, Felix, it's cool. Take some time to yourself. We can talk later."

"There is no later, Kyle. Not for us. I owed you one. Hell, I owed you more than one. But this time pays for all. We're even and we're done."

"You're just upset. And fucked if you don't have a right to be. But in a few days…"

"You think time is going to make this right? Nothing makes this right, Kyle. Going in there and telling the cops the truth doesn't make it right. It might provide the Hardys with a bit of justice, but I don't even know what that means anymore. And frankly, that's the only thing keeping my mouth shut right now."

"I'm sorry, Felix. I don't know what else to say."

"This is the part where I'm supposed to say, 'You changed, man. You used to be different.' But the fact is I always knew this about you. I knew if you started taking on these types of cases, someone would get hurt, someone would die, and it wouldn't be you. Never you."

"I'm a survivor, Felix. You are, too. We're the same."

"Fuck, I hope not. If we are, I might as well go home and eat my gun." I pointed my finger at him. "I don't want to see your face ever again. Don't come by my place or my office. Don't call or e-mail or send me a smoke signal. If I get so much as a Christmas card from you, I'll come back down here and tell them the truth."

Kyle looked away. "No, you won't."

"Excuse me?"

"If you told them the truth, you'd be admitting that you lied."

"Are you threatening me?"

Kyle shook his head guilelessly. "You're threatening yourself. You're part of this now, Felix."

"That sounds like a threat."

"I'm only saying it like it is."

"That's all you ever do, right? You're not the bad news, you're just the messenger."

"That's right," Kyle said. "That's what we are, Felix. That's why we're the same."

"Like hell," I said.

"Like heaven or hell," Kyle retorted. "It doesn't matter. We're not going to either place. You remember Ross Macdonald? The night streets are our territory, and will be till we roll in the last gutter."

"I'm not like you," I said. "I wouldn't do what you've done."

"Give it time, Felix. You may surprise yourself."

"Stay away from me. I'm serious."

I started walking away. Kyle shouted after me.

"We're the same!"

Enfield signaled one of the STAR guys to check the door. The man trotted over and pushed it open with a steel-toed boot so as to keep both hands on his gun.

A little girl was standing there, about eight years old, eating a popsicle. Banana, it looked like.

"What do you want, kid?" the STAR officer asked brusquely.

"I'm here for the party," the girl said. She was wearing a dress with a pattern of toucans and coconuts on it. The straps of a backpack were slung over her scrawny shoulders.

"There's no party here," the STAR officer said, and kicked the door closed in her face.

"Who the hell was that?" Enfield asked.

"Some kid looking for a rave or something," the STAR officer said.

"What's a kid doing here in this fucking wasteland?" said one of the other suits.

"Did she have black eyes?" I asked.

Enfield looked at me. "What?"

There was another, louder knock at the door. I looked over at Kyle. He was still backing toward a hallway that led deeper into the building. "What did you do?" I asked him.

Kyle shook his head without looking at me. He was looking at the door.

I turned and watched as the same STAR officer repeated the motion of pushing the door open with his boot. The girl was still there, but something about her was different. I couldn't tell what it was at first because it wasn't anything about the girl herself. She looked the same, still eating her popsicle, still wearing the same toucans-and-coconuts dress. Then my gaze drifted upward to take in the long metallic appendage rising out of her back. No, not her back—her backpack.

At first, I thought it was an antenna of some kind. But then the girl raised her left hand—the one not holding the popsicle—and I saw the small, cylindrical object like a roll of coins with a fat red button protruding from the top.

Bomb! I thought frantically. She's a bomb!

I didn't have time to turn these thoughts into words before her glitter-nail-polished thumb clicked down on the trigger.

There was no explosion. And the object sticking out of her backpack was no antenna. It was the metal arm of a swing lamp that was now blasting three hundred watts of light into the STAR officer's face.

He recoiled backwards, holding up a gloved hand to block out the glare.

The girl stepped inside the building, the lamp bobbing above her like a second head. She mimicked the gesture of the STAR officer, raising her hand up in front of her, then higher, where it became a starfish-shaped silhouette against the light. She held it there for a moment, her head tilted in a speculative way, then her fingers clenched into a tight fist with an abnormally loud cracking sound. It wasn't her knuckles popping, or even her bones breaking. The sound didn't even come from her hand. When the STAR officer swung around, we all saw it had come from his face.

It was like the man's brain had turned into a black hole whose powerful gravity had caused his head to implode. The cracking sound had been caused by a combination of the man's goggles breaking along with all the bones in his face. Blood poured in freshets out of his ruptured eyes and half a dozen fissures where shards of broken skull pierced his flesh. He couldn't scream because his jaw had snapped in two; the broken pieces clacked like an insect's mandibles while he gagged and choked on the blood spilling down his throat. His hand came up—the same one he'd used to block out the light—then fell to his side. Then his knees unhinged and he collapsed to the floor. Ever the good soldier, his other hand remained gripped around his weapon, even as he died.

The girl took the final bite of her popsicle and tossed the stick aside. "Now it's a party," she said, licking her fingers clean.

Enfield stared at the fallen officer. "Sweet Christ," he muttered.

The other STAR officers had their guns pointed at the girl. They started shouting at her to get down, get the fuck down on the floor, and don't move.

She did neither of these things.

She didn't get down and she didn't stop moving.

She advanced on them, laughing.

It started out as a little girl's laugh, then it fell through the octaves until it became something thick and guttural, barely recognizable as a laugh at all.

One of the STAR guys looked to Enfield for instructions. "She's not human," Enfield said. "Drop her."

It was like a repeat of when Kyle and I first entered the building. Except this time the blinding flash of light was accompanied by an ear-shattering crescendo of submachine gun fire.

The girl bore it all, every fine-precision shot, and managed to stand her ground. It was impossible. As all the creatures from the Black Lands were impossible.

She was still laughing as she raised her hand up in front of the lamp—which hadn't been struck by a single bullet, so perfectly focused was the STAR team's aim on her body—and swung her arm in a broad sweeping motion.

The shadow that leaped across the room was as thick as a redwood trunk—and as strong. It struck the STAR officers and sent them flying like bowling pins.

The girl raised her other hand in front of the light and snapped it outward in a halting gesture.

Another shadow shot across the room, striking one of the PIA suits and crushing him against the concrete wall. His body exploded like a water balloon, leaving a bloody Rorschach blot in its wake.

Then the girl raised both hands in front of the light and flung her arms out wide.

A pair of long shadow arms spread across the room like black tidal waves and struck the standing lamps, knocking them over and shattering the bulbs. The only light now came from the lamp hanging over the girl's head like a demonic halo. The rest of the room was filled with shadows. Her shadows.

Then Enfield drew his pistol and shot the girl's light, casting us all into darkness.

. . .

"I don't know, Kyle. It doesn't feel right."

"Trust me, Felix. I've been doing this a long time. Longer than you. When you get to where I am, you'll understand."

"I hope not."

Kyle gave me his smile, the one that managed to be both humble and condescending at the same time.

"Don't be such a Boy Scout," he said. "There's a war going on out there. It's not human vs. human. It's human vs. supernatural. Don't let them divide us. That's what they want."

"It's against the law."

"The feds don't even follow their own laws. So why should we?"

"Two wrongs don't make a right."

"That's Boy Scout talk. This is the real world, man. Time to cowboy up and pick a side. You think the feds are going to help us?"

"They seem to be doing an okay job of holding the line."

"Sure," Kyle said. "For themselves. They're making a Brave New World all right, but not for us. We have to stick together. Remember what I said?"

I grinned in spite of myself. "Dicks stick together. Just don't rub them together."

Kyle shrugged. "I'm a fucking poet. Sue me. That's my wisdom."

"Some wisdom," I said. "I'm better off following the teachings of Jacques Cousteau."

"We're on our own, man." Kyle spread his arms. "The portals are open for business."

"I didn't become a P.I. to get rich."

"No, but you need to make a living, right? We all do. And people out there need our help. Nothing's free in this world, Felix. We provide a service, and every service, whether it's plumbing, electrical, or private investigation, costs money."

"This is different. We're not talking about insurance fraud or divorce cases anymore. These are supernatural entities, demonic possession, and every other paranormal problem we can imagine. And even more that we can't!"

"You started it, man. You think I became a P.I. so I could walk around packing wooden stakes and silver bullets? I was perfectly happy snapping pictures of guys cheating on their wives at five hundred yards with a telephoto lens. You changed the game, pal, not me."

"That's your problem. You still think of it as a game. But it's not. This is serious. And if we really are on our own, then that's more reason to protect ourselves."

Kyle shrugged. "I can't protect others unless I protect myself first. If I wanted to inspire people with my death, I would've gotten my martyr's license instead."

I shook my head. "You have to be more careful, Kyle. Next time, you may get someone killed."

I couldn't see a thing, and when the hand grabbed my arm, I almost screamed.

"It's me," Kyle hissed. "Come on, we've gotta get out of here."

He dragged me away, presumably in the direction of the hallway he'd been retreating toward when the girl showed up. I clipped my shoulder on a doorway and almost went spinning to the ground. Kyle caught me and hoisted me back to my feet. "It's okay, buddy," he said. "We're going to make it."

That was more than could be said for Enfield and the others. As Kyle led me away, the silence behind me was ripped apart by screams and gunfire. I looked back long enough to have my vision blinded by the staccato flash of muzzle fire, overlaid with an eerie red light that made me think of a photographer's darkroom, then it was gone.

We stumbled down a hallway of some indeterminate length. Kyle pulled me abruptly through a doorway and I tripped up a flight of stairs.

"Wait," I said breathlessly. "The others."

"It's too late for them," Kyle said. "Too late for us, too, if we don't haul ass. It's not like I trust them."

"What are you talking about?" I said. "What the hell is going on?"

"Talk later, buddy. For now, just climb."

We went up and around, up and around. I counted three flights of stairs. Then we went down a hallway and into a long room with a row of windows along one wall that presented a view of the city. The lights seemed very far away. Like stars.

Kyle went over to the far end of the room and started messing with one of the windows. "Come on," he grunted. "Where the fuck is it?"

"What?" I asked.

"Fucking fire escape," he said. "I thought it was on this side of the building."

"Why didn't we go out the back?"

"It might be covered."

"Covered by who?"

"By more of those things," Kyle said. "Like that little bitch downstairs. Paramental freaks or true Black Landers. Who the fuck knows."

"You planned this," I said.

"Bet your ass I did."

"You set me up."

"I'm saving your ass," Kyle said. "In case you didn't notice. I could've left you in the dark down there, but I didn't."

"What about Enfield and the others?"

"Fuck 'em," Kyle said. "What have the feds ever done for us anyway?"

Something clicked in my head. "You didn't set me up. You set them up. Why? Because you've got a hate-on for the PIA?"

"I didn't want them," Kyle said. "Not all of them. Just Enfield.

I didn't know he'd bring his buddies and a whole fucking STAR team with him."

"I guess that makes him smarter than me."

"Don't play the innocent with me, Felix. It's not going to save you tonight. If you want to get out of here alive, you're going to have to get dirty."

There was another blast of gunfire from below, muffled by the floors between us, but not so much that I couldn't hear the scream that came right after.

"You're alive," Kyle said. "I did that. Which is more than can be said for those pigs downstairs."

"They're dying because you led them here."

"I didn't know!" Kyle shouted. Then: "It was only supposed to be Enfield. He's the one they want. Seems you were right about him. He must be as good as you say for the Black Landers to want him so bad."

"And what about the others?"

Kyle shrugged. "More meat for the grinder. Plenty more where they came from."

"You're a real piece of work."

"Hey," Kyle said. "There's only one me and that's who I've got to take care of."

"I've heard this bit before."

"It's not like that," he snapped. "I didn't have a choice."

"You always have a choice."

"I got in too deep, okay? I wasn't lying when I said I know things." He sighed and ran a hand through his hair. "I've been to one of their meetings."

"What meetings?"

"I didn't think they saw me, but… they must have. I don't know. Maybe they knew I was there the whole time. I thought I was protected. The point is, they said they'd let me live if I gave them Enfield."

"And you believed them?"

"Of course not. That's why we're not going out the back door. I don't fucking trust them. The only one I trust, Felix, is you."

"That's comforting," I said. "What about your ex-wife and your brother?"

"I don't give a shit about my ex," Kyle said. "As for my brother…" He shrugged. "I don't have one."

It made sense to me then. When Kyle had broken down in my office the other day, the tears had been real. But they hadn't been for his ex-wife or his non-existent brother—they had been for himself.

So I hit him. For the lies, for getting me into this, for what was happening to Enfield and the others. One punch wasn't enough. Not nearly enough. But nothing, not even killing him, would tip the scales back.

"I'm going back to help them," I said. I was telling myself as much as I was telling Kyle.

"Oh yeah?" he said, wiping his bloody lip. "With what? They took our guns, remember?"

I barely heard him. I was down the hall, running back to the stairs, back into darkness.

"I almost shot you," said the guy in the rumpled trench coat. Then he held up the camera. "With this. Who figured that Carswell broad would hire two P.I.s to follow her philandering fuck of a husband. But I guess she's got the bread for it, eh?"

I eyed him skeptically. "You're a private detective, too?"

"Don't let my stereotypical attire confuse you," he said. "The clients expect Sam Spade and I try to deliver as best I can. Except for the fedora." He reached out and thumped his finger against my chest. "Never let me see you wearing one of those fucking things. Fedoras are for assholes."

"Noted."

"You're Felix Renn, right?"

"How do you know that?"

"I'm a detective," the man said, and flashed a crooked grin. "I'm Kyle Burke."

We shook hands.

"How long have you been peepin'?" Kyle asked.

"About a year," I replied.

"Who'd you do your apprenticeship with?"

"Madeline Ferine."

"Mad Maddy Ferine?" Kyle sounded impressed. "I didn't know she'd taken anyone under her wing."

"She's sly like that."

"You don't have to tell me. I tried to tap that once, and she almost put me in the hospital."

"I'd believe it."

"You don't see a lot of female dicks, but Mad Maddy's all right."

"She is," I agreed. And if she ever heard you calling her Mad Maddy, she'd probably remove your lungs with an ice-cream scoop.

"Don't get me wrong," Kyle said. "Nothing wrong with a broad being a private license. I don't discriminate. But it's really a man's game. We're wolves, Felix. Lone wolves. But we can help each other out from time to time, okay? Everybody needs someone to watch their back every now and again."

"That sounds fine by me," I said.

"Dicks stick together," Kyle said. "Just don't rub them together."

"I'll keep that in mind," I said.

"And I'll keep you in mind," Kyle said. "We're the same, kid. Never forget that."

The screams and gunfire had stopped by the time I reached the main floor. I didn't take that as a good sign.

I crept slowly toward the front entrance. I could only see an area of space about three feet in front of me. On my left and right, rectangular pools of deeper darkness marked the empty offices that opened off the hallway.

I reached the end and glimpsed a scene of bloody carnage that was tempered, mercifully, by the darkness of the room. Despite that, I could see enough detail for a year's worth of nightmares.

One of the STAR officers was lying on the ground near my feet. He appeared to have grown a tail. As my eyes adjusted, I saw it was his spine, half-ripped from his body and left hanging out. Another man had both of his arms torn off. A third appeared physically intact except that his head was twisted around backwards.

I didn't see Enfield or the other suit, but they might have been there. In whole or in pieces. I didn't look long enough to be sure.

I was retracing my steps down the hallway, thinking about taking my chances going out the back, when a hand reached out and pulled me into one of the empty offices. I reached for my gun, remembered I didn't have it, then started flailing with my fists. A pair of powerful arms wrapped around me and squeezed until I was still.

I smelled sweat and fear and knew it wasn't one of them. I let my body sag until the arms released me.

It was one of the STAR guys. His helmet and goggles were gone. He looked incredibly young. His eyes were wide and scared. Blood was smeared across his left cheek, but I didn't see a wound. It probably wasn't his.

"They've got us surrounded," he said in a trembling voice.

"How many?" I asked.

The STAR guy shook his head. He bent over at the waist and started sucking in deep breaths.

I touched his shoulder. "What's your name?"

He looked up at me. "Torrens."

"Felix," I said. "Nice to meet you."

Torrens gave me a shaky smile. "Right."

"What happened out there?" I nodded toward the main entrance.

"A slaughter," Torrens said. "The little bitch took out three of us with those fucking shadow puppets of hers. I've seen paramentals before, but none like her."

"But Enfield shot out her light."

Torrens shook his head. "She must've brought a spare." He looked off, remembering. "It was red."

"Then what happened?"

"The light went out and the girl was gone. Larson and Wong went to check the back and I heard them screaming. I was going to help them, but…"

Torrens turned and looked toward the back of the room. I followed his gaze and saw a man in a suit sitting on the floor with his back against the wall. He wasn't moving.

"I couldn't leave him," Torrens said.

I squinted my eyes. "Is that Enfield?"

"No," Torrents said. "Agent Deschamps. His skull's crushed."

"Where's Enfield?"

"Don't know. Lost sight of him in the commotion. If he's smart, he bailed."

"Larson and Wong never came back?"

Torrens shook his head.

"Have you seen anything else out there?"

"No, but there must be."

"We can't stay here."

Torrens nodded grimly and straightened up.

I nodded at his MP5. "You got a spare?"

He reached behind his back and produced a handgun—my Ruger. "You watch my back," Torrens said. "I'll watch yours."

"Deal."

We stepped back out into the hallway. I was trying to decide which was the better escape route—the rear entrance or the fire escape—when I became aware of a low hissing sound. It might have been there for a while, but I didn't notice while I was talking to Torrens.

"What is that?" he asked.

I shook my head, realized Torrens couldn't see the motion in the dark, and said, "I don't know. You got a light?"

"Yeah," he said, sounding surprised, and clicked on the flashlight clamped under the barrel of his gun. He panned it down the hallway toward the front entrance and the grisly tableau on display there, then quickly snapped it around in the other direction.

There was a man at the end of the hallway.

At least, I thought it was a man. The little girl and her shadow show had called off all bets.

He was man-shaped. I could say that much.

His head was on fire. The flames were blue. As they grew in intensity, I saw it wasn't his entire head that was on fire, only his mouth. His lips were black and cracked like burnt parchment paper. The fire dimmed and flared in a steady rhythm. Because he's breathing it, I realized. That was where the hissing sound was coming from.

I tried to pull Torrens back into the office, but it was like trying to move a marble statue. He was fixed to the spot, staring at the man with the blue fire in his mouth, perhaps hypnotized by those eldritch flames. His gun sagged in his hands.

The hissing sound rose to a high-pitched whistle that felt like ice picks stabbing into my ear drums. I fell to my knees—and ended up saving my own life. Torrens wasn't so lucky.

It looked like a flare. A blue one—shooting down the hallway like an errant comet. It struck Torrens in the face with a wet fizzing sound and his entire head was engulfed in flames. Blue flames.

I could smell his hair burning. I climbed to my feet and reached for him, but he went tearing off down the hallway toward the place where the rest of his friends had fought and died. Torrens was screaming and slapping at the flames dancing across his face, trying to put them out, but succeeded only in spreading the fire to his hands. He fell to the floor and start rolling back and forth, perhaps remembering the old safety technique. But it was too late for that. The fire continued to move even after Torrens had stopped.

I looked back at the black-lipped man. He was advancing slowly down the hall. Flames flickered in his mouth. His lips burned and he inhaled the smoke and snorted it out again. He was smiling.

I darted back into the empty office as the second fireball came flying at me. I saw it go sailing past the doorway, dragging a tail of smoke behind it.

I swung back around the corner with my gun arm straight. I fired three shots. The first one missed. The second one clipped the black-lipped man's shoulder to no effect. The third shot slammed into his chest and he faltered to a halt. The smile left his face. His eyes were slitted against the smoke drifting out of the corners of his mouth… and from the wound in his chest.

A tiny rill of smoke poured out like steam from a kettle. He let out a breathless cough and slapped his hand over the hole. Then he raised his eyes and gave me a look of such black hatred that I almost dropped my gun.

Instead, I fired three more times.

The first shot hit him in the stomach, but the next two struck him square in the chest, puncturing the infernal engine that dwelled within his lungs.

Smoke billowed out, and the black-lipped man didn't have enough hands to cover the holes. That made me think of Kyle's comment to Enfield about fingers in the dyke. I wondered if he made it down the fire escape and got away. Probably. Dirty guys like Kyle always seemed to get away clean. There was no balance in this world, or any other.

The black-lipped man was now doubled over. He began to retch, but instead of vomit he was throwing up fire. Great burning globs of blue napalm. He was choking on the stuff. And it burned him. But not in the way it burned Torrens. The black-lipped man was melting.

I went down the hallway past him. I kept my gun on him even

though it was empty. He didn't know that, and I didn't think he'd care if he did. He only existed now in his own world of pain. I left him to it.

I reached the stairwell, then decided I didn't want to follow Kyle's path. I'd take my chances going out the back.

I stepped out into the night. The sweat that covered my body encased me in a cold cocoon. I swung my empty gun around, feeling like a fool, but there was no one there to laugh at me. No one alive.

On the ground lay the smoldering remains of two men who had to be Larson and Wong. Even their mothers wouldn't have recognized them now.

I went around the side of the building and propelled my legs into a stumbling run. My car was a distant silhouette against the endless sprawl of cracked parking lot.

I didn't see the girl until it was too late.

She was sitting on the hood of my car with her back against the windshield. Her dress had been ripped to shreds by the STAR team's gunfire, but her skin was completely flawless. She clicked the trigger in her hand and the lamp over her head came on. The red bulb spilled its bloody glow across the pieces of Kyle's body that she had laid out for me to find. He was all there, from head to toes, but nothing was attached anymore. He was no longer human. He was a jigsaw puzzle.

I stared at his eyes, laid out on the ground next to his decapitated head. I followed the bloody filaments of the optic nerves all the way back to their empty sockets. I thought, *All the king's horses and all the king's men.* Then I turned and vomited on the ground.

I saw light out of the corner of my eye. I turned my head and saw the office building was in flames. Blue flames. The fire department was going to be scratching their heads at that one. Who was I kidding? The fire department wasn't coming down here. No one was. I was very much alone.

"Pretty," the girl said.

Almost alone.

I wiped my mouth, then turned and looked at her. She could've been talking about the fire or Kyle. Or maybe the puke on the ground.

I heard the growl of an engine and leaped out of the way as a car came screaming into the lot. There was a harsh screech of brakes, then the passenger door flew open. Enfield was behind the wheel.

"Get in!" he yelled.

I leaped inside without a backwards glance.

Enfield peeled away. I waited for an enormous shadow-fist to crush us like an egg, but it never happened. He pointed the car at the lights of the city and slammed his foot on the gas. I would have gotten out and pushed if I thought it would have made us go any faster.

"You came back for me," I said.

"I came back for Deschamps," Enfield said.

"He's dead. They're all dead."

Enfield didn't say anything.

"You knew it was a trap."

"No," Enfield said. "But I knew your friend."

"He's not my friend," I said. "He's dead, too."

"He was a piece of shit."

"Not always."

"Always."

I looked at Enfield. "If you knew what he was, then why did you come?"

Enfield looked at me. "Why did you?"

Neither of us seemed to have an answer to that question.

From Space & Time #134, Fall 2019

Ian Rogers is the author of the award-winning collection *Every House Is Haunted*. His works have been selected for The Best Horror of the Year and Imaginarium: The Best Canadian Speculative Writing and as a finalist for the Shirley Jackson Award. Ian lives with his wife in Peterborough, Ontario.

A MAGAZINE OF FANTASY & SCIENCE FICTION

DREAMF RGE

DreamForge is a speculative fiction literary magazine founded in 2019 by entrepreneur, author, and video game developer Scot Noel and graphic artist Jane Noel.

By design, the magazine showcases characters who bring meaning and value to the world, whose actions are of consequence, and whose dreams are the vanguard of things to come.

In 2021, *DreamForge* transitioned to a digital-only publication, adding essays on the craft of writing as well as a look inside the minds of the authors featured in each issue to discover how they conceived and crafted their stories, especially the editing and improving processes.

DREAMFORGEMAGAZINE.COM

FANTASY • HORROR • SCIENCE FICTION

Founded in 1966 by a high schooler named Gordon Linzner who published his brainchild on a mimeograph machine he purchased for $25, *Space & Time* is now the world's longest continuously running semi-pro speculative fiction magazine.

After publishing short stories and poetry for well over fifty years, *Space & Time* was rescued and revamped in 2018 by the publishing team of Angela Yuriko Smith and Ryan Aussie Smith, and is once again a must-read for true fans of the strange and unusual.

S P A C E A N D T I M E . N E T

Also from Uproar Books:

ASPERFELL by Jamie Thomas (Gothic Fantasy)

Named one of *Booklist*'s Top Ten Debut Speculative Fiction novels of the year, Asperfell is a must-read for fans of Jane Austen who always wished she'd dabbled in blood magic.

ALWAYS GREENER by J.R.H. Lawless (Dark Comedy)

In the corporate dystopia of 2072, the world's most popular reality show starts a competition for world's worst life, and now everyone is out to prove just how bad they've got it.

FORETOLD by Violet Lumani (Y.A. Contemporary Fantasy)

As if OCD isn't bad enough, high schooler Cassie Morai discovers she can also see the future—and must join a strange secret society of psychics to prevent her best friend's death.

THE WAY OUT by Armond Boudreaux (Sci-Fi Thriller)

When a virus necessitates the use artificial wombs for all pregnancies, two fearless women discover the terrifying truth behind this world-changing technology.

WILD SUN by Ehsan Ahmad and Shakil Ahmad (Epic Sci-Fi)

This old-school science-fiction epic follows a handful of native slaves as they strive to find a way to strike back at the soldiers of the interstellar empire that conquered their home world.

For more information, visit uproarbooks.com